FOURTH DOWN

FOURTH DOWN

Dave Klein

FORGE®

A Tom Doherty Associates Book *New York*

This is a work of fiction. All the characters and events portrayed in this novel are either fictitious or are used fictitiously.

FOURTH DOWN

This book is printed on acid-free paper.

Design by Bonnie Leon-Berman

A Forge Book
Published by Tom Doherty Associates, LLC
175 Fifth Avenue
New York, NY 10010

Forge® is a registered trademark of Tom Doherty Associates, LLC

Library of Congress Cataloging-in-Publication Data

Klein, Dave.
    Fourth down / Dave Klein.—1st ed.
       p. cm.
    "A Tom Doherty Associates book."
    ISBN 0-312-86370-5 (alk. paper)
    I. Title.
  PS3561.L3442F68   1999
  813'.54—dc21   99–22196
                                                 CIP

First Edition: September 1999

Printed in the United States of America

0 9 8 7 6 5 4 3 2 1

TO MY FATHER,
who is living in wait

ACKNOWLEDGMENTS

For the help I received, with great doses of love and friendship, I would like to thank 323. Both the love and the friendship are there—then, now, and always.

The early help provided by Michael Seidman is gratefully appreciated.

The later help, from Tom Doherty and Melissa Ann Singer, even more so.

And the nicest thing about this book is that in its writing not a single animal was harmed.

January 1999

FOURTH DOWN

ONE

. . . **ABOVE** all, no matter what else would come to mind seconds after anybody asked him how he felt about football, his first thought, his first visceral memory, was the heat.

And the grass drills.

He had never experienced heat like that, but even if he had, he absolutely never would have considered putting himself through such intense physical strain in the midst of the worst of it. Grass drills? Devised, clearly, by some equally warped and perverted descendent of the Marquis de Sade.

The football players, already having gone through intense strength-draining practice sessions for up to three hours, were lined up in sweating, panting rows and, at the sound of a shrill, nerve-jangling whistle, began to jog in place. The leader of this little experiment in terror would suddenly shriek, "Hit the grass!," which required all the sweating young men to throw their bodies to the ground, belly first, and jump right back up again, almost as soon as contact had been made, to resume jogging in place.

The torturer would then scream, "On three!," meaning on every third jog-step the "hit the grass" procedure would be repeated. But then he'd change it to "on four," or "on six," sometimes "on two," and those who failed to keep up not only physically but also with the math would be forced to go through extra sessions of grass drills before they would be allowed to stagger off into the nearby woods and puke.

But that was the way things were in 1968. It seemed college campuses slightly out of the way, like the University of

Oklahoma at Norman, were divided into two groups of male underclassmen—those who couldn't play football and therefore spent their time either studying or protesting (rarely both) and those who did play football and didn't have time for much else, especially to give a damn one way or another about their nation's involvement in Vietnam, which was some obscure country halfway around the world that specialized in growing rice while starving its young.

It was hot because preseason practice was held in August, when the temperature and humidity both fooled around with and finally married each other, becoming, for all time, the nineties twins. And Ed Buck played football at Oklahoma. This was truly surprising, since he was a walk-on, no-scholarship unknown whom nobody from Oklahoma had scouted or even heard of and, of all things, a Jewish kid from the streets of New York. Neither category, walk-on nor New York Jew, had been represented in the storied Oklahoma football program for nearly a decade, and never had both afflictions been present at the same time in one athlete.

The fact that Ed Buck was matriculating at OU at all was equally inexplicable. He had attended Boys High in Brooklyn, played football there only because he had been able to hide it from his parents, and through a variety of subterfuges somehow managed to deal with the problem of being too good until the *Daily News* named him to its All-City team. In itself, this didn't really present an insurmountable problem, because the only newspaper ever read in the Buck household was the *Times*. But then too many of his parents' friends began calling to congratulate them, and he was able to save himself from eternal Jewish Parent Purgatory only because he had found time to earn sufficiently high grades to rank ninth in his graduating class and soon after was accepted by Cornell, Colgate, and Tufts, three of the four colleges to which he had applied at his parents' urging. Princeton had turned him down, thereby reinforcing their solid conviction that Albert Einstein had been the only Jew to spend any time there, because the desperate White Anglo-Saxon Protestants had harbored a sinister plot to mystically excise a few of his intelligence genes while he slept.

Ed was also accepted by the University of Oklahoma, to which he had applied on his own. His father, Sheldon Kalman Buck, whose father's last name had been Buchhalter, had with predictable precision determined that Cornell produced more doctors than Tufts, which in turn produced more lawyers than Cornell, and that both produced more of both than Colgate. So he and Ed's mother, Dora, during one of their "official" meetings in the kitchen of their apartment on Avenue J, decided, after long and soul-searching study, that Ed accept the admission offered by Cornell.

Which was exactly when Ed said, "Oklahoma."

The battle raged for a month. Ed wanted to go somewhere else, to see some other part of the country. Besides, in a truth known only to himself, standing six-four and weighing 250, he harbored just enough ego to want to try his hand at major college football. But that could never be mentioned as a factor, for he had barely begun to convince his parents that he had not already suffered irreparable brain damage from his bout with high school athletic insanity. Instead, he argued that it didn't matter where he went to college because he wanted to be neither doctor nor lawyer but writer, author, a man of words like his two heroes, Ernest Hemingway and Jack Kerouac. It was undeniable that writers learned by doing, by traveling, by coping with unusual, perhaps even threatening, situations.

Sheldon Buck, a certified public accountant, was convinced that writers wound up broke and depressed, probably drunk, certainly divorced, and alone. Dora Buck said she had known only one other woman to have raised a lunatic son, Molly Goldman, whose Nathan had turned down the chance to use his hard-earned dentist's degree by going in as a partner with Dr. Paul Katz, a family friend. Instead, Nathan had run away to Southern California, where he sold paper tax shelters to rich actors and actresses, an endeavor that invariably made them less rich while at the same time adding to Nathan Goldman's clearly ill-gotten gains. Dora sulked, pleaded, and finally settled on old-fashioned, healthy mourning, convinced beyond a doubt that her Edward was going to be killed and eaten by Christians or Indians, after which they would sell his typewriter and electric shaver for far less than they were worth.

Sheldon persevered, correlating for his confused son Cornell with a guaranteed high future income, Tufts with permanent financial security, Colgate with at least a chance at professionalism. Ed listened patiently because he loved his parents, tolerated all their arguments and all their threats and all their warnings of doom, and wound up leaving by train for Norman, by way of Oklahoma City, ten days before the fall semester of 1968 was to begin. Sheldon formally shook his hand at the platform in Penn Station and surreptitiously slipped Ed five twenties neatly folded in half.

Dora, wiping her reddened eyes with a finely embroidered handkerchief made decades ago by her mother in Russia, managed to insert two twenties and a ten in her only son's jacket pocket when he bent for a final kiss, knowing in her heart that he would discover it in times of great need, hopefully before he ever thought to send the jacket to a dry cleaner.

The freshman year was a piece of cake. The high school education he had mastered under the then-strict guidelines of the New York City Board of Education had put him at least a year ahead of the demands placed on college freshmen by OU. Freshman English was a cupcake; basic algebra was almost embarrassingly easy. The American history professor was well ahead of the class, which added some interest to that course, and Introduction to the Novel, which Ed had to beg to be allowed to take as a freshman, was his favorite. But Ed's high point came as a result of spotting a notice on the bulletin board in the student union center, which he had started visiting to earn quick money at the snooker tables.

FOOTBALL TRYOUTS. OWEN FIELD. MONDAY SEPT. 2. 9 A.M.

OU did not need to conduct tryouts—indeed, did not want to—and seldom, if ever, were any real players ever turned up during such charades. The team was stocked with High School All-American types from Oklahoma, Tennessee, Texas, California, Arkansas, and Nebraska. In addition, the nation's most highly prized high school quarterback, Adam Benson of Oliphant, Pennsylvania, had broken recruiters' hearts at Penn State, Syracuse, Florida State, Ohio State, Notre Dame, and Miami by deciding, as Ed had, to see what Oklahoma was all about.

But since the university had been founded under federal land-grant conditions, certain formalities had to be maintained, just as the Grambling University sports program, traditionally all-black, had to have at least one white athlete on scholarship to satisfy state of Louisiana requirements. At OU sports teams had to hold open tryouts, all male students were required to participate in some form of ROTC training, and blacks had to be accepted according to some nebulous but nevertheless quite real formula. It was argued by some students that the one over-riding factor in the formula was overwhelming athletic ability. No one disputed the theory.

So the morning arrived and, armed with nothing more than shorts and a pair of low-cut cleats, Ed Buck jogged the two miles to the field, found the open gate, and approached the first man he saw with a clipboard, an assistant coach named Harvey Joe Bigelow.

"Buck, Ed, freshman," he said.

"Ah don't seem to find your name on my list heah," said Harvey Joe, nervously eyeing this obviously fit, visibly well-built freshman. "What's your position, son?"

"Offensive line, sir. I mostly played tackle in high school, but I spent some time at center."

Harvey Joe shrugged. "Well, it sure don't matter. I'll find your name sooner or later. Get over there with the offensive line; ask for Coach Johnson."

Coach Frank "Pop" Johnson didn't have Buck's name on his list, either, and didn't like being surprised. But what he did like was the size of this kid, the clear eyes, and the implied toughness in that New York accent.

"Do we know about you?" Johnson asked, his sun-leathered, weather-beaten, lined face creasing easily into a smile. "Do we know you're here?"

"No, sir, but it said you were holding tryouts and I just got here and I'd like to try out. OK?"

"You play?"

"High school."

"Any good?"

It was Ed's turn to smile. "Yes, sir. Real good."

Pop Johnson had been around the whole thing twice. He was sixty-two years old and had played pro football when it was little more than a barnstorming carnival. He had coached high school teams and college teams, at the highest levels and at those places where football was still just a game. He even coached for a while in the National Football League, but that wasn't what he wanted. Pop Johnson loved to work with kids, make them better, watch them improve. Right now, he was getting a tingle, a feeling, about Ed Buck.

"Look, son. We have to hold these tryouts, you understand? Every year a couple of kids show up, mostly just for the fun of it, and we let 'em work out with the team and take a few hits and then they go back to being students and they leave the football players alone. From the look of you, you'd have to play offensive tackle on the freshman team. Now, in addition to being the offensive line coach for the varsity, I am the freshman coach, and I make damn sure to take care of myself, you understand? I have got one freshman tackle who was a Scholastic All-American and three more who were All-State. The All-American is six-six and weighs two hundred and seventy pounds and he has a thirty-eight-inch waist and a fifty-four-inch chest.

"So, now I'm gonna ask you again. You any good?"

Ed Buck looked the old man right in his eyes. "Damn good, coach. Watch me."

Pop Johnson watched. When the daylong workout had ended, he ambled over to Ed, who had more than held his own, who had even blocked Raymond McClelland, the Sooners' junior All-American defensive end, four consecutive times during skeleton passing drills. McClelland didn't like that, especially from a freshman nobody knew about, so after the third time he jumped up, threw a roundhouse right, and caught Ed just under the breastbone.

"Don't you fuck with me, you freshman piece of shit," snarled Raymond McClelland, standing tall and lean and almost religiously outraged over the prone body of the upstart maverick.

When the five-man offensive line and the two receivers shuttled back to the impromptu huddle, Ed was seething. "Call the same play," he hissed to the freshman quarterback, the prized recruit from Pennsylvania, the heroic Adam Benson.

"You got it," smiled the rock-hard coal country kid, who was thinking that he might have just made a friend.

Same formation, same objective: to free a receiver over the middle. Raymond McClelland, who had guffawed with his friends in the defensive huddle, now smiled benignly, and with great confidence, across the line of scrimmage.

"Watch me, boy; I'm comin' through."

Ed said nothing at all. His face was white, his body taut. The ball was snapped, Ed stutter-stepped backward, setting up for pass-blocking duties, and McClelland came roaring across the line—to be met by Ed Buck's left hand, an uppercut that seemed to start from the ground. It caught the All-American smack on the point of the chin and lifted him about six inches off his feet before he fell to the ground in a heap, an unconscious heap.

Everything stopped. Jim Lee Hudson, the nationally famous head coach of the annually powerful Sooners, rushed toward the scene to see whether his defensive star was all right and to kick the ass of this unknown freshman, but Pop Johnson caught him by the elbow.

"Hold on, Jim Lee; I got a feelin' about that boy. You been watchin' his feet? He's quick. He's smart. You just saw that he's tough. And he won't back down. Before you get all over him, maybe you ought to find out how come your All-American is pukin' on the ground, you know?"

Hudson smiled. "You're right, Pop. Who is that kid?"

"Walk-on. Named Buck, Ed Buck. Freshman. From Brooklyn-New-Yawk, if you please."

The smile broadened. "Get him signed up, Pop, and if any-body asks, tell 'em we knew about him all along, that a friend, maybe some high school coach up there, tipped us off. Who do we know in Brooklyn? Some scout?"

Johnson nodded his head. "We'll find somebody. Golly, coach, you sure are one smart sumbitch, ain't you?"

Jim Lee Hudson smiled broadly. After all their years together, he kept finding new reasons to like old Pop Johnson.

Ed Buck made the freshman team. He started, then spent the next three seasons with the varsity; he could not hide from his parents the fact that he played football because he was a junior and senior All-American selection and was drafted by the Chicago Bears in the third round of the 1972 draft. He signed a contract, got a $50,000 signing bonus, was prepared to earn $105,000 in his rookie season, and then, playing in the now-extinct College All-Star game against that year's defending NFL champions, the Green Bay Packers, tore his right knee, suffering extreme damage to the medial collateral and cruciate ligaments, and knew with absolute certainty that his football career had come to a tragic, premature but unquestioned end.

So he came home and became a sportswriter for the *New York Express*. It came as no surprise to him or anyone else that he was assigned to cover pro football in general and the New York Giants in particular.

Now, a dozen years later, his weight down to 240, his reputation as one of the nation's best sportswriters assured, the author of half a dozen "airplane book" novels that probably would have pleased Hemingway and infuriated Kerouac, with enough money to do what he wanted to do, a divorce now seven years old, and completely healed, he was comfortable, secure, pleased with his life. Sheldon Kalman Buck, had he lived, would have been happy, not to mention surprised, that all writers do not end up desolate and drunk. Dora Buck, had she lived, would have continued to insist that Ed got out of Oklahoma just in time.

It was football season. The Chicago Bears were coming to town, and that meant a long-awaited visit with their star quarterback, Adam Benson, the six-time Pro Bowl selection, holder of many NFL career records, the "old man" of the league's quarterbacks, the Scholastic All-American from Oliphant, Pennsylvania, and OU—and Ed Buck's best friend.

As a professional, Benson had made as much of an impact off the field as on it. He had taken the Bears to their first-ever Super Bowl championship three years earlier despite having been picked up and booked for disorderly conduct in Miami Beach and spending four hours in a one-man cell, providing the *Miami Herald* with a prizewinning photograph of Benson signing autographs for the local police while sitting on the cell's threadbare cot next to three as-yet undrunk bottles of beer. He and one of the second-string defensive linemen had decided that Super Bowl Week had made too much of an imposition on their social lives. So they got themselves roaring drunk and before being arrested were cruising down Collins Avenue in a convertible, throwing official NFL footballs through storefront plate glass windows.

The league commissioner had considered ruling Benson ineligible to play that day. For about three seconds. Then wiser heads prevailed, advisers who reminded the commissioner of the television ratings, the enormous amounts of money at stake, and the almost certain publicity damage, the fact that this was going to be, beyond doubt, the biggest Super Bowl attraction since the underdog New York Jets had stunned the haughty Baltimore Colts in premerger days.

The official announcement at noon on Super Sunday, five hours prior to the game, was that Adam Benson, released and in the care of his team, would be summoned to New York the following week for a "frank discussion" with Commissioner Paul A. Davis. The unfortunate second-string defensive tackle, however, would not be allowed to play that day. It had been "learned" that he (and the commissioner had managed this with a straight face) had been the one to "lead Benson astray" in the first place.

The media chuckled, convinced that "frank discussion" meant another attempt by another authority figure to show Benson the "proper" way to represent himself and the league. Ed Buck, who had spent four years with Adam, chuckled most of all. Ed knew it was hopeless, that a capricious, uninhibited spirit like Benson's would never respond well to society's bonds. If at all.

Adam had finally married, three years ago when he was thirty, to a legitimate centerfold girl, tall and willowy and flat-out gorgeous. Her name was Sherri Novak, and with her looks and his reputation they immediately became a celebrity couple for the entertainment pages, invited to the California and New York parties and offered off-season roles in movies that wouldn't demand too much in the way of acting skills.

Adam had called Ed late the previous Wednesday night, eager for their reunion—it had been almost a year, and they hadn't gone that long since leaving Oklahoma together—and while Ed thought Adam's old bubbling enthusiasm was missing, he chalked it off to the pressures of the game, the recent slump that had dropped him to the lower half of the NFL's quarterback-efficiency charts the previous season, which had never happened before, and his obvious struggle so far through the seven games of the current season.

Sherri wasn't going to make the trip. The Bears would arrive in New York late Friday afternoon. Ed would meet Adam at the team hotel, and Saturday night would be dinner, just the two of them, at an out-of-the-way but exceptional steak house on Manhattan's Lower West Side, the Old Homestead.

Pro football weekends in New York City, with the weather crisp and clear, were among Ed Buck's favorite things, and adding to that the pleasure of seeing his old friend again simply heightened the anticipation.

Ed even started to feel some of that old football excitement that had been missing lately. All things considered, Ed was anxiously looking ahead to this meeting.

TWO

ADAM Benson looked terrible.

Haggard was the first word that came to mind; *pale and drawn* followed almost immediately.

They sat at the bar of the Metro-Plaza Hotel, two old friends pulling at their drinks. Ed smiled and nodded and feigned interest in what Adam was saying, but his mind was casting about for some explanation. *He's not old,* Ed thought, *and he's not sick, because he's playing regularly. It can't be emotional, because that would affect his performance, and even if he was struggling, what was a struggle for Adam Benson represented a high-quality season for most other quarterbacks in the league.*

But he looked so awful.

Finally, Ed had to ask. "Adam, what's wrong? You look like two trucks have been taking turns running you over at night. Man, I mean, you look like hell. You losin' weight, too?"

A shrug of the shoulders, and the Benson smile flashed through. "Hey, it's a jungle out there, Jane," he laughed. "This is the National Football League, Eddie, and my offensive line sucks. I need you at one of the tackles, you know? That big kid, the first-round draft choice, Lange? Well, my friend, he's a turkey. They made a mistake and they know it, but they can't cut him loose yet because it would make them look stupid in public. He's got no heart, Eddie, just a lot of size and no balls. I told 'em if I can't count on a guy I can't play with him, and they know that, but then the owner tells the coach to keep him in and that's the way it's going to be.

"Also, Bill Jillian, the center? He's workin' with a bad back.

The guy's got all the heart in the world, but he can't move because of the back. But Michael Lee Reasons, the guy who plays behind him, is a coward. Can't do the long snap, either. So Jilly has to play, and he gets the ball to me and most of the time he gets the job done, but then there are certain nose tackles . . . like the guy the Giants have, Blake? . . . the small, quick ones . . . who show him one move and then cut across and get past him the other way, and he can't do anything but scream in pain. So now I'm keepin' both backs in to block, and that cuts down my passing choices."

Talking about the Bears' deficiencies visibly depressed Adam. "I been thinkin' it's gettin' time to retire, maybe," he said. "I mean, two years ago I had the best damn offensive line in the entire league, and then Slaby and Webster retire, Jamieson gets smart with the coach and winds up in Buffalo, for God's sake, and Pownall gets himself elected union president and they cut his ass the next week. All I got left is Jillian and a bunch of shit. This is takin' more out of me than it's worth, Eddie. Even the game we won, it took me three days to shake the aches. I am really taking one unbelievable pounding, you know?"

Having worked himself up, apparently getting a rare chance to bitch to somebody who would understand, Benson made a fast emotional comeback. Wiping his sweating forehead with a cocktail napkin, snapping his fingers for another round, he laughed.

"Did I tell you I got to meet Burt Reynolds, at his house, and he had my picture waitin' for me to autograph? I did, down in Florida; guy's got a house like a small town. We sat around all afternoon, maybe half a dozen of us, talkin' football. He knows something about this game, you know? Oh, and Sherri isn't here because she's auditioning for a part in one of those horror movies for teenagers. You know, like *Halloween*? She says there's a pretty good chance she'll get it, too."

He rambled on for a while, drinking three more beers, growing more animated. Color flooded his cheeks, his eyes sparkled again, and he looked just like Adam Benson was supposed to look.

"Hey, Ed, I'm gonna be late for another team meeting," he

suddenly said, glancing at his watch, slapping two twenties on the bar, pushing the stool away behind him. "Tomorrow night, the Homestead, eight o'clock. Right?"

They shook hands and he was gone, hitting the hotel lobby in a half-skipping, half-running motion, just slipping into an elevator car as the door began to slide silently shut.

Ed was smiling as he left the hotel, and a little flushed from the beer, too. Since it was reasonably warm for late October, he decided to walk the twenty blocks back to his apartment. Tomorrow he would knock off his Sunday column, put the finishing touches on the advance story for the Giants–Bears game— using exclusive quotes from the star quarterback, of course— and maybe see Leigh for a few hours in the afternoon. Usually, Saturday nights at home were for her, but she knew that when Adam Benson hit town she'd better find other plans. Still, Ed had thought about taking her with him, to meet Adam, because he felt it had come time to do that. But the mysterious way Adam was behaving convinced him to let it wait for the next opportunity.

He felt a twinge when he opened the door to the apartment, for maybe the thousandth time, knowing no one was home. Maybe he'd think a little harder about what Leigh had been trying to sell him. Marriage. Lord, he swore he'd never marry again, not after the ordeal that was spelled *Suzanne,* as in Suzanne Chait-Buck; now, thank God, Suzanne Chait-Feldman. No kids, no alimony, but best of all, no Suzanne. No wondering who she was with when he was on the road, who had been sleeping with and sweating on and fucking his wife in his own bed. There was an old line from the late Hugh Vanbrock, Hall of Fame quarterback, later a head coach, offered when someone asked if he cheated on the road:

"Cheat on the road? Son, when I close my suitcase I get a hard-on," he had said, laughing.

In Suzanne's case it had been slightly different. When Ed closed his suitcase, she got horny.

Saturday morning woke up raining. Ugly, dirty gray clouds spitting down on the streets of New York City. Always a good day to work. Ed brewed coffee first. Coffee was one of his great weaknesses, and so he allowed it to be one of his great extravagances, like Knockando, the best of the single-malt scotches, and Ketel One, the top of the vodka line. He bought the coffee in compact eight-ounce boxes from a specialty company that imported it from Holland. Sure it was expensive, but the powdery rich brown grinds, which resembled talcum powder more than coffee, made the best cup he'd ever had. At the equivalent of eighteen bucks a pound, it better be good. The Knockando and Ketel One he got in the biggest bottles he could find. Same story. Expensive but worth it.

Something in Adam's behavior still bothered him, still hovered just beyond awareness, taunting and teasing. He was . . . what? Too changeable, too unpredictable? Just different, a new Adam Benson that Ed simply wasn't accustomed to seeing? How often did they really see each other, three, four times a year? It was the past that bonded them together, a comfortable, familiar friendship grounded in what life had been, not in what it was now. So Adam was different. So what? The last time they had met was in January, at the Super Bowl in Phoenix. Ed was there to work, Adam to party, mostly, to represent a beer company at the cocktail hours and NFL-related functions. *That was ten months ago. So he's different now. Who isn't?*

Ed shrugged, poured the first of what would be many mugs of hot, black coffee, flipped on the switch of his laptop computer—hooked right in, it was, to the newspaper's system; instant story, without an editor, even, in Ed's case—and began to work. Shortly after, he sat back and smiled, wondering how he could ever work during the day without coffee and Marlboros and how he could ever work at night without vodka and Marlboros.

It was simple and easy, a smooth transition between the column, opinion—remember, the readers want to know what you think so they don't have to think for themselves—and the game advance, which was as useless as all game advances, free publicity for the team, in effect.

The Giants are playing the Bears today, at the stadium, at one o'clock, here are the starting players, here is the

situation as it affects both teams in their divisional
standings, here are a few of the more noteworthy statistics achieved so far by some of the individual players,
and here, you should pardon the expression, is the way
I have chosen to present this information to you, in the
form of some gimmicky, often contrived hook:

"The difference between the Giants' 6–1 record and the
Chicago Bears' 1–6 is only eighteen points," he wrote. "The
Giants have won five games by a total of nine points, while
the hard-luck Bears lost five by the identical margin. The
fact that both teams are virtually even in talent and experience
will become obvious on the field, where it should be a far better
and more closely fought game than the two records might in-
dicate."

Once, as a community service to the team's owners, in a time
when stadiums weren't always sold out, the city newspapers,
as in the rest of the country, ran these advances as an attempt
to spur some last-minute Sunday-morning ticket sales. Now advances were real crap, but the copy filled the hole, and it was
precisely what the sports editor. Willie Moss, who had been in
the position for almost half a century and was the best newspaperman Ed would ever know, insisted was part of the paper's
job in covering the team.

"You can't just ignore a game and then go cover the damned
thing and come in with a front-page story and a column," Willie
had always said. "If it deserves that kind of treatment when they
play it, then it deserves some kind of announcement that it's
going to be played that day. Final. That's it. Anybody who
covers a New York team for this paper while I'm the sports editor, any team, any sport, is going to do game advances or wind
up taking high school box scores on the telephone Friday night.
And remember to always fill in with the good kind of crap between commas. That's what the readers want, even if they don't
know it."

The point was well made and well-taken. Game advances
had become a way of life. Boring, perhaps, but nevertheless automatic, and the trivial material that made the players turn from

names on a broadsheet into real people became part of Ed's writing.

The fourth mug of coffee and maybe the fifteenth Marlboro later, at four in the afternoon, Ed punched the key to "SAVE" what he had written, picked up the desk telephone, dialed the newspaper's incoming transmission number, got the required *beep,* and pushed the transmit button on the mini-computer. The answering beep told him the machines had joined in perfect, if only temporary, union, and since he had written the equivalent of seven old-fashioned pages of paper, the transmission process would continue for approximately four minutes.

He leaned back, watched as each line blinked and disappeared (not forever, though the first time he had watched the process in operation it had almost brought his heart to a stop), put a match to yet another Marlboro, and closed his eyes. *Beep . . . beep . . . beep . . .* Line after line went whirring into the telephone cable, to be gobbled up by the monster at the other end, to be turned into type of a preprogrammed style and face, to be made ready, justified, balanced, and paginated, for the editor who would be in soon to study Ed's offerings, as well as those of all the other writers on the staff, on his video display terminal for final changes and headline work.

Old-fashioned typewriters were still in his blood, but Ed had quickly come to rely on the speed and ease of editing offered by these new machines. You don't like it, you just push a button and everything disappears, electronically erased, and you don't have to roll fresh blank paper into the carriage, type all the same headers and codes, then find you made the same error again and had to go through the process yet another time. Still, typewriters were real; these things were probably produced by George Lukas and used by Mark Hamill or R2D2. Or maybe they *were* R2D2.

The final *beep* told him that both files had been successfully transmitted. Glancing at his watch, he figured one of the editors would already be in the office, since all deadlines were earlier on Saturday nights to handle the rush of extra Sunday editions.

He pushed the proper combination of number-buttons, heard two rings and then: "Spawwwts."

That was Howard Weiss, the best editor in the city, the guy who could turn sows' ears into silk paragraphs.

"Hey, Howard, Buck here."

"We got 'em both," Weiss snapped. Conversational amenities had never been part of his repertoire. "Column's real good; advance is a piece of shit."

"Advances are always a piece of shit, my prizewinning editor friend," Ed said. "Let Moss say the word and there won't be a dry eye in the house when we kill the bastards."

"I'll fix it, save your ass another day. It's busy. You done?"

"Yeah. And my compliments to your speech teacher, you silver-tongued devil, you."

Flipping on the television, Ed had the chance to see the tail end of the UCLA–Ohio State game, unconsciously hoping UCLA was winning because the coach, a nice guy named Walter Raye, used to coach the Giants, winced when the announcer's voice told him there were three minutes to play and the Buckeyes held a two-touchdown lead, turned down the volume, and made a mental note to call Los Angeles sometime the next week to talk to Walter Raye, find out what he thought about the Giants from his new vantage point. He had virtually handpicked his successor, the current Giants' coach, Duane Charles, who had been not only his defensive coordinator for four years but also his closest friend, best man, and godfather to his first child.

However, in the past few months, with the Giants doing better and better, it became obvious to those who knew how to look that Charles was growing more sensitive to the references that this was "Raye's team," seeing as how it was virtually unchanged in terms of the offensive and defensive units put in place—especially over the last two years.

Charles was visibly uncomfortable when asked to talk about Raye or to explain just how things were different when the cast of characters had remained virtually unchanged. Perhaps that would be an interesting dimension to explore.

But now it was past five, and it remained for Ed to shave,

shower, make a few telephone calls, perhaps sit back with his feet up and his legs propped for thirty minutes, carefully nursing the first Ketel One of the day (with shaved ice, of course, in a fat-bodied, squat pony glass).

At seven-fifteen he strode out of his apartment on East 72d Street, waited no more than five minutes before a taxicab cruised past and stopped, and was in the lobby of the Old Homestead at seven-fifty, shaking hands with the owner, Mike Muldowney, an old friend, looking around for Benson, then telling Mike that tonight's guest was the noted quarterback Adam Benson and that a slightly out-of-the-way table, like in a corner or against a wall, would make the night much easier for his neatly uniformed waiters, who would not have to wait while a small crowd of autograph seekers clogged the aisles.

Mike understood perfectly, made a few marking-pen flourishes on the oversize desk blotter used as the reservations chart, and smiled. "All done, Ed." Snapping his fingers at the nearest waiter, Mike added: "Take Mr. Buck to table seven, Mario, and nothing he or his guest orders is to be billed, do you understand?"

Mario not only understood but smiled. He knew, since this had happened the last time, and because Ed really didn't like the no-charge courtesy, that Buck was going to leave sufficient cash on the table, after he argued with Muldowney, who would refuse to accept payment. And one way or another, that cash, which figured to be about a hundred bucks, was going to wind up in the pocket of the extremely grateful Mario Cress.

He led Ed to the table, assured him that he would bring his guest as soon as he arrived, and asked whether Mr. Buck would like his Knockando mist. Mr. Buck would, and Mr. Buck was impressed that Mario remembered.

But it wasn't until Mario delivered the second Knockando that Adam arrived, twenty minutes late. "Sorry," he said, easing himself into the chair against the wall. "Meeting ran late. Damn coach thinks we can beat this losing streak by having meetings. Been here long?"

Ed shook his head. "Nah, couple of minutes. You drinking?"

It was Adam's turn to shake his head. "Game tomorrow. Just a light beer."

Mario heard, and it arrived, in a frosted mug, moments later. "You gonna beat our Giants tomorrow, Mr. Benson?" He smiled. "I remember last year, you beat us good, and I had a hundred bucks on the Giants. But I don't hold a grudge. Just lay down tomorrow so I can get my money back, OK?"

Adam's practiced public smile vanished as quickly as Mario did, and he turned to Ed, his face devoid of color.

Now Ed was sure something was wrong. He looked directly into his friend's eyes and quietly spoke two words: "Tell me."

Adam nodded, almost imperceptibly. "OK, I will. I have to. This is as far as I go." He paused, drew a deep breath, motioned with his head over his right shoulder in the direction in the waiter had gone. "What he said, that waiter? He was right. It's in the bag. I am gonna lay down tomorrow. The Giants are gonna win. I have made the Bears losers in three of the seven games we have lost this season, and tomorrow is supposed to be another one. I am supposed to throw at least three interceptions, and if we get inside the Giants' twenty-yard line I am supposed to fumble a snap. I have been throwing games for two years, Eddie. I think I'd be a lot happier dead."

A humorless, dry laugh. "And if I don't do it, I *will* be dead. Worse yet, if I don't do it, Sherri will be dead. I don't know what else to say. Shit, what else could be this bad?"

Ed stood up, pushed back his chair, and dropped some money on the table. "Not here, Adam. My apartment. Now."

Benson nodded, also rose, and followed his friend out to the entrance hall, where Mike Muldowney grew panicky. They assured him nothing was wrong, that they'd be back soon, that Benson had forgotten an important errand that had to be done immediately.

In less than thirty minutes they were in Ed Buck's apartment, sitting on facing chairs separated by a glass coffee table.

"The whole thing, Adam. All of it, now. We got all night, and the hell with your curfew."

Another ironic smile played with Benson's lips. "No curfew

this trip," he murmured. "Coach Parr thinks we need to kick our heels a little, stay out late, maybe get laid, get loose, and win one. It's OK. Shit, it's expected of me, considering my reputation, you know? Funny, nobody really knows what they're saying when they talk about Adam Benson's reputation."

For the next hour, almost without pause, the quarterback spun out a story of sensational partying, random sex, high-level gambling, multimillion-dollar drug deals, addiction, manipulation, intimidation, and, finally, fear. Adam dealt with a man called Whistle, a common thug, who told him which games were to be fixed, how much he was going to receive, and what would happen to him and his wife, especially his wife, if he changed his mind or if, for whatever reason, things didn't come out the way they had been structured.

"I made six hundred thousand a game last year. We arranged three games. It's easy. I fumble the snap, or I change my cadence, just once a game, to draw one of my own linemen offsides, or I throw the ball just a foot too far or to the wrong side. Simple. Nobody knows; nobody suspects. It's a game of inches and breaks, and who can blame the quarterback for those things? I feel lousy, Eddie. I've been crapping on the game and my career and everything I ever got out of football."

Ed nodded in agreement. "You're right, Adam, and nothing anybody says is gonna make that come out any different. But why do it at all? What made it something to even consider? You didn't really do it just for the money, did you?"

"Hell, no. I make too damned much and I'd probably play for expenses, food, and a place to live if somebody asked. It was the cocaine, Eddie. I got myself an addiction, and that costs more, and the longer you do it the more you need, and that runs up the price, and it's absolutely true that if you can get all you need without worrying you can play well enough so that nobody will think anything's wrong. I use an untraceable masking agent when we take the urine tests. I couldn't do this for another whole season, and I am cutting way down, but this is no problem at all."

"So what happened? Why the guilt now, after all the damage

has been done? This is starting to sound like some fucking soap opera, you know?" Ed knew he sounded more indignant than he wanted to, than he had intended, and was still trying to remember that Adam Benson was his friend, that they went back a long way, that according to his ever-increasing sense of perspective that seemed to go hand in glove with the years old friendships were to be cherished and preserved.

"I just don't want to do it anymore," Adam whispered. "I don't want to lose; I don't want to be on somebody's string. I'm still a great quarterback, and I want to go out as one. Not like this. Not like some slug that crawls back under a rock after he dirties something good and clean. I'm going to be putting my ass on the line, and worse yet, I'm going to be jeopardizing Sherri, but I can't live with myself anymore. That's it. I am going back to playing quarterback, and the bad guys are going to have to find themselves another boy. I told them. Last week. I said we will probably lose the game to the Giants, but if we do, it won't be because I didn't try to beat their brains out first. Hey, what can they do, sue me? Report me to the police?"

"No, you asshole, they can kill you."

"Never. They're gamblers, not murders, not Mafia guys with flat noses. Forget them; it's over. All I want to be able to do now is play football and get out of this without people knowing what a shit I've been."

"They can and they will kill you."

"I know none of this gets in the papers, Ed. I know that. It's why I decided to tell you. You're my friend and I had to get this out, had to share it with someone I trust. I hope you don't think I'm just another prick, but I am and if you did, you'd be right. And I'm sorry. I know what football means to you, and believe it or not, but it's my life and I don't want to fuck it up. It just happened. I got trapped by the good times and then it was too late and I was in too deep to get out. Or so I thought. But I'm out of it now and I'm going to stay out of it. I'm going to be the best damned quarterback you ever saw."

Ed shook his head. "You always were, Adam. You always were."

Adam nodded, moved as if to leave, then suddenly grabbed Ed in an impulsive bear hug before turning and walking out of the apartment.

Ed walked aimlessly from room to room, the silence painfully loud, his mind swirling with confusion as he tried to fit things into the logical, newspaper style of organization that was the only way he could ever feel comfortable. Finally he went to the counter between the kitchen and the dining room that he used as a bar and poured a vodka, straight. It didn't much help; it was without taste. He sat on the couch, staring at nothing but the dark. It wasn't over. Things were never that simple, especially with such danger present and so much at stake. Where were the responsibilities and obligations this time? According to the rules by which he lived, he should have had no problem. He should have called his boss, the department head, and demanded a meeting with the overall editor of the newspaper, perhaps with the publisher and the corporate lawyers as well, to determine a course of action, since such a story had to be printed.

Had to be printed.

But it wouldn't be, not yet, anyway, because Adam Benson was his friend, because he felt his friend's life was at risk, and because he would do nothing to adversely affect that. It was a long time before Ed slept, and when he did, it was fitful at best.

THREE

IT was October 29, the anniversary of the crash of the New York Stock Exchange, but unlike that suicidal day in 1929, this one was sunny and crisp, the morning light more golden than pastel, extending the promise of that special kind of autumn day so rare as to perfectly define the season.

Ed had slept poorly, but sitting on the couch staring out into the blackness of Manhattan had done nothing to provide answers to those questions concerning his professional ethics and responsibilities. He had no idea how he would handle the story of this game, but in the end that was of secondary significance. He was still worried for his friend, now more than ever.

But perhaps things would work out just as Adam had suggested. A game scheduled to be fixed would instead be played honestly, and by the best quarterback in the league. To whom, indeed, would the fixers complain? Besides, as Adam had also posed, there was a chance no one would ever know. The Giants were far superior to Chicago, and even if Benson was able to call upon his magic again, even if the offensive line suddenly became capable of blocking and protecting him, the Giants had more than enough offense, more than enough defense, and there seemed no doubt that they were going to make this season one for their fans to remember. Maybe the Bears would lose by more than the required margin; maybe the man Adam called Whistle would shrug, convinced that the quarterback had merely been shooting off his mouth and wouldn't have the nerve, at crunch time, to really renege against such dangerous men. Maybe.

Being a New Yorker, a status conferred only on those who

live and work in four of the five boroughs that make up the largest city in the nation—Staten Island is far too suburban and removed to count and should be part of New Jersey anyway—Ed Buck didn't own a car. In fact, he had allowed his New York State driver's license to lapse several years ago. So going to a game at Yankee Stadium meant using the subway, the IRT train from the Lexington Avenue stop at 77th Street for the forty-five-minute trip.

There was no commuter crowd at ten o'clock Sunday morning, few suspicious-looking travelers whom Ed would associate with muggings and violence, and certainly no reason for delay. The trip was without incident, but the unusual peace and quiet of the underground, although it gave Ed more time to think, got him no closer to resolving his personal conflict. Adam Benson had put him in an untenable position, and he resented it.

By eleven-fifteen he was sitting in a quiet corner of the press lounge, sipping coffee from a plastic cup, thumbing through a week-old copy of the *Giant,* an independently produced tabloid-sized fan's newspaper that had dramatically increased in circulation and impact over the last few years. Most of the sportswriters assigned to cover the team were paid for freelance feature articles, and six months earlier the owners had managed to lure one of the best newspapermen in the area, an unrelenting Giant fan from the *Daily News* named Al Savill, to become the publication's first full-time editor. He had immediately injected a new look and verve, as well as some controversial content, to the extent that the team had begun to pay attention and show annoyance at editorial opinion with which it didn't agree. That was par for the course.

Vinnie Gordo and Stan Bradley, the "Double-Team Team" from the *Daily News* who spent the entire season with the Giants, on the road and at home, wandered into Ed's corner, carrying briefcases, portable computers, and cups of coffee.

"Hey, reading up on what's new and breaking?" asked Bradley, a tall gangly black man who had played basketball at Fordham while majoring in Obnoxious 101.

Ed smiled. "You bet, Stanley. I tried to find out what's new and breaking in the *Daily News* this morning, but then I made a mistake and read your story. So I didn't learn a thing."

Gordo laughed. He was short and stout, a student of the game who still, down deep, was in awe of Ed Buck the former All-American football player. "They win today by four touchdowns, Ed," Vinnie said. "The way the Bears are playing, we can start writing our leads by halftime."

"What? And miss those vintage hot dogs? Today's are from 1958. You remember what a great year that was for dog meat, don't you?"

The repartee was forced. Ed was uncharacteristically silent, and as soon as his two visitors realized it, they drifted off to find better company until the game started. Ed went back to the *Giant*, not even knowing what he was reading, just marking time until the next part of the day, the one he felt might turn out to be far more important than the game but one he wished he didn't have to view, began to take shape.

At twelve-forty-five he took the elevator to the press box on the fourth level, which actually was too high. But the Boland brothers, who owned the team, weren't about to pass up the chance to rake in exorbitant prices from three thousand of the best seats in the old stadium they had arranged for the city to renovate into luxury suites at the taxpayers' expense by holding out the threat of taking the team to the Jersey Meadowlands. Besides, the Bolands had never much cared about the newspapers, and it was universally felt that this lack of concern was easily explained: they couldn't read them, so why help them?

The high school band of the week, invited without an offer of expenses and "paid" with the worst, field-level, end zone seats, tooted its way through the national anthem. Four Chicago captains met at midfield with six New York captains, and after introductions were completed the Giants won the coin toss and chose to receive. Harland Vares kicked off for the Bears, Spider Keyes took it at the fifteen-yard line and returned it to the forty-five, great field position, and the capacity crowd, even before most had reached their seats, began its rhythmic, patented chant of: "*Score . . . score . . . score . . .*"

The Giants' quarterback, Gary Feller, went for it all on the first play. And he got it, throwing a deep sideline pass to the right flanker, Billy Joe Booker, who snatched the ball away from the Bears' left cornerback, Horace Jacobs, recklessly cutting across the receiver's path, looking for the interception. Booker, who possessed world-class sprinter's speed and had been an Olympic silver medalist three years earlier, had no trouble losing the frantic outside linebacker as well as the free safety, who had been caught totally unaware and never had a chance to catch the speedster despite having the angle. Jacobs simply stood at the sideline, head down, kicking at an imaginary divot in one of the league's last real grass-dirt fields, nothing artificial, not AstroTurf or TartanTurf or SmurfTurf.

With just fifty-three seconds elapsed in the game, Vares' extra point made the score 7–0. The anticipated rout evidently had begun. Ed relaxed, certain that Adam Benson, even on his greatest day, couldn't stem this tide.

The Giants kicked off. Chicago's James Truman took the ball at the goal line, eluded one tackler at the ten, sidestepped another at the thirty-three, and suddenly, impossibly, streaked between two Giants at midfield and was untouched, alone, uncatchable, all the way into the end zone. The scoreboard clock, which had read 14:07 when Feller threw the fifty-five-yard touchdown pass to Booker, showed 13:40. The score was tied.

Now the Bears kicked off. Keyes was snowed under by a gang of tacklers at the Giants' twenty-four, and three plays later Billy Anderson had to punt out of trouble. Finally, with possession on the Bears' forty, Adam Benson took the field.

Ed had seen Adam play for too long, had been there when the fire began to stoke itself, had been part of the electricity when he got himself psyched to play, and was able to tell, just from the bounce in his step and the almost spastic motion of his hands, that this was going to be one of those days. Ed had often ruminated over a theory he knew he would put into practice if ever he coached Adam Benson. He had even mentioned it once to Walter Raye when he took over as the Giants' head coach. They were talking about Ed's days at Oklahoma and Raye's at Alabama—they were approximately the same age, and

in fact, Raye had been a senior at Alabama when Ed was a freshman at Oklahoma—on a late-night coast-to-coast flight. "Honest, Walter, I remember when we got a good quick start," Ed
said, "he'd get all excited and damned near jump up and down
and play his ass off the rest of the game."

"Yeah, I remember, especially when you guys beat the piss
out of us in the Orange Bowl. I thought that was about the best
game I ever saw a quarterback play, you know?"

Ed had smiled, clearly recalling that 30–27 victory so long
ago, when Alabama had taken a 24–9 lead into the fourth quarter.

"So what would you do, Ed, if you were his coach?"

"Shit, Walter, the first play I'd call would be a short pass, a
little baby pass, two yards to the sideline. Just so he gets to
complete his first one. I mean, the man goes absolutely out of
his fucking mind. You can see it. He comes back to the huddle
talkin' a mile a minute and jumping up and down and all excited to get the next play called. I mean, he almost fucking stut-
ters and wets his pants, he's so keyed up."

Raye had nodded and, like all coaches, filed away the information for possible future use, either for the day he might find
himself coaching Adam Benson or, more likely, for a day when
he might have to coach against Benson in a crucial game. Besides, it was a tip from another football player, someone who
had been there, who knew, who wasn't just another asshole reporter.

Ed saw the signs. He knew Adam had decided to forget that
this game was supposed to be lost. He knew, with a mixture of
excitement and fear, that Adam Benson was about to stick it to
the gamblers, the guys who control the money and the drugs
and who sometimes choose to put an end to a life without feeling a twinge of conscience.

Adam knelt on one knee in the huddle, one of his trademarks.
Ed could see Adam's hands drawing diagrams in the air, his
head bobbing, his body tensing and relaxing, tensing and relaxing. *He's going to have one of those games,* Ed thought. *He's
going to tell the bad guys to shove it.*

The Bears broke the huddle. Benson crouched behind the

center, barked signals, barked again, again. The forty-second clock counted itself down, and just before it would have expired Adam took the snap, dropped back, faked a handoff to the fullback slamming up the middle to buy another few seconds, then veered to his right, apparently heading for the sideline, suddenly braking, almost skidding to a quick stop, and firing a line drive across his body, to his left, to the other side of the field.

It is the most difficult pass for a quarterback to throw, demanding not only timing and touch but also incredible arm strength and a large dollop of acting skill. Benson had it. Benson had also fooled the entire Giants' defense, because no one was there to defend against Ronnie Barnes, the halfback, who had slipped off to the left sideline and virtually walked downfield, waiting for the play to break.

Barnes caught the pass in stride, suddenly running full-speed, and was in the end zone before half the Giants knew what had happened. The play was so spectacular that the crowd, almost involuntarily, began to cheer, then, as if realizing it had happened against the Giants, choked off the noise. Ed Buck, sitting at his press station, felt his legs tighten, as if he were on the field, sharing in the excitement, basking again in the glow of a magical Adam Benson performance, feeling almost grateful to be allowed to be a part of it.

The Bears held the lead, and after a deep kickoff and some inspired defense they had the ball again, too, on their forty-seven. The first quarter was winding down, but Benson wanted another touchdown. He was having fun again, enjoying the lead, pleased with the play he had called to catch the league's best defense in high school embarrassment.

Adam handed off to Barnes after faking a toss to the fullback, and the play gained seven yards. Now Adam dropped back, stumbled, seemed about to be covered by hard-charging Giant defenders, and suddenly threw the screen pass to Barnes, who had stationed himself at the line of scrimmage. The right guard and the tackle, having allowed the defensive players to crash through, suddenly pulled out and set up a convoy for Barnes, who took the ball down to the Giants' eight-yard line before a desperate ankle-high tackle brought him down short of the goal line.

There was very little noise in the stadium now, although those who appreciated the rare talent they were watching were too enrapt to make any noise. They were studying Adam Benson, because few men had ever been able to lift quarterbacking to this particular state-of-the-art level.

From the eight, hands cupped tightly together underneath the center, Benson bellowed the signals. Ed could almost hear him on the field in Lincoln, Nebraska, or the Los Angeles Coliseum, or the Orange Bowl in Miami, could picture those games with the Sooners when Benson's genius hushed the crowds, when those rabid fans of the home team were forced to pay their respects to a genius. And it was happening again, right here in Yankee Stadium, in a game that should have been a pushover for the home team. Against their will, against their wishes, more than sixty thousand fans found they were forced to recognize a master.

Lifting his head from the possession chart he was filling in, Ed studied the Giants' defensive formation. Benson was spitting out signals, staccato, shrill, a voice Buck would have recognized anywhere in the world, anytime. And suddenly, perhaps because of nothing more than a gut feeling, perhaps because of the way Benson was almost fighting to keep his feet planted, Ed knew what he was going to do. It was a bootleg, the naked bootleg that even Benson's own players didn't know was coming, for that was the only way to keep it pure, to make it work. He had done it against Georgia once, and another time against Oklahoma State.

Jillian, the center, snapped the ball. Barnes, the halfback, had been set in motion, cutting back across the grain, just behind Benson, moving right, and Ed knew how surprised he was when Adam put the ball in his belly and then pulled it back. But Barnes was a professional, and it didn't take a fraction of a second for him to know he was the unsuspecting decoy. He never broke stride but clutched the imaginary football to his stomach and kept right on running.

The linemen, aware only of the play that had been called, a misdirection comebacker to the halfback in motion, had taken that first false step to their left and then cut-block the Giants by color, mowing down any blue uniform in their area of responsibility, generally no bigger than one yard square. It was called zone blocking, and it was especially effective in short-yardage situations. Nevertheless, what made it work was the natural execution by the other players, who sincerely believed in the play and therefore had no reason to show any brief glimpse of nervousness, which as a result would almost certainly tip off the real intent.

Adam Benson had the ball. Now, with the nerve of a gambler and the guts of a cat burglar, he tucked it tight to his right buttock and just for a second stood there, motionless, watching Barnes move to what everyone thought was going to be an attempt to score.

And then Benson began to amble to his left, gradually gaining speed. There was an instant flash of recognition on the face of the Giants' right outside linebacker, Tommy Taylor, when Benson swept past him. Right then, but forever too late, Taylor knew he had been duped, knew the entire defense had been duped, knew that Adam Benson had the ball and was going in for the touchdown, and knew there wasn't a thing in the world any of them could do about it. They had been suckered by an expert. For the second time in two consecutive series they had been set up by the master, then chopped in half by a classic opportunist.

Benson scored, and the Giants, reacting that split second too late, charged after him. So, too, did his own linemen, suddenly aware that they held a two-touchdown lead and now concerned with protecting their quarterback from the kind of punishment meted out by those who have been made to look foolish in front of their own.

The pileup was gigantic. It took a full minute to clear it, the officials pulling and tugging at the bodies, helping them off, getting them away, breaking up one minor skirmish between a Giant linebacker and Chicago's tight end.

But Adam Benson loved it, rolling over on the grass in the

end zone just over the goal line, laughing so loud the paying customers in the first few rows of the end zone seats could hear him distinctly. Football hadn't been fun in a long time, but today everything was right. Today beating the heavily favored Giants in New York, not only making it look easy but also subjecting the Giants to some real humiliation in front of their fans, made everything right. He had reason to laugh. It was the joy of a boy coming through the frustrations and worries of a man.

In the press box, the noise level grew as the clock ticked off the final seconds of the first half, and the grin on Ed Buck's face was hard to wipe off, even when fat Fred Harris, the Giants' business manager and an old friend of the owners, walked past.

"Hey, Buck, you rootin'?" he asked. "I don't see anything that damned funny."

"You wouldn't, Fred, because it's happening to you. Don't you see? Adam Benson is the best quarterback in the league. Remember three years ago, when the Bears were trying to trade him? Might have been a good idea if you had said yes, you know?"

Harris walked off grumbling about the front-running, ungrateful sportswriters who don't give a shit about the team but eat the free food and drink the free beer. Fat Fred was primarily concerned with that food and beer and, in fact, related most things in his life to a stuffed face and a bloated belly. That he knew next to nothing about football, that most of the other teams in the league wanted to trade with the Giants because they could almost always fool the guy, was a truth that didn't seem to matter, because he worked cheap and did exactly what the Boland brothers told him to do, and they really didn't care that much about whether the team finished as champions or in fourth place, just so long as the television revenue kept escalating. Besides, Fat Fred had played for the Giants years earlier, and the Bolands always rewarded such men, assuming it didn't cost much.

The Bears held a 21–7 lead, but there was ample reason to believe that the Giants would be able to come back and perhaps still win with convincing superiority, so there seemed no sense in starting to write the first-edition story. Ed confined himself to doing the running account of the first half, storing it in the computer for use only if the game should go into overtime and some type was necessary to fill the space for the street sales. The running was little more than a play-by-play recap of the four scoring drives plus some of the more noteworthy individual statistics. The afternoon-paper reporters didn't have to deal with such tedium; they had taken the elevator back to the lounge area, watching halftime highlights from other games on the television monitor or snacking on fat Fred Harris's cheap hot dogs.

Benson had gone through the roof, statistically, showing seven completions in eleven attempts for 204 yards, scored the two touchdowns, and thrown no interceptions. It had been a long time since Ed had seen his friend this good, perhaps not since that Super Bowl year when he won every award possible and set a league completion percentage record—78.2—that might stand forever. This was going to be a fun game to write, and because there was no one in the press corps who knew Benson (or football) nearly as well as Ed did. No one was aware that Adam had found all the glitches and holes in the Giants' highly publicized (and too unbending) semirevolutionary three-two-six defensive alignment and that such a masterful job of "industrial espionage" couldn't be wiped out during a brief halftime meeting. The Bears were going to win this game. That was guaranteed.

The second half had already started when the last few stragglers returned, mostly the radio guys whose microphones weren't necessary until afterward (and then just barely), who really showed up at the games to look for jobs and, of course, to see the action from the vantage point of "privileged citizen." The Giants kicked off, Chicago took over deep in its own territory, and Benson's problems with his offensive line became apparent. Jillian let the nose tackle through almost untouched, and Burton leveled Adam with a nine-yard sack.

Then the rookie tackle, Billy Lange, showed why he wouldn't stay long in the game, flat-out quitting (Ed saw it, but then Ed had been a tackle and knew what to look for) when the Giants' left defensive end, M. T. Marshall, hurt him with the only forearm shiver he was allowed, as part of his initial move at the snap of the ball. Marshall sluiced past the kid, showing incredible speed for a near-three-hundred-pounder, and Adam was down again, this time just as he was setting up seven yards deep in the backfield.

With third and twenty-six on the Bears' four-yard line, Adam chose caution as the greater part of valor, calling a simple fullback slam into the middle and giving the huddle up to the punter. The ball went to the Giants' forty-eight, Keyes wrestled for two yards on the return and Feller set the Giants in formation at midfield. It took five plays, the longest being the thirty-one-yard touchdown reception by the rookie halfback, Phil King, who had come in on third-and-seven as a blocking back but set off on a short circle pattern out of the backfield when the Bears didn't blitz but dropped into a seven-man coverage umbrella.

The score was thus narrowed to 21–14. The Giants' offense, at least, had made the proper adjustments. It was about to become evident whether the defense had a clue as to what it would take to cool off the white-hot Adam Benson. The Giants kicked off; Truman took it on the Chicago eleven and was cut down at the twenty-one. The crowd began to come alive, realizing that if the defense held here, the offense seemed more than capable of getting the tying touchdown.

The Bears' offensive players took the field, their orange-and-white uniforms already bearing the expected "Christmas tree" stains—green for grass, red for blood.

Benson was still on fire. On second-and-ten, he found the tight end clear across the middle for a twenty-one-yard gain to the Bears' thirty-two. On first down he threw a strike to Barnes, circling out of the backfield, and it was a twenty-two-yard gain, to the Giants' forty-six. Ed watched as Benson bounced and jumped and grew hotter still, keeping the ball on first down— almost unheard of in the NFL, considering the low-percentage nature of the call—and made six yards behind Lange, the rookie who couldn't play offensive tackle.

The ball was on the Giants' forty. The defense had been no more effective than tissue paper in a hurricane. This latest Bears' drive was the easiest yet, almost humiliating in its thoroughness, and the crowd had begun to boo. From the forty, Adam crouched behind the center, barked his signals, built in a long pause in an attempt to draw somebody offsides and get a bonus of five free yards, then took the snap and darted back on his toes, eyes scanning the defensive formation as it unfolded before him. He pump-faked once and took the Giants' left cornerback out of the play, waited for the wide receiver to make the cut to the inside, a deep, diagonal pattern, and let it fly. Connection! Completion! Only a spectacular knee-high tackle by a swiftly pursuing Taylor saved the touchdown, on the Giants' two.

No matter. A touchdown was inevitable, and the crowd knew it. A pallor fell across the field, giving Adam the chance to bark signals in such quiet that his voice could be heard in the press box: "On two, bingo, fourteen, six, twenty-eight, hut-hut-hut." On the final "hut," Jillian snapped the ball. Lange came down on the defensive tackle, jammed him laterally across the line of scrimmage; Jillian hesitated to allow the traffic to clear in front of him and then went searching for a blue shirt, finding the middle linebacker and mowing him down, creating the beginning of a massive pileup in the end zone. Adam Benson had the ball, of course, had followed Jillian's block, had waited with unnatural patience while Lange made his clearing, sealing block, and then drove headfirst into the end zone, realizing that he had scored when he saw the white goal line marker under his right shoulder.

The players on the Bears' sideline were up on their feet, jumping and waving upheld fists, knowing now for certain that they were part of a stunning upset.

The officials had blown their whistles, stopping the clock, and with the help of a few of them the players had begun to get back on their feet and allow those underneath to do the same. One by one they unpiled, the Bears running joyously to their bench, the Giant defenders, thoroughly confused, trudging with heads down to their sideline.

Ed Buck felt an inner satisfaction for his friend and watched the end zone to see how Adam was going to react now. He had taken the game by the nape of the neck and shook and shook until it came out right. There was virtually no chance that the Giants would be able to mount a comeback; one more Bears' score, even a field goal, would put this one out of reach. The gamblers and the fixers were fucked. Benson had told them that he was going to do it and he was doing it.

Adam was still lying across Bill Jillian's legs, motionless. Jillian was saying something to the official, old Jack Reader, hovering over them, who then bent and stared into Benson's face. Reader turned to the head linesman; Jillian scrambled out from under the quarterback and then gently turned him over on his back. Adam still hadn't moved. Ed saw the rolling gurney being trundled out from under the stadium tunnel in the opposite end zone, pushed by two white-coated paramedics, while the two team doctors sprinted for the end zone and arrived almost simultaneously, almost comically, to kneel on either side of the motionless player. Now they helped move him—gently, gently—to the stretcher, which had been lowered almost to ground level and was raised only after Benson had been carefully strapped in, helmet removed.

Ed thought it might be a spinal or head injury, considering the care with which the doctors had supervised the movement of his body. Now even thoughts of the fix, of the point-rigging scandals, of the threat to his friend's life were gone. This was injury, that most dreaded of events to a football player, and this seemed to be serious injury, perhaps career-threatening, especially at Benson's age. But Buck couldn't storm down to the training room; he was a member of the media and thus was expressly banned from the training room or the locker room proper, for that matter, when players and coaches were on the field. He would have to wait along with the others until an announcement was made.

The score was 28–14 when Vares kicked off for the Bears, and the ball bounced once at the Giants' nine before skidding into the end zone, where it was downed. Feller put the team in play from the twenty and netted only six yards in three plays against the fired-up Bears' defense, and the Giants had to punt.

But Ed's concentration was slipping. He had to know what was wrong with Benson, but repeated requests to both the Giants' publicity director, Don Carson, and his Chicago counterpart, Rick O'Donnell, had been fruitless.

"We'll make an announcement as soon as we know something, Ed," Carson said. "We can't get any word from their locker room yet."

"Fucking phone not working again?"

"No, it's working fine. They're just not answering it."

Ed went back to his seat, tried to pay attention, tried to keep up his charts, but his interest had waned appreciably. There was an undercurrent of unease throughout the press box; Ed could feel it.

Gordo, sitting near him, leaned over and put it into words: "The longer it takes, the more serious it must be, you know?"

"Yeah, I know, and there's nothing we can do. Drives me up the wall."

On the field, both teams had reached that point—which seems to arrive at least once in every football game—of total inertia. The Giants' defense had stiffened, or so it would appear, but the Bears' offense had flattened out, with a young and rarely used quarterback, Solomon Black, trying his best not to throw a pass, to keep the ball on the ground, clearly under orders, and allow the clock to finish the job that Adam Benson had started.

The fourth quarter was halfway over, the Bears still holding the 28–14 lead and moving downfield slowly but inexorably. The crowd had already begun to thin out, and with each first down in the ground-dominated drive more of the faithful got to their feet and made for the exit ramps. Ed stood up, perhaps for the first time in a year deciding not to wait for the end of the game and a complete chart. He was going downstairs, into the catacombs under the old stadium, to wait outside the visitors' locker room until he could get in and see what had happened to his friend.

There was already a crowd queued at the elevator, the "PRESS ONLY POSTGAME ELEVATOR" that the working press almost never got to use, it being crammed with friends of the Boland brothers, such as a local (not network) news anchorman, prematurely gray and prematurely senile, and his five friends, at least half a dozen of the more extravagant spenders among the advertisers, girlfriends (and their friends) of the Bolands (both of whom were married), and as many television cameramen and day-off personalities as could squeeze into the overworked car.

"Hey, Ed, how are you?" bellowed the news anchorman. "Come on. Push in here; we'll make room for you."

"Nah, thanks, Jim, I'll just hit the steps. You know I don't like to interfere with your parties," Ed snapped. "Have a safe trip."

There were three sets of stairs and two ramps that one could use to get to the basement entrance to the stadium, and Ed knew the route by heart. The paying customers seldom used this way out, even those few who were aware of it, and so there was no delay at all in reaching the ground floor. Pushing open the small door at the base of the final set of stairs, Ed half-trotted down the ramp and was in the corridor under the stadium, a roughly circular passageway off of which were locker rooms, ushers' changing rooms, ticket-counting facilities, support areas, three darkrooms for the photographers, and a large press working room, complete with folding wooden chairs and cinder-block walls.

About fifty feet past the press room was the visiting team's locker room, where a small cluster of press had already gathered, mostly the sidebar writers, the columnists, and a few photographers and cameramen.

Ed sidled up to Chuck Nolan, the Newark paper's rotund little columnist. "What's going on?" he asked.

"Not a damned thing, Eddie. It's spooky. No noise, nothing."

"Anything? Anybody come in, go out? Nothing?"

"Not a fucking thing. It's like the damned room is empty, you know? They're gonna open the door and there won't even be stools."

The sound of the crowd insinuated its way into the basement corridors, and Ed always marveled at the fact that the officials' whistles sounded louder down here, echoing and reverberating, than they ever did on the field. Finally the gun—the game was over. In a few minutes, the Bears came tramping down the field ramp, yelling, clapping backs, clapping hands, dirty and scuffed, uniforms grass-stained and blood-blotched, whooping with the thrill of a soundly administered beating of a heavily favored team.

Behind them came the coaches, the trainers, the equipment men, then O'Donnell, the publicist.

"Just give us a minute, guys," he said. "I'm sure this door will open soon. We won, right?"

The door closed. For a few more seconds there were the normal sounds of a team shedding gear, popping beer cans. Then, at once, silence, followed almost immediately with a keening, moaning sound that reached its icy fingers out into the corridor through the door and chilled the heart and marrow.

Ed knew.

The door opened and it was O'Donnell, accompanied by the team's owner, Johnson Dillard, a good-old-boy type with a red face and a broad girth, but now his eyes were red, his speech tentative.

"Gentlemen," he began, "it is with the utmost sadness that I must inform you that Adam Benson has suffered a fatal heart attack. He died the way he would have wanted, as a winner, with the ball in his hands and a touchdown on his final play." With that, Dillard broke down completely, leaving it to the equally red-eyed O'Donnell to fill in some of the necessary details.

"Dr. Thomas Mannion examined Benson on the field when the players realized he wasn't moving and exhibited no signs of life. Dr. Mannion was unable to get a pulse, determined that Adam was not breathing, and administered mouth-to-mouth resuscitation. To no avail. Oxygen was administered in the locker room, as was a derivative of adrenaline, by injection directly into the heart. At 4:34 P.M., Eastern Standard Time, Adam Benson was pronounced dead of cardiac arrest. His body has been taken to St. Vincent's Hospital, where an autopsy will be performed tonight. His widow, Sherri Benson, has been notified and will arrive at seven o'clock tomorrow morning from Los Angeles. Funeral arrangements are incomplete at this time."

The ground began to sway, and Ed fought for balance and control. *Adam Benson dead? Never. No man had ever been more alive, more in love with life. Dead of a heart attack? A joke, a macabre joke played by a fiend. Adam Benson dead? No one with such skills, with such verve and daring, could just stop living. No one, especially not Adam Benson. Remember? The games won when all was lost? The special magic that poured out of him and enclosed everyone around him? Come on, God, stop screwing around. A bad joke, baby. Make him live again. Make this nightmare stop. Adam Benson can't be dead. He's thirty-seven years old, an athlete, a man for whom such things as the Hall of Fame and megadollar contracts were invented. Dead?* "Bullshit!" Ed Buck screamed, and then the pain wrenched his body and the sobs constricted his chest and he wailed at the loss of a friend.

Gordo, who knew the relationship, who knew the closeness, came to Ed and put an arm around him. "Come on, Ed; let's go get a drink. Come on; I'll drive you home."

"No, I want to go to the hospital. I want to wait there until somebody he knows gets there. I'll call his father. I knew him pretty well. Vinnie, can you get me to St. Vincent's?"

Vinnie nodded. "Sure, Ed, but aren't you going to write?"

Like he had been slapped in the face, like ice water had been poured on him while he was sunbathing asleep, Ed Buck was jolted into control and composure. "Yeah, first we write; then the hospital. If Adam is really dead, he's gonna be that way a long time. Thanks, Vinnie. Let's go upstairs."

The story was of the death, not the game. But the story of the death in no way mentioned the information Adam Benson had given Ed the night before. This was not the time. This was not the way to bury a friend. There would be time for investigation and research, but not now. Now was time to mourn.

FOUR

LEIGH Crespino knew better. She had been involved with bachelors before—several of them, in fact—and she recognized that the longer they lived with themselves and their bachelor status, the better they liked it, the more accustomed to it they grew, and the harder it was to convince them that marriage was even a semiviable alternative.

But while those others all had been nice guys with something decent or meaningful to bring to a relationship, Leigh had escaped being stricken with that malady called love—until Ed Buck. She knew she was in deep trouble with this one, because she wanted to be with him no matter what, marriage or no marriage.

That wasn't how it all started out, of course. But so what? It was exactly how things were now. She knew where she was with him, knew all about the weird hours and the unexpected trips and the hardening status of his bachelorhood. It wasn't her idea of satisfying, but she had already told herself that whatever the structure of their relationship, she had no choice but to accept it. She did love him, and somehow, she hoped, there would be marriage in their future.

He called at two in the morning, but when the telephone rang she already knew who it was and what it was about. She had heard about Adam Benson, of course, and had tried to reach Ed with no success, realizing after an hour of dialing his apartment that he'd still be at the stadium or the office or even the hospital or morgue. She knew he was hurting, knew he was in pain, had no idea where to find him, and so she waited. Just waited. Leigh

Crespino had been doing a lot of waiting for the past year, all in the name of Ed Buck.

She reached for the phone, also knowing that she was the first person to whom he had reached out, and that pleased her very much.

"Ed? Where are you?"

"Downstairs, here. Can I come up?" His voice was thin, fragile, shaky.

"Of course. Wait a minute." Leigh put the receiver back in its cradle, then dialed 0323, the code built in to the apartment's security system that opened the double doors, extra-thick and bullet-proof, to the elevators. She tugged on jeans, slipped on a sweater, left her feet bare, and walked into the living room, arriving at the door almost at the second Ed did, opening it and then her arms, holding him close, tightly, while silent sobs, without tears, more like muscle spasms, took control of him.

Then it was over. Abruptly, as if he had once again looked at himself and, despising weakness, pulled himself away from his emotions, creating an artificial sense of calm and dispassionate involvement.

"You heard?"

"Yes, I heard," Leigh said. "The radio said heart attack. Is that what it was?"

"So far that's all we know." Ed headed for the overstuffed soft leather couch, kicking off his shoes as he fell back into it. "I waited until his father showed up. You remember me talking about Andy Benson? The toughest old man I ever met? He wasn't so tough when he saw me at the hospital, Leigh. That old guy just fell apart, cried like a baby, held onto me, and . . . damn, it was terrible. I was trying so hard not to do that, not to come apart, and then that old man broke up and I went with him. We just held onto each other in the lobby and cried and cried. He's alone, old Andy Benson. His wife died about six years ago and he moved from the farm they had to Scranton and now he's got nobody. Adam's brother lives in Florida, and his sister is married to some Oregon dentist. They put him in a room there, gave him something to make him sleep. I'll go back tomorrow when Sherri gets in from California."

Leigh went to him again, sat next to him, and just held on, saying nothing, just being there. Ed gripped her hard, embracing her warmth, her silence, a confirmation of sorts that life and breath still existed.

"Coffee?" she asked. "Or a drink?"

He managed a wan smile. "Coffee, baby. I've had enough tonight."

She padded into the small kitchen, her jet-black hair tumbling around her shoulders and partially across her face, found the coffee canister without turning on the overhead light, and measured enough for a full pot. She had a feeling this was going to be an all-night catharsis, and she was ready for it, for it meant drawing even closer to Ed. While the coffee was dripping into the pot, she took a bottle of Ketel One, ice cubes, and two pony glasses, stacked them on a tray, then grabbed two mugs from the cabinet over the sink. By the time she had collected spoons, the sugar bowl, napkins, and the mugs, the coffee had finished dripping, and balancing the whole assortment, she arrived back in the living room to find Ed staring into space, looking out at nothing.

She poured, and still he said nothing. She pushed the mug at him, touched his arm, and caused him to look around; just for a fraction of a second, he was surprised to find her there, confused at where he was. It was just a fleeting look, crossing his face the way a shadow might, and then he seemed to register his contacts and looked at her with a sad, small smile.

"I've got to talk to you about something," he said softly. "I don't really want to, and I probably shouldn't, but I've got to tell somebody and you're it."

"Shoot," Leigh said. "I can take anything."

He shook his head. "No, this isn't funny. This is dead serious, and I don't know why I just don't go to the police, which I probably will. But I need your opinion. You have the best mind I know, and I want your input. This is dangerous, and before I start, I want to you know that it's OK if you tell me not to say anything, that you don't want to hear this stuff, any of it. I love you, Leigh, and I want to include you, but I love you so much

I don't want to be the cause of you getting hurt, either. So quickly, say it, before I start talking."

It was her turn to shake her head. "You look here, you dope," and her voice was louder and more strident than she wanted it to be, and her voice shook with more emotion and frustration than she could have expected. "You look here, you fucking idiot. I love you. I want to marry you. I don't want to be your girlfriend, you moron, I want to be your wife, and that means for the whole deal. If there's something you can't tell anybody in the world, you can tell it to me. If there's something you want to do so awful and so horrible that nobody in the world will let you do it, I'll let you. I love you, you idiot. Now tell me what you have to say so that you can be finished and I can take you into my bed and fuck your eyes out."

That, finally, brought the smile to his face.

"On one condition."

"Oh, you infuriating man. OK, what?"

He smiled again. "The condition is, that if I tell you all this terrible stuff, and if I tell you what I'm going to do about it, then you have to marry me, because a wife can't be forced to testify against her husband. OK?"

She was totally without the ability to speak, but a shriek came from her lips and she clutched him around the neck so tightly that for a minute he feared for his windpipe. "Marry you? What the hell do you think I've been talking about for a year? Marry you? Only somebody as crazy as I am would even consider it. Marry you? Yes. When? Tomorrow? Wednesday?"

Their next embrace was for a much longer period of time, and it wasn't necessary for them to speak, yet in that fearful, trembling embrace both of them said all that can ever be said and all that ever need be said.

They withdrew then, took their coffee mugs in hand, and with Leigh staring directly into his eyes, Ed Buck told her everything Adam Benson had told him. Everything.

"And so maybe you can see," Ed said hours later, when he had finally finished, when he had cried and remembered the old times at Oklahoma, when he had cried and admitted that his best years were gone, when he had cried and lamented his lost youth, "so you can see, maybe, why I don't think I can believe a heart attack. Adam was beating the shit out of the Giants, but more important, he was doing a million-dollar number on some very bad people. I know, I know. It's impossible to kill a football player on the field during a game. It's impossible. He wasn't shot and he wasn't stabbed and I know it's absolutely impossible, but he's dead and he was too young to die and not that way, for sure, and it's just too much of a fucking coincidence."

His voice was hoarse by now, his words cracking, barely audible. He paused, drew in one more large gulp of air, and said, "Leigh, somebody killed my friend. I'm going to find out who, and how, and you have to help me."

She nodded her head, her cheeks damp with tears. "Yes, I will," she said. "Now let's go to bed, and one day soon, when this is over, let's go and get ourselves married. OK?"

"OK," he said.

They cried again, together. And then they made love, and it was never that good before, and as Ed drifted into sleep, as the sky over Manhattan was turning pink-orange, he heard Leigh say, "Good night, my husband," and he thought he'd never heard anything quite that perfect in his life.

They slept for only a few hours and felt more tired than before when they awoke, and with a gripping sadness Ed realized that all of what had happened the day before was not only real but forever. Adam Benson was still dead.

FIVE

HER face streaked with dry and drying tears, Sherri Novak Benson looked across at the man sitting behind an ornate mahogany desk.

"He didn't have to die, Billy. He didn't have to die."

The man was short and squat, a fire hydrant with arms and legs, no more than five-feet-five, but he weighed every bit of 250 pounds. He fiddled with an enormous gold pinkie ring, twisting it around and around his stubby finger while he talked.

"Yeah, he did. He was gonna turn us in. He made a deal with us, he took the money, he knew how it was, and he was gonna fuck it all up and turn us in. You know that. He told you." He looked up at her, smiled a chilling smile, and added: "He told you, and then you told us. Remember?"

Adam Benson's widow began to cry again and started to get up from the chair to leave, but the big man standing behind her, the only other person in the room, reached out and put a hand on her shoulder. She sat back down.

"You have to go to New York," the man, Billy DeSalvo, continued, pretending not to hear her cry or to have seen her attempt to leave. "You have to be the perfect widow. You are going to get your husband's body and bring it to wherever you want it buried, and there is gonna be a funeral and all the newspapers and television and the radio stations are going to be there and you are going to cry and look pretty and keep your mouth shut and that is going to be the end of it. You knew what he was going to do, and you know what you want, what you need from us. You know it wasn't really a personal thing; he just made a mistake and we had to stop him from making a bigger one. Hey, chickie, you didn't have much of a marriage anyway, remember?"

Sherri Novak nodded slowly, still crying, as much for her complicity and her charade with Adam as for the death of the man to whom she had been married for just two years. He was dead. That was fact. But she still had needs, and Billy DeSalvo was going to meet them. All she had to do was mourn, and then keep quiet. But Adam was dead, the most exciting man she had ever met, ever, in all her twenty-six years. He was kind and decent, too, and she hadn't known a man like that since her father died. She had been seventeen then, and in less than six months she was out of the house in Buffalo, first going to Miami Beach, then Las Vegas, finally Los Angeles, always trading with her body, eventually meeting up with people like Billy DeSalvo, ultimately finding her answers in the drugs that made her need more and tied her to DeSalvo and all the ones before him.

In the last year, she had come to admit to four needs in her life, and three were still within reach if she played her cards right: she wanted to be in the movies; she wanted all the cocaine she would ever need without worrying about how she was going to pay for it; she wanted lots and lots of money, fuck-you kind of money; and she wanted to stay married to Adam Benson. Now he was gone, but the other three goals were there, right in front of her, close enough to touch. She nodded her head again, reached out for the airplane tickets DeSalvo held out to her, as well as a small plastic bag filled with white powder and a set of credit cards. But for a long moment he kept them just out of her reach.

"It's nine o'clock now," DeSalvo said, grinning again. "The red-eye leaves at twelve. The credit cards are in your name, the tickets are first class, there's enough shit in the bag to last you two weeks . . . even you, baby . . . and in the ticket envelope you got ten thousand bucks in cash." He completed the short instructions and leaned back in the reclining leather chair. "You go to New York, buy whatever you need, spend whatever you want, take care of all the questions, but don't really say nuthin' to nobody and get back here as soon as you can. First thing, no fuckin' around or stopping off someplace. We got what you want, the movie deal is about to get made, and you may have to start workin' in less than a month. You know, you might be a star yet, and with a dead football hero for a husband it could happen even sooner. You got all that?"

Sherri nodded. "Yeah, Billy, I got it," she said, her voice tight, controlled. "I got the money and the tickets and the shit. And I got no husband now, but I got you, and dipshit over here"—she nodded at the big man still hovering behind her chair—"and I got whoever you want me to have, right? What else do I need, right, Billy?"

He said nothing.

"I also got more on you than you want anybody to know, Billy, so how do I know you don't plan to blow up the damned plane tonight? How do I know that, Billy? How do I know that, my friend?"

The chill become a real and palpable presence in the room. "You don't, you stupid broad; you don't. But it wouldn't look good to make you dead now, see? Too soon. It wouldn't be smart. The fucking football player drops dead in a game and the same night the widow's plane explodes when she goes cross-country for the body? Too soon, too stupid. Maybe we'll get around to you in a month, two months, six. Maybe a year. You know, we got people who can make you wish we only wanted you dead, especially a nice head like you. You know why else we ain't gonna kill you? Because we can use you. Because you are the nicest-looking piece of ass I have ever seen and guys will turn over their mothers to us just to get close to you. Because you can even act. Because we have already invested a bunch of dollars in your ass.

"But mostly, because Mr. Assante likes you. Me, I could kill you in a minute. I could watch somebody else kill you. I could take fuckin' Polaroid pictures of it and save 'em. You know why? Because to me you're just another broad. There are great broads all over, you know? Prettier, sexier, bigger tits, great legs, and they would do anything, and I mean anything, to get where you're goin'. And they have. You know what else? There are even great broads who don't have to put shit in their noses every four fuckin' hours, too. But see, we got you to need it, we made you need it, and now we know you're comin' back, and we know you're gonna keep your mouth shut, too. We own you, and you know it."

He stood, walked around the desk to the chair where Sherri Benson was sitting. He leaned down and spoke right into her face, inches away, close enough for her to smell his breath, to feel the flecks of spittle as he raised his voice, to see the dilated pupils in his black, hateful eyes. "We own you, don't we?"

She nodded her head, weeping.

"Answer me."

"Yes, Billy, you do. You own me. Mr. Assante owns me. Anybody else you want to own me owns me. Billy, please, I'm hurting; can I use some now?"

Billy DeSalvo smiled. It was going to get worse. She knew it. "Not yet. First there's something I want you to do for me, now, here." He nodded at the big man, and big, stupid Rico Scalzi walked around to the front of the chair.

"Billy, for God's sake, Adam's dead. Today. Billy, not now. Please, Billy, don't make me."

"Now, damn it!" he barked.

Sherri Novak Benson stood, the silk dress clinging to her body. She reached her hands up behind her neck, unbuttoned the collar, and shrugged the dress off her shoulders to the floor. She wore no bra, and her breasts, nipples already hardening, thrust upward, as fine as any Billy had ever seen. She stood in her high heels and skimpy bikini panties, then bent, hooked her thumbs in the elastic and slipped off the whispering fabric, it, too, falling to the carpeted floor.

DeSalvo stood back and gazed at this most erotic of bodies, the front of his trousers already tenting. With no expression showing on her face, Sherri Novak Benson began to pinch her breasts, then lifted them gently, pushing them together, then dropped her hands to the wispy blond curls at her pelvis and softly inserted a finger into her vagina, the fingers of her other hand caressing herself.

"Sit down," he said, and she did.

Billy nodded again, and Rico Scalzi undid his trousers, letting them fall around his ankles.

DeSalvo handed Sherri Benson the small plastic bag. With one hand she worked Scalzi's already-rising organ into a full erection; with the other, she tapped out a measure of the white powder onto its purplish, rigid head.

"Go ahead, Mrs. Benson, snort your coke," DeSalvo said, "and when you get the high, make sure you show Rico just how grateful you are."

Sherri Benson bent to her task, and neither man noted or would have cared about the new flood of tears that blurred her vision. In a minute, neither did she. The rush, the high, was all she wanted. The rest would pass.

SIX

"I'VE got a friend in the police department," Ed said, turning to Leigh in bed shortly after seven o'clock.

They had managed to sleep for a couple of hours. She looked up, saw his drawn, pale face, and realized nothing was going to be all right until his friend was buried and the murderer identified and caught; although she had serious doubts that it was murder, she kept them to herself. She also realized that getting married would have to wait, but that was all right. They were going to be married, and that was all that counted for the time being.

"Are you going to call him?" she asked.

"Yeah, I think so. But that's not the first thing. I have to go to the hospital and check on Adam's father, and his wife should be landing any minute. She might need a place to stay, somebody to be with. I don't know what to do first. The hospital, I guess."

"Do you want me to go with you?"

"I'd love it. But don't. Stay here. I need to know I can call you. Can you stay home today? Not go to work?"

"Of course. How about your friend? The policeman?"

Buck nodded. "He's not a cop, exactly; he's a detective. Not exactly a detective, either, but he used to be. He's assistant to the chief of detectives. I think he can pull enough strings to find out what happened."

"Should I call him?"

Ed nodded. "Yeah, that's a good idea. See if he can meet me tonight, at my place. His name is Gerry Keegan. Lieutenant Joseph Gerard Keegan, working out of the Foley Square head-quarters building."

"OK, darling. But let's make it here tonight, not your place. In fact, let's make this place your place. Permanently. How about if I go over to your apartment later and find some clothes and stuff?"

He smiled, nodding his assent.

They got out of bed then, showered together, and while Leigh set up the coffee machine Ed shaved and dressed. She was on the telephone, her back to him, when he walked into the kitchen.

"Tell Dirty Dave that I can't come in today, or tomorrow, or maybe the rest of the week, Doris. Tell him I don't want to get fired, but if that's how he feels, maybe I'll just quit. This is more important."

But she was smiling. David Drexler, founder and president of one of New York's most successful advertising agencies, might not even realize that Leigh Crespino was missing for a day or two. She was one of his staff of four secretaries, but he was so seldom in the suite of offices that her absence might be covered for a week. On the other hand, the last thing he'd want to do would be fire Leigh Crespino. With her quick mind and natural instinct for where to advertise which product she had quickly become a valuable asset to DD Ads, Inc.

"I'm here for as long as you need me to be here," she said, smiling, when Ed walked up behind her. "Coffee?"

He gulped half a mug while standing at the window, looking out at Second Avenue and the cords of traffic already coiling and snarling. "I just can't believe he's dead," he said. "I'll call," he added, returning from wherever he had so briefly been, and was gone.

Leigh sat at the small pedestal kitchen table, sipping coffee, trying to sort through at least those things near the surface of her consciousness. Ed's friend was dead, a spectacular event in terms of who he was and where it had happened. Ed had been privy to confidential information about gambling and game fixing, and in his mind the coincidence was too neat, too pat.

He was going to need her over the next few weeks, for both emotional support and help. She wouldn't fail him.

Leigh reached for the phone and dialed 411 for information. "Yes, operator, New York Police, Foley Square precinct, please. No, this is not an emergency."

She waited, finally heard the electronic, metallic voice, and copied down the number spit out by the computer. She dialed, and a male voice, interspersed with the intentionally audible regulated beeps of a recording device, informed her that she had, indeed, reached "Foley Square, New York Police Department, Sergeant Quinn."

"Is Lieutenant Joseph Keegan in, please?" she asked.

"Hold, please. Who's calling?"

"My name is Crespino. Leigh Crespino. He won't know me, but tell him I'm calling for Ed Buck. They know each other."

A pause. Static hummed in her ear, as well as the faint sound of someone else's conversation, not loud enough to make out the words but, because of the extremely overworked and overloaded New York telephone system, not an uncommon occurrence.

"Keegan," a man said, deep-voiced, cutting through the not-quite-noiseless silence of holding on.

"This is Leigh Crespino, Lieutenant Keegan. Ed Buck asked me to call. He thinks we're going to need your help. Unofficially, at least for now."

"We? Miss Crespino, have you finally gotten Big Ed to pair up? Congratulations. Tell that jerk it's about time. Now, what can I do? What does he . . . I'm sorry; what do the two of you need?"

"I don't know, Lieutenant," she began, thinking that he had the timbre of voice that made you like him, at least at first, "not exactly—"

He cut through her sentence. "It's Gerry," he said. "If you're the girl who has finally put a collar on Eddie Buck, we've got to be on a first-name basis. OK, Leigh?"

She smiled. She was sure she liked this man. "OK, Gerry. I'm not sure what Ed has in mind, but you heard about the football player who died yesterday?"

"Yes, Adam Benson. I imagine the whole country has heard about that. How is Ed involved?"

"Well, he isn't, Gerry, except that he and Benson were good friends. They played together at Oklahoma, stayed in touch all these years, and had dinner the night before the game. Saturday night. And Adam told Ed some things that make him suspicious now, after the death. I think he wants to see you, but off-the-record. Can we set that up?"

"Sure. Where and when?"

"Tonight, nine o'clock, my place. It's 200 East 68th Street, fifth floor, Apartment 515-B. And yes, Gerry, it's about to be our place."

She could hear him smile. "Just invite me to the wedding, and make sure it's Orthodox. His grandmother will refuse to come unless the food's kosher."

Lee Crespino was Italian, but she had already promised herself that if Ed Buck wanted to live in a Jewish home, under Hebrew laws, or Hindu or Buddhist or WASP, it would be her pleasure to learn the rules and put them into practice.

"We believe in great vodka and scotch, imported beer, and dinner, if you like," she said, smiling into the phone, "Gerry," she added.

He laughed. "I'm pleased to know that Ed found a girl without going outside his religion, either," he said. "Nine it is, but don't bother with the dinner."

SEVEN

BILLY DeSalvo was frightened, but not physically, not the way he used to be in the neighborhood when the big kids went after him.

This fear was different. This was the kind that comes when somebody very important is angry at something you did, when that important man can inflict severe pain and humiliation and can even instruct others to end your life.

Billy was stricken by that kind of fear because Adam Benson wasn't supposed to die, because Adam Benson wasn't supposed to do anything but continue to arrange the proper results of certain selected NFL games involving the Chicago Bears.

Billy was afraid of a man he had never met, whose real name he didn't know, and a man he would never know. But in the world in which Billy lived everybody knew of this man, a mystery to all but a few, a man truly to be feared because of who he was and the power he commanded.

The only name ever needed was Assante, and it was enough to cause even the most arrogant to pause and reflect. Once, only once, Billy had received a telephone call from Assante. It was almost seven years ago, when Billy had moved into the Los Angeles sports betting circle and made a few quick hits, reaching a few of the pro basketball players and realizing enormous profits from their subsequent efforts. What had amazed him the most was the relatively inexpensive toys and inducements he really needed.

The center of the Los Angeles Hoops, a seven-footer named

Marcellus Malone, wanted $25,000 a game for each game in which he would be asked to shave a few points. Billy DeSalvo, who had learned the art on the streets of Brooklyn, stalled. "It's too damned much, Marcellus; my people can't afford it. Come on; you'll make an extra grand a game and nobody is gonna know nuthin'. What's so bad about that?"

Marcellus was adamant. Billy allowed him to convince him to try, to let him believe that there was another "boss," a shadowy figure who had the power to make the decision, when in reality it was just Billy.

"I'll have to make a call," he said, finally, allowing himself to show just a trace of fear and a lot of reluctance. "You stand next to me. We'll either do it right now or it's no deal, never."

Malone couldn't wait. The two of them went into Billy's private office in the no-profit bar he had bought in a rundown section of LA, never intending for it to make money, and dialed, with great show, the local number for weather information. While the electronic voice droned on about clouds and humidity, he spoke to those anonymous people of his. "Yeah, that's right, Mr. Spencer. Marcellus says he won't do it for less than $25,000 a game. . . . Yeah, I know; we'll have to cut down the games. . . . I know. . . . No, sir, I don't think he'll do it for less." At this point, Billy looked over at Malone, who shook his head. "Right, that's what he says. . . . Well, OK. I think it's the right decision, Mr. Spencer. . . . Yes, sir, absolutely. We can trust this man."

He put the phone down slowly, looked at Marcellus Malone for a long, silent moment, then smiled broadly. "Well, you did it, big guy!" he shouted. "You got him to back down. Good job, 'Cell."

The fix stayed in place for two seasons, during which time Billy DeSalvo arranged for a total of ten games to be fixed. It wasn't too many, because Billy had learned a long time ago the penalties of greed. It cost him, as the sole operator of the scam, a total of $250,000 for Marcellus Malone. Billy made that much the first game, and by the time all ten had been played out, with only one "accident" along the way when Malone shot so badly he had been taken out of the game near the end and his replacement, trying to impress the coach, had scored the last eight points, Billy DeSalvo had taken in just short of $1 million bucks.

And the beauty part was that nobody else knew. Just Billy and the big spade, who finally crumbled under his cocaine habit and now was pushing a rag in a car wash.

It had been Billy's deal, Billy's plan to meet the player, to get friendly, to slowly work in the thought that there was money to be made, big money, without the Hoops even losing a game. "Just don't win by the spread," Billy had explained. "I'll tell you which games we want, I'll tell you what the number is, and you make sure the other team loses by less than that number. That's all. Nobody gets hurt; nobody has to lose a chance at a championship; nobody knows nuthin' but peace and quiet."

He sealed it by arranging regular visits by one of the most beautiful young girls he had ever seen, an eighteen-year-old named Sherri Novak, whom he had led into a major-league coke and heroin habit, and who, as a result, had developed an incredible lack of conscience and inhibitions.

And even she had no idea what was happening. She just did what she was told and Billy DeSalvo made sure she had enough shit. It was the sweetest deal ever. Big, big money and nobody knew.

Then Billy's telephone rang. Somebody knew.

"Billy DeSalvo?" a deep, hoarse voice nearly whispered.

"Yeah, who wants to know?"

"This is a friend of your father's, from New York. My name is Assante. I want you to stop dealing with the black, the basketball player."

Billy could still remember the way his hand shook. Damn, Assante. Everybody in the business knew of the Boss. Billy was no different. He knew all the things everybody else knew, had heard all the stories of violent, absolute vengeance, and had no interest in finding out whether he was "important" enough for Assante to assign someone to convince him.

"Yes. I understand," he said. "How can I show my friendship?"

Assante was pleased. Very pleased. The exercise of power

always pleased him because it, too, was an absolute. "We will share this," he said, the voice soothing now, calmer, less strident. "We will share this not because I desire the money, but because you will prove yourself to me with this sacrifice. Later, you will see, this gift of yours will be repaid several times over."

Of that Billy DeSalvo was certain, and he knew that the telephone call was, all things considered, a blessing. Better to swim with the shark and benefit by its protection than to be pursued and devoured.

So the deal with Marcellus Malone was split, 75 percent of the take going to the mysterious Assante, the remaining 25 percent staying with Billy. But Assante's people had managed to infiltrate another team, had "bought" another player and presented Billy with 25 percent of that money, too. A bond had been established, a tie had been formed, and when Billy really thought about it, which wasn't often, he knew that the Assante organization had hundreds like him on the streets, around the country, turning in huge sums of money only because of the implied threat so subtly framed in explaining what might happen if an agreement wasn't reached.

"The best day of my life," he had once said to his bodyguard and only friend, Rico Scalzi. "It was the best day of my life when Mr. Assante called."

There was no reason to assume that Assante was a surname, that it was even a true name, but Billy felt better, more comfortable, by making it appear to be a business arrangement between two men, not between a man and an organization so large and so powerful that no one, no person, no corporation, no police department, no government, could mount a serious threat.

Rico had nodded, his trust in Billy DeSalvo almost religious. He had been brought up in the slums of New York City, his people were Assante people, and when there was trouble one prayed first to Assante, then to God. To work for a man who worked for Assante, who received money from him, who shared in business transactions with him, was all too much, much more than Rico Scalzi could have expected. It was unimportant to say that he would kill for Billy DeSalvo, because he already had. Twice. For Assante. It was more important, more significant, to say that Rico loved DeSalvo, beyond any reluctance to act instantly to satisfy any of his whims, to fulfill any assignment, and, if necessary, to die in the effort. Gladly. With honor.

Gradually, Assante's sources moved DeSalvo higher in the organization. He was trustworthy, if not overly intelligent. He was loyal, if only because of fear. He was dependable, because he knew the consequences of irresponsibility. He loved money, more than anything but food, gargantuan amounts of it. He was ruthless in his own way, or perhaps *without conscience* was more accurate. Women were unimportant to him, except as tools, as currency, and he was clever enough to know how to use them properly. The young blonde he had used to nail down the basketball player was more than just useful. Assante had plans for her—rather, for what she was able to make others do.

In all, Billy DeSalvo, the runny-nosed kid from middle-class Brooklyn Heights, had carved a considerable niche for himself in Los Angeles. He lived in Bel Air, secluded, in a house valued at more than $4 million. He drove a Bentley, kept an old Rolls Corniche in the garage, had a small fortune on deposit in a bank on Grand Cayman Island, and, of course, offered to do anything he could for the Assante organization.

Billy brought a smile of amusement to Assante's face on the few occasions he and Scalzi spoke of him. He was insignificant but for the things he could arrange, the money he produced, the loyalty he displayed at every opportunity. Assante knew he was rock-solid—Scalzi told him, once a month, in a private home overlooking the ocean on Pacific Highway in Malibu Beach. He liked Rico. He had liked Rico's two older brothers, who had been equally loyal soldiers in New York, both of whom, sadly, had died in the service of the organization.

Maria Scalzi, the bereaved mother, had been sent to Florida, had been set up in a palatial home in Golden Beach. She was part of Assante's history, part of his childhood, and she was among the few who knew everything there was to know about him, about his business, about who his boss, his only boss, really was. Her husband, Enrico, had served well as a master engraver, had worked for six full years engraving the plates that produced the AT&T bearer bonds with which Assante had almost brought Wall Street to its knees, flooding the financial marketplace with $100 million of the virtually flawless, as well as worthless, copies.

When old Enrico died, before the two sons had met their bullet-riddled destinies, those in attendance at the High Mass funeral service in St. Joseph's Church caught the law-enforcement clowns off guard. They never expected the superstars who appeared, and even had they staked out the High Mass, which they did not, there wouldn't have been time to properly arrange the kind of surveillance needed.

They had no idea Enrico Scalzi was that well respected in the organization, and so they spent the next year trying to find out exactly what it was he did. They failed, as they usually did when they began to dig into the Assante organization.

Rico Scalzi had been brought to Assante himself after the death of his brothers, when he was already a man of twenty-five. He trembled with awe. He stammered his words. He mumbled, mostly, eyes cast down at his shoes, at the ground, anywhere but at Assante.

"I have a new interest in Los Angeles," Assante had said to Rico, his voice friendly but also full, powerful, resonant. "There is a man there, a fat man, a stupid man, but he has proven his loyalty and his respect and he is going to do business with me. For me. For now. I want you to be his right hand, and my eyes. I owe much to your family. Your father was a great man; your brothers were loyal and brave. It would honor me to have another Scalzi in my employ. Will you take the job?"

Rico knelt on one knee, reached for the old man's right hand, and gently pressed his lips to the large ring. His acquiescence promised all that it implied. He was employed for life. He would never reveal any information about the organization, and especially, above all else, he would never reveal anything he knew about Assante. Death itself carried less fear—much less— than the shame of informing, the disgrace of weakness.

Two years earlier, Assante's spokesman had reached Billy DeSalvo at his home, ringing his unlisted telephone at 3:00 A.M. It was not as if Billy had been wakened. He and Rico were counting money, money in tens and twenties, the old-fashioned way.

It was for the laundry, and the next night Rico would fly to Grand Cayman, to deposit the wrinkled bills collected from Billy's drug salesmen in the Grand Cayman National Trust and Bank and watch it turn into perfectly clean, absolutely untraceable entries on anonymous ledgers for some anonymous empty corporation that listed fictitious people as its officers and a post office box in Sante Fe, New Mexico, as its home office.

"Yeah, hello," Billy said, annoyed at the disrespect of some people.

"It is a message from Assante," said a cool, cultured voice. "We must discuss something important."

"When?" Not why. Just when.

"In the morning. At ten. Please keep an appointment you have made at the Key Systems Building on Wilshire Boulevard. Your appointment is with Arthur McDonald, and his office is on the nineteenth floor, Suite Forty. Thank you, and good night."

Billy didn't sleep. Not at all. No chance. This was his first contact since the Malone thing, the first opportunity to serve as more than just a collector of money and a dispatcher of same. He was ready well before ten o'clock, shaved and bathed, neatly dressed, Rico sitting downstairs in the Bentley, not his own anonymous gray Chevrolet.

The directory in the entrance lobby listed some of Southern California's most prestigious firms. Under "M" was the entry for "McDonald, Arthur R., Investment Counseling." The elevator whispered its way up to the nineteenth floor; an arrow clearly visible upon emerging from the car pointed to the right for Suites 1930–1955. Billy DeSalvo opened the door, was greeted by a middle-aged woman who smiled at him. "Good morning, Mr. DeSalvo. Mr. McDonald is waiting for you in his office. Thank you for being on time. He has an extremely busy day today."

She rose, led him down a corridor, and opened a large mahogany door, unmarked, letting it swing open as she stepped back. DeSalvo entered. The woman reached for the doorknob and silently swung the door shut.

Seated at a large desk, bare but for a telephone, was a man

Billy DeSalvo did not know and had never seen. Behind the desk, drapes fully open, was a floor-to-ceiling glass wall, and the glare from the streaming sun temporarily blinded Billy and made a full study of the man's face impossible.

"Hello, Billy," he said. "I believe you know Miss Novak."

Billy glanced to his left, in the direction of the man's extended arm, and saw the peachcake he had used to get Marcellus Malone's attention. "Yeah, I know her," he said, strangely uncomfortable, annoyed that the girl should be there before he was, that he wasn't told she'd be there at all. "You McDonald?"

The man smiled. "If you like, yes, I am Arthur R. McDonald. I deal in investments. Please have a seat," and he gestured at a maroon leather armchair to the right of the desk. Billy DeSalvo sat quickly, already aware that he had been rude, that this might, in fact, be Assante himself. "I'm sorry for my behavior, Mr. McDonald," he said. "It wasn't an easy night, and we found some traffic before we could get here."

McDonald smiled broadly, openly. There was genuine warmth in his face. "Yes, of course. I know how Rico dislikes traffic. When you leave, please be sure to give him my best wishes."

It had to be Assante. How the hell could he know so much?

"Well, we are here to discuss a business venture in which our friend has a very strong conviction," the man began. "Miss Novak has been promised a role in a major motion picture for her time and certain of her sacrifices. Not to mention, how shall we say, the continuation of supply of certain chemical substances her system requires. You, Mr. DeSalvo, will profit in amounts of money thus far withheld from your activities with our friend. He has been highly pleased by your continued support and allegiance. He is now prepared to show his gratitude, in return for your efforts as the, shall we say, manager of this particular project."

Billy's hands were shaking. This was it, the major kill, the big time for sure, say good-bye to the penny shit forever, Billy Boy.

"Hey, you know I'll do anything, Mr.—our friend, I mean— asks me to do. Just lay it out for me, OK?"

McDonald smiled again, clearly pleased. "I can tell you that our friend is going to be very happy, Billy," he said. "Fine, then, let us begin."

They began talking about Adam Benson, the National Football League, the Chicago Bears, Sherri Novak's film career and her drug habit, and how Billy DeSalvo and Rico Scalzi were going to manage the entire affair.

Only Sherri, of the three people present, seemed less than agreeable, but at one point, when her voice had become strident in its refusal, the elegant, splendid Arthur R. McDonald had half-stood, reached out, and slapped her face with the palm of his hand, a crack so loud it echoed in the still office. That this man had done such a thing, that it was so totally out of character, surprised her more than the blow.

She would nod her mute agreement to everything that was said after that.

Two hours later, when they all left the empty shell of an office, the deal was set, the arrangements had been made, Billy DeSalvo was going to run the operation (and be solely responsible for the heat, although he couldn't know that), Sherri Novak was going to ensure her success in the film world and her ability to acquire all the money and drugs she'd ever need by marrying this football player, and Assante was going to make millions more dollars through the tried but until then unsuccessful method of fixing the results of NFL games.

And Adam Benson didn't know a thing about it or any of the people involved.

EIGHT

DETECTIVE Joseph Gerard Keegan, just Gerry Keegan when he was with friends, was . . . well . . . with friends.

He had arrived promptly at nine o'clock, liked Leigh from the minute she opened the door and smiled at him as if they had been meeting each other like this for years, and was further pleased to see just how close she and Eddie Buck seemed to be. The casual brush of a hand on his cheek, the straightening of a lock of hair that had slipped down on her forehead, Gerry was sure he had never seen this kind of natural togetherness when Eddie was married to Suzanne, a woman who had a decided leaning to the shrewish, who was able to express disappointment and bitter disapproval with a look and a glance, a motion of her head, that no one in the room could mistake.

He remembered that from the time he had been married to Marsha, and even though that was a lifetime ago, his stomach still tightened just a little when he thought of that sad, unhappy woman.

He entered the apartment and gave Leigh his jacket, and Ed appeared from the kitchen, pony glass in his hand, just the right mix of vodka and shaved ice. Gerry Keegan, at least in Ed's mind, was the inventor of the "Ketel Mist," and while he thought the fast dilution of such an outstanding vodka was somehow to be avoided, it was what Gerry Keegan drank, and after all, how much worse was it than those millions of amateurs who took one of the great single-malt scotches and mixed it with tap water?

"Well, it's not the best of times, and I'm sorry I haven't tried

to get us together when there was no other reason but social,"
Buck began when they were seated, "but my friend is dead and
I'm convinced he was murdered."

Keegan put down his glass, empty, and when Leigh moved
to refill it he motioned her away. "One for now," he said. "More
when it's strictly social, OK?"

She nodded, silent, allowing the two men to conduct what
she was certain would be a quick discussion of Ed's almost ir-
rational conviction that Adam Benson was somehow murdered.

"Gerry, they killed him. They had reasons, and I know they
did it, but they are so damned smart that nobody could even
think it was anything but accidental. But I know it was done to
him and I need you to help me prove it."

Keegan nodded, and because he was unusually tall and unusually thin, and because one leg was crossed over the other
and his arms folded across his chest, the simple action of nodding his head seemed to cause all his extremities to move as if
they weren't all connected to a common torso. "Tell me what
you know."

Ed told him.

"You got a tape of this, in his voice?" Keegan asked.

Ed shook his head from side to side. "No, no tapes. Shit,
Gerry, I didn't know what he was gonna be telling me. He was
my best friend and I promised him it would just be something
between us. He came to my apartment Saturday night, before
the game, spilled it all, and felt like he had a friend he could
admit anything to without worrying about the guy's memory,
you know? I didn't even take notes. I wasn't working, you understand? I was busy being his friend."

Keegan looked disappointed. "Shame," was all he said, so
quietly that it was barely audible.

"Why?"

"Because if I had a concrete reason, if I had evidence, then
what I'd want to do would be a lot easier to accomplish. Because
if I go to the coroner's office and demand a full work-up autopsy
his family is going to complain, and maybe somebody in the
family is mixed up with what you think got him killed, and if
they bitch loud enough I'm going to look like an asshole because

he isn't a guy found murdered someplace, because it really isn't any of my business and sure isn't in my jurisdiction, and because then I'll have to explain about my friend the sportswriter and his crazy theory that nobody can prove or even think of a way to try to prove. That's why it's a damned shame, Eddie, because if you had a tape or if you had been wired or something, anything I could hold in my hands and show the official jerk-offs, it would be possible. As it stands now, I can't do a damned thing. And even if I thought you had a chance of being right, which I'm not sure I can say, I'm afraid my hands are tied."

"But, Gerry, what if he was murdered? Just for a second, for the hell of it, let's pretend we both know for sure that it was a murder. What would you do then, with no proof, no evidence, nothing else but what you feel? How would you deal with it then, if you were absolutely, positively sure-as-shit convinced that Adam Benson was wiped out because he told the gambling syndicate in this country to fuck off?"

Keegan said nothing. He stared out at some point above Ed Buck, silent. Then Keegan said, "Well, if I had that sure a gut feeling, I guess I'd tell the coroner to do the full work-up autopsy and not give a shit who bitched, because he's an old friend and I think if I made it the one all-important favor I was ever going to ask him he'd find a way to do it without anybody else knowing and then cover it all up so nothing would ever be known if he didn't find anything. And if he did, of course, then it wouldn't matter who knew what we had done because it would be legal and there'd be an investigation and all that stuff. But that's only what I'd do if I had a strong, 100 percent feeling. I don't, Eddie, and you haven't convinced me I should."

He paused, saw the tight, stubborn cast to his friend's face.

"OK, I asked you to tell me why I should be as sure as you are, and you told me. Now convince me you're right, Ed. Tell me how a guy could be murdered in front of seventy-four thousand fans in a public stadium in broad daylight, on a field with twenty-one other football players and six officials and sidelines full of coaches and players and photographers and television technicians? Tell me who did it? How? There was no bullet hole, no knife wound. He wasn't poisoned, because every player on the team ate the same pregame meal and it was served in the hotel at a buffet table—yeah, we did that much asking, anyway.

"So we have ruled out guns, knives, and poison. He was not involved in a hit-and-run auto death. A fucking safe didn't fall on his head. He wasn't caught in a fire; he didn't die of smoke inhalation. What did it to him, Eddie? Some incantation mumbled by some mafioso's mother sitting on her veranda in Italy looking out at the Mediterranean? Who did it? How was it done? I don't even give a shit why, because if you can make me think there's even a chance you're right . . . Yeah, you don't have to convince me, just make me think there's a one-in-a-thousand chance that you're right. Well, go ahead. Give me a reason to put my ass on the line after twenty-five years of unblemished service. How did they kill Adam Benson? You don't even have to tell me who 'they' are. Just how did they do it?"

Ed began to lose his temper, not at Keegan but at the futility of proving something that was apparently impossible to begin with. How, indeed, could a guy be killed on a football field, in Yankee Stadium, without a mark on him?

"Damn it, Gerry, I'm not the detective. I'm not the cop. And I'm sure not some kind of mystic psychic weirdo you guys sometimes use when nothing else seems like it makes any sense. Maybe that's what we need, some kind of Uri Geller doll, a guy who's gonna smell Adam's coffee cup or comb or something and tell you exactly who had him killed and exactly how they did it. I don't know. How the hell am I supposed to know how? All I know is what he told me, that yesterday was the day he was gonna shove it up their asses, and now he's dead. I know that my friend is dead and I'm the only one he told this story to and I can't even find anybody who wants to help me get him some justice. I'm sorry I asked. Thanks for coming, and maybe next time we'll be at some silly cocktail party and we'll talk about the fucking Giants and the Super Bowl. You know, something important."

Keegan blew up. "You damned fool, why do you think I'm here? Because I want your fucking autograph? Because I want inside information on which games you're gonna pick the wrong way Sunday? I'm here because I'm your friend, because

I know you longer than you knew Adam Benson, because you asked for help in an area in which I am an acknowledged goddamned expert, and so here I am. Cocktail parties? You don't get invited to the important cocktail parties. How could I see you at one of those? Now talk to me, you stupid shit, or I am going home. I'm tired."

For the first time in the conversation, Ed smiled. His face relaxed, he laughed. "Important cocktail parties? My, my, you are going places in the crooked New York City poli-pol circles, aren't you? I'm sorry. You're right. I'm a shit."

Leigh couldn't restrain herself. "Gentlemen," she said softly, "without trying to sound overly feminine or stupid, what the hell is poli-pol?"

Keegan smiled back at her. "That's his word," he said, nodding at Ed. "See, paranoid old Buck here is sure that the police and the political animals in this city are in collusion and have been since the city got running water and flush toilets, that nothing goes on or is allowed to go on, which is probably the point of his argument, unless the mayor and the police commissioner, who has to blow the mayor because that's who gave him the job in the first place, first have a little meeting and exchange promises and get about six nephews and cousins easy jobs. I used to laugh like hell. Now, as I move up a little higher. I'm not so sure he's wrong. Anyway, that's poli-pol."

Leigh smiled, satisfied, and leaned back. Ed, too, leaned back, looked at his friend the detective, and began speaking.

"Gerry, you know there are ways of killing somebody without leaving a trace, not a goddamned hint that anything wrong happened. I read a novel once where some Japanese guy visited his friend in jail and the guy was really unhappy about being there, you know? He had lost face, and he was an old guy to whom face was everything. So he asked his friend to kill him, but not to have to pay the price or get caught."

He paused, and Keegan could see the brightness in his eyes, as if he had just unlocked a wondrous secret. "Gerry, this guy took a pencil from his pocket, just a regular everyday pencil, and pressed it against his friend's temple, in some special spot only these Japanese ninjas knew about, and in like fifteen seconds this old guy smiles, nods his head, and keels over, dead as a fucking mackerel. And the friend gets up, bows his farewells, and leaves the old guy neatly arranged on his bed, looking just like he was asleep. No wound, no blood, no sign. Just an old guy who died in his sleep. It was perfect."

Gerry Keegan suddenly became Detective Joseph Gerard Keegan. "So what are you saying? That the bad guys dressed up like football players and carried a pencil in their uniforms, and when there was this big pileup they pressed it against Adam Benson's temple and made him to go sleep forever? How about Tinkerbell shows up and nobody can see her and she fucks him to death on the goal line? Come on, Eddie; isn't that a bit contrived?"

"Sure it is, and you're right," Buck said. "But something like that is possible, and I think you know it, and all you asked me to do was convince you there was maybe a one-in-a-thousand shot and you'd try to find somebody or something. I did, damn it; I did."

Keegan nodded. "Yeah, you did," he said. "Maybe there's something I can do, ask around, call in a favor, something. Give me a day to think about it, Eddie. I need to think about it."

He rose from the couch, clearly no longer in a social frame of mind. "Leigh," he said, "it was nice to meet you. If you are really going to marry this guy, I'm a little suspicious of your taste in men, but perhaps you'll invite me to the wedding anyway, so I can have one final chance to make you see the light." The smile on his face was genuine but fleeting.

"Ed," he said, turning to his friend. "I don't know if you have anything right going for you except this woman, but I agree what you've given me does have a one-in-a-thousand chance of being accurate and I am going to try to find out something. I'll call. You stay out of it, don't bother me, and above all don't call anybody else to find out what I'm doing, because anything I do right now is going to be unofficial. Don't get my ass in trouble by being a prying reporter. OK?"

Ed Buck smiled. "OK, Gerry. No trouble, I promise. But let me know what's happening, because I can't keep a promise like this forever, you know?"

Keegan left the apartment, got into his private nondescript black Ford sedan, and drove home slowly, thinking about where to start, what to do, how to handle this special favor, and whether there really could be anything to it. Hey, fixed games in the NFL would be too massive a story to handle quietly. A star quarterback getting killed because of it, and because he was involved, would only make it worse.

By the time Keegan reached home in newly safe Brooklyn Heights, he had decided that the first thing to do would be speak with George Laskey, the assistant medical examiner under whose temporary care rested the body of the late Adam Benson, quarterback. George owed him a favor, a big one. He was going to ask for something in return, finally, six years after he had made a record of a homosexual pandering arrest disappear, one concerning Scott Laskey, George's son and only child.

NINE

THERE were two things Dr. George Laskey did probably better than anyone else. He was as clever and gifted a forensics expert as could be found in New York City, where all the good ones worked. He also could drink more vodka than any man alive, at least in the opinion of those who had tried to drink with him, and it might well have been the reason that he was the assistant medical examiner and not in charge of the department. The guy who was, Dr. Kenneth Huff, should have retired by now, but the mayor was reluctant to pull that particular trigger because he'd have no choice but to elevate George Laskey to the position. The mayor had been at an important political gathering two years ago at the dedication of the newest wing at St. Vincent's, and George had picked that night to get drunk for the first time in a decade.

"Cheap vodka," he said the next day.

But George Laskey was reliable, consistent, and dependable, an aging Boy Scout with pallid complexion, wispy light brown hair that failed miserably in his attempt to cover an ever-widening bald spot. The perpetual smirk on his face, coupled with his lack of height, too many pounds, and the bald spot, reminded most people he met of an aging leprechaun. The fact that George was forty-seven came as a surprise; he looked older. He was quick to laugh and smart as a whip, and if he drank . . . well, so did a lot of people who couldn't hide it nearly as well and because of it were totally unable to function anywhere near George's level.

Detective Joseph Gerard Keegan always deserved Laskey's attention. He owed Keegan for saving his son from a stupid mistake, saving the embarrassment and probable career-killing reaction his "accident" would have brought about. The kid was twenty-three now, certifiably gay, and so what? He was bright, attentive, and on his way to first-year residency at Manhattan Memorial, a huge private hospital on the Upper East Side. Scott Laskey was going to be a surgeon, and as George would say to his friends, "the only difference is that he cuts open live people and I cut open dead ones."

None of it would have been possible had Gerry Keegan not intervened, not put his own career on the line and somehow found a way to squash the stupidity. Scott, then eighteen, and his friend Chuck Grossi, both of them newly thrilled with the bravado they had exhibited by admitting to their homosexuality, had been picked up for soliciting an undercover detective on Third Avenue, offering the services of both for a hundred bucks. The second they described what they had in mind and said how much they wanted for their services the handcuffs came out and the two were taken into custody.

Keegan made the incident disappear.

George Laskey owed him. Big-time.

So when Keegan's voice turned up on Laskey's answering machine, he called right back. And when Keegan said he needed some time, Laskey told him to come right over, meet him in the lobby of the New York City Police Forensics Lab on Varick Street near the Holland Tunnel.

Half an hour later, they were shaking hands.

"Gerry, how can I help?" George asked when they were seated in his tiny cubicle of an office just beyond the huge room with more than fifty stainless-steel operating tables lined up, complete with the stainless-steel sinklike drains to suck away the blood, a rolling cart of surgical instruments, a scale to weigh various organs, a computer terminal and screen, and an overhead microphone/tape recorder with a foot-pedal activation switch.

Keegan always had trouble drinking coffee when he could look through the glass door and see all this, but it never bothered Laskey, nor did it ever dawn on him that it might bother someone else.

"I need a favor, George."

"Name it, Gerry. Scott starts his internship next month."

Uncomfortable, Keegan tried to shake that debt. "George, look, it was just a favor, an easy one. I'm glad for you both. I did what I would do for any friend in the department. Nobody was hurt; nobody had charges to press. The kid made a mistake. Done. Let's drop it. You've done fifteen favors for me that might have put you in a spot since then. We're more than even. OK?"

Laskey smiled. "Fine, so how can I help?"

"I need you to do an autopsy without anybody knowing you're doing it." he said. "This is a major-league favor. You could lose your job and your license. If it was me, I wouldn't do it. But if I'm right, we'll all come out of this with citations and maybe promotions."

Laskey brightened. "Gerry, the only promotion I can get I can't get, at least until Mayor Moron is out is out of office." That was what most of the city employees called Mario Marone. "But if you need it done, then consider it done. Where's the body?"

"You have it. Came in last night."

"Yeah. So did sixteen others. You got a name or should I cut up all of them until we find the Easter eggs?"

"Adam Benson."

"Holy shit. The quarterback? What am I looking for?"

"I don't know."

"Well, that's helpful. What happened?"

"Don't know."

"What do you think happened?"

"Murder."

"Yeah, right. On a football field in the middle of a game. In full view of . . . Jesus, Gerry, what do I look for? Where do I start?"

"That's why you get the big bucks, George. But remember, nothing to nobody. This is just between us."

"Yeah, sure. Then I'll tell his widow somebody got him confused with the floater we found in the river and cut him all apart before the mistake was . . . oh, shit, I'll find a way. Call me to-night."

Keegan stood, again those long limbs making him appear more like a marionette than a man. "Thanks, George. May your scalpels always be sharp."

"Get the hell out of here," Laskey said, laughing.

It was later that day, well past six, which was later than George Laskey ever liked to stay in what he called the Vault, that he put down his scalpel, surveyed the results of an exhaustive autopsy, and virtually whispered into the overhead microphone something that he had never had to say before.

"The guy is still alive," he said. "Nothing killed him. He's not dead and he is as healthy as a horse."

There had been no sign of the easy symptoms. No heart attack. No drug overdose, although there were obvious signs of what the medical fraternity calls "extended recreational cocaine usage." No severe trauma to the head or the neck. No aneurysm in his brain, no embolism anywhere else in his body. No internal injury from a sudden impact during the game that might have punctured a lung or cracked his larynx.

Nothing.

Adam Benson wasn't dead, except for the inescapable fact that he was. He was the healthiest corpse George Laskey had ever seen.

He didn't call Gerry Keegan until he got home and had a drink, which put the time at about nine.

"What do you mean, nothing killed him?" the detective yelped. "He's dead; something must've killed him. What do you think he's doing, sleeping?"

"I know," Laskey said. "I know. But I don't know. To find out, I'll have to run much more sophisticated tests than we normally do for the drunks and the vein poppers. But nobody is supposed to know I did this. The widow said no autopsy. So what am I supposed to do, Gerry?"

All detective now, Keegan studied his options. "Make it official," he said. "This is an autopsy ordered by the New York Police Department. Do whatever you have to do, but find out what killed the guy, and for God's sake keep it away from the press."

He slammed the receiver down, picked it up again, and dialed Ed Buck's apartment.

"Listen; this is Keegan," he said when Buck picked up. "We've got a case. Sort of. I asked for a favor and we did an autopsy. Your friend shouldn't be dead. Nothing killed him. The only way to find out what really happened is a much more intense study, and I authorized it. If I have to, I'll put this under suspicion of first-degree murder. I'll keep you informed."

"Thanks, Gerry. I'll try not to be a pest."

"Yeah. Sure you will. Talk to you tomorrow."

TEN

SHERRI Novak arrived the next morning, her face tear-stained, haggard, grieving. She hugged Ed when she arrived at the hospital, in the lounge area reserved for VIP attendance, and Ed was struck again by her beauty.

"Eddie, what am I going to do? I don't know how to bury a person; I don't know how to be a widow. What do I do first?"

Forced to set aside his own mourning for the moment, Ed Buck became friend of the family, that one efficient person who seems to materialize when a crisis bursts open.

"His dad is coming in today," Ed told Sherri. "I would think he'd want Adam buried in Oliphant, unless you and he had already decided things like that." As he said "he," he realized how foolish it sounded. People as beautiful and alive as Adam and Sherri Benson didn't think about burial plots and wills and estate planning. Normal people did that. Ordinary people.

"No, we didn't have any plans," Sherri said. "Whatever Mr. Benson wants is fine. Ed, where is he? Where is Adam? I want to see him."

Where indeed? Did Ed tell the newly minted widow that her husband's body had already been opened by a police order? Did he tell her that the New York City Police Department, at his urging, had begun handling this case as if it was premeditated murder?

"He's in the morgue," Ed managed to say. "They did an autopsy. Standard procedure for this kind of thing. But now that you're here, they'll release the body to you, arrange for you to have someone pick him up. Or we can just wait for his father."

Sherri stiffened, almost imperceptibly. Her eyes opened wide. "Autopsy? Why would they need an autopsy?" she asked, and Ed Buck wondered whether that was shock or fear just on the other edge of her voice.

"Any public death, Sherri. Anything like that. Anything suspicious. They just automatically do an autopsy. Routine."

"Suspicious? What's suspicious about it?"

"Sherri, the guy is the quarterback of a team and right there during a game he just dies? He scores a touchdown and he doesn't get up when they unpile? Don't you think that looks a little suspicious, that some people might be a little suspicious about why he died, how he died?"

She looked thoughtful for a moment, her mind frantically racing, then nodded her head. "Well, yeah, of course it does," she said, "but how else could he have died except from something like a heart attack?"

"I don't know, but the detective I spoke to said that's why they do these things."

Sherri looked at Ed, right into his eyes. "Did they find anything? Anything at all?"

He shook his head. "No, and that's why it's still suspicious. No sign of a heart attack, an aneurysm, a stroke. No head injury. No broken rib that punctured a lung. He didn't swallow his tongue and suffocate. Nothing. He's just dead and nobody knows why, or even how it happened. They can't just let it hang like that, you know?"

"Well, I can," Sherri Benson snapped, angry now, the grief fled from her face. "They aren't going to do anything else to Adam. Nothing. That's it. I'm the wife . . . and I can stop it, can't I?"

Gerry Keegan appeared at her side. He introduced himself and, taking her hand, said, "I'm afraid not, Mrs. Benson. You can't actually stop the procedure now. Once we get involved in something like this, it has to run its course. We'll release the body as soon as we can. I've asked the doctor to meet us. And I am very sorry at what happened. I was a fan of your husband's for a long time."

Ed and Keegan led Sherri Benson to a couch and tried to answer questions for her while they waited.

George Laskey finally came across the lounge and was introduced to Ed and Sherri. "My deepest condolences," he said to her, bowing ever so slightly, an almost European touch. "I conducted the autopsy myself. I was the only one who touched him. I am truly sorry, Mrs. Benson. Your husband seemed to be a man in better than reasonable condition, a little wear and tear, a few old scars, but nothing out of the ordinary for a professional athlete."

"Then who—I mean what—killed him?"

"We don't know yet," he said. "Detective Keegan has authorized a more complete examination, the kind we conduct only when foul play is suspected. To tell the truth, though, I don't know what to expect to find. I did a normally thorough job and I couldn't find a thing to attribute his death to. That in itself is suspicious, of course. People just don't die without a reason, without a cause. It is not within the parameters of the definition of death."

Sherri looked stricken. Ed was puzzled. Keegan nodded, stared at the woman for a long minute, then turned to explain in layman's terms.

"Look, a man dies of a heart attack, there is evidence of damage to the heart. A man has a stroke, you find the spot. Gunshot, poisoning, bludgeoning, choking . . . all those more normal causes of death are easily found, targeted, and studied.

"But Adam Benson shouldn't be dead. There isn't a mark on him. There is no evidence of foul play. No poison. His oxygen wasn't cut off. Nothing, nothing, nothing. And then more of the same. Nobody dies from being too healthy. Dr. Laskey here will find it. He will need more time, and when he is finished we will have an answer. We owe it to your husband, Mrs. Benson, to find out exactly what happened. It is a little difficult to imagine a man being killed in front of a packed Yankee Stadium crowd and not finding a mark on him, wouldn't you agree?"

She nodded, face pale, lips thin. "Do what you have to do, Detective Keegan," she said. "I will be . . . Jesus, I don't know where I will be. Probably in a hotel. The Warwick, probably. I'll let Ed know."

They said good-bye. Keegan got into his unmarked car and dissolved into the steady flow of traffic. Ed and Sherri went back inside to wait for Adam's father.

They didn't have long to wait. Andy Benson arrived, nearly filling the doorway to the waiting lounge. He knew Ed from all those years ago, of course, and grabbed him in a great, burly bear hug, tears running down his cheeks. "All the way up here on the train I couldn't stop crying, Eddie," he said. "I'm a grown man. A tough old man. And I couldn't stop crying."

He turned and saw Sherri.

"I am Andy Benson," he said. "It is nice to meet you."

For a second Ed thought the old man, who he knew to be well past seventy, had simply blocked a memory. Of course he would have met his daughter-in-law by now. Of course he would.

But Sherri nodded, extended her hand, and said, "Hello, Mr. Benson. I'm so sorry we couldn't have met under different circumstances."

Adam and Sherri had been married for three years and he had never brought his new wife to see his father? Had never flown the old man out to California or down to Florida or wherever the hell it was they lived to see his new wife?

Ed was stunned.

"Mr. Benson," Sherri said, "I understand you have a family burial plot back in Oliphant. I'd like to have Ed buried there, if it's all right with you."

He nodded. "Sure," he said gruffly. "He'll rest next to his mother. Thank you for that. Who do I see to make arrangements?"

"We can't do anything yet, Andy," Ed said. "They aren't finished with his body yet. They don't know what killed him. I asked a detective friend to look into it and they're treating it like a suspicious death. As soon as they're done, they'll let us know and we can take the body."

Andy Benson nodded. "I'll wait," he said.

"Andy, it could take days. You can't wait. Why don't you come home with me?"

He stood, hat in his hand, pain on his face. "I won't be in anybody's way? You're sure? I don't think I'd like to be alone in New York City right now. Thank you."

"I'll call Leigh," Ed said to Sherri, "my fiancée. She'll come and take you back to her place until you get settled."

Sherri nodded.

"I'd like to see you tonight, for dinner," Ed said to her. "I'll bring Andy to Leigh's place and we'll stay there for a while. Is that all right with everybody?"

They both nodded their assent. Ed went to the pay phone, and half an hour later Sherri Benson was on her way. Ed sat with Andy Benson for a long time, neither man talking. Finally the old man, eyes still red, looked over at his son's friend.

"You think it's kind of strange that I never met her, don't you?"

"Yes, Andy. I do. I know Adam was proud of her, and I know how much he loved you. I don't understand it at all. Do you?"

Andy nodded. "It was her," he said. "Adam told me she didn't want to get involved in any family stuff. That she had grown up alone, that her father and her brother had left as soon as they could, and that she had lived with her mother for a while, until the woman killed herself with drink and drugs. So she didn't want to get too close to another family, even her husband's. And she told him, too, that she never wanted to have a kid. Imagine that."

His shoulders started shaking again and that awful sound of a proud old man's heart breaking came through in muffled sobs.

"I never met her until today, Ed," he said. "I don't like her and I don't trust her."

With that, they got up, wordlessly, and walked out onto the street to hail a cab.

ELEVEN

ED helped Andy Benson, with his one overnight suitcase, out of the taxi and into his apartment building. They spoke mostly about Adam and their college days at Oklahoma; Adam's high school exploits, which Ed had heard about in the time they had spent together; and a few things he never knew and never would have known had this tragedy not happened.

For instance, that Adam had named him, Ed Buck, as executor of his will. Not his father. Not his wife. That the will was in Andy Benson's possession, not in his wife's; that there was more than $3 million in Adam's estate, which included property on Cape Cod and Key West.

"He gave you the real estate," Andy said. "Adam had a problem telling people how much he loved them. I always had the same problem. But, Ed, you were his best friend. I don't think he had another."

Pouring another pony glass of Ketel One, with Andy Benson nursing a second beer, Ed learned more about his friend, the kinds of things that Andy, without knowing why, had to talk about to provide some sort of catharsis for his grief. That once, at the age of sixteen, Adam got into a fight over a girl and sent the other guy to the hospital with a fractured skull and that his mother was so upset at the thought that the boy might die that she refused to sleep or eat for six days, until the doctors said a full recovery was likely. That by the time Adam was thirteen everybody in Oliphant and soon the entire state of Pennsylvania knew he was one of those miracle athletes and that he could have gone to college to play basketball or baseball, not just football.

But he said he didn't want baseball because he didn't think he could make it to the major leagues as a pitcher, "and if I can't have the ball every play, be in charge, I'm not interested."

The old man finally went to take a nap and left Ed sitting in the living room, staring out at the busy street, holding a half-full glass of watered-down vodka and wondering what the rest of the story would be by the time the mystery of Adam Benson's death was solved.

And why didn't Andy Benson like Sherri? What was there? What had happened? Or was it just an old man's instinct, a dislike of the flashy and the extravagant?

TWELVE

ED must have dozed off, too. The jangle of the telephone woke him an hour later, and in reaching for it he toppled the glass that had been set down on the table next to his chair.

"Ed, it's Sherri. I have to talk to you. I'm at Leigh's, but I can't talk to you here. Or on the telephone. Will you meet me?"

"Sure. Listen, if you just go out and turn left, there's a place on the corner, kind of a pub called the Knickerbocker. Go there. Get a booth in the back. Tell the guy at the bar, probably Rob Knox, that you're expecting me. I'll be there in half an hour."

Quickly showered and dressed, Ed hailed a taxi and in twenty minutes was at the Knick, as all the locals called it. Sherri was there, in the back booth, and considering the time of day, the middle of the afternoon, there wasn't much in the way of a crowd.

He slid in opposite her, told Knox to bring him a mug of black coffee, and sat studying Sherri's face.

She was gorgeous, the rare kind of beauty that cosmetics cannot create and often obscure. She was beautiful but hard, no softness in her face, rather angles and sculpted lines, and although Ed never knew her and had never really spoken to her, he sensed more of an intelligence than she would ever allow to be seen.

"What's up, Sherri? What do you need that needs to be secret? Is there something I can do, something I can help you do?"

She stared at him and the sadness in her eyes was palpable. "I want to ask you to find the bastards who had him killed," she said. "But that isn't necessary. I know who they are. I need you to prove it and to make them pay. I don't know how it was done, but I know who ordered it done, and I'll tell you everything I can to find a way to get even for Adam."

Was that the floor opening under him? "So you know—"

"Yes, of course. It's why he's dead, Ed. There's another reason, too. Me. He's dead because of me. Our marriage was arranged. They needed him to help them make a lot of money; I needed them to get where I thought I wanted to go. I didn't love Adam when we married. Oh, he loved me. He was crazy in love with me. And I kind of liked him, too."

Ed's left hand shot out, and he had to stop its motion at the last second before it crashed into the side of her face. All the pent-up anger and anguish at the death of his friend was threatening to boil to the surface, unleashed. How could this woman so casually address the death of the man she had married with, "And I kind of liked him, too." Ed was unsuccessful at hiding the motion of his left hand; Sherri noticed and flinched.

"You kind of liked him? You kind of liked him?" he said, voice hard and rigidly in control. "You kind of liked the guy? He was your husband. He loved you. What the fuck does that mean?"

Sherri began to sob, very quietly, almost unnoticed but for the erratic movement of her shoulders and the fact that she had turned her face away from him, toward the wall. "It means," she whispered, "that I married Adam because they told me I had to, and it means that once I did, I fell in love with him. I knew about the gambling; I knew about the cocaine. I hooked him. I got him into it. And I agreed that gambling, fixing the games, was the best way for him to keep it coming and stay out of trouble. But I never, never thought they'd kill him, Ed. He told me he was going to stop it and I begged him not to. I knew what they were capable of doing. And they did it, in the one place in the world where no one can commit a murder. Witnesses? There were almost seventy thousand of them, and not one of them saw a thing."

She looked up at him, face tear-tracked.

"Please, Ed. Think whatever you want to about me, but help bring these people down. Do it for Adam. Not for me. I don't count here and I think maybe I never counted at all, to anybody. Not ever. And especially not to myself. But I loved him. So did you. Please help me.''

THIRTEEN

ED told her about the conversation with Adam Saturday night. My God, was it only that, only two days ago? He told her that Adam had been both frightened and belligerent, embarrassed for what he had done to the game that had provided him with everything and in fear of what his sudden reversal would do to her, to his wife.

"He loved you very much and always seemed to consider himself especially lucky that you would even agree to talk to him. When you said you'd marry him, I swear he thought it was some kind of joke."

Sherri's eyes misted again. "It was, at least at first," she whispered.

Sherri Novak Benson was twenty-six years old. She had been born Sheila Novaczenski in Buffalo, New York, to a mother who drank and a father who worked too hard to have much time for her.

Sheila had a brother, Johnny, two years older, and by the time she was fourteen Johnny had sexually abused her and, worse, humiliated her by forcing her to make it with his friends, each watching and taking turns. The news that Johnny Novaczenski had been killed in a botched holdup of a convenience store came as no surprise and brought little regret to Sheila. By then her mother had been institutionalized and her father, working harder than ever, had mourned for a day or two and then gone back to his job as a maintenance man for the big hospital, Saint Theresa of Mercy.

Sheila left Buffalo as soon as she graduated from high school, hitched to New York City with a truck driver who said he would charge her twenty bucks but took a blow job instead. Sheila knew that was coming and was surprised the guy didn't insist on the money, too.

It took less than a week to change her name and get work in the big city. She became Sherri Novak, an escort girl, and learned one thing, that her looks made up for everything, her beauty and sexuality were her tickets out of the garbage can, and, above all, she had to preserve her looks and her body.

Her pride went first; her sensitivity followed. There was nothing she wouldn't do for the money, less she wouldn't do for someone she thought might be of help later on down the road. Which was exactly how she met Billy DeSalvo.

It was a Christmas party in Queens, and the local low-level hoods had hired several girls to spice up the festivities. It was a celebration of sorts; more money had been made that year in prostitution, gambling, and drug sales than ever in their little group; more than $5 million by the end of December would be salted away for sharing later on.

So Sherri, hired along with three other girls from the escort company, agreed to earn 1,000 bucks for the night's work. What work? "Anything any of the guys asks you to do," said Dominick Valentine, who put the party and all other "major" deals together. "If you don't think you can handle that, back out now."

For a thousand bucks Sherri would do most anything, and by 5:00 A.M. she had. But by far the sickest and most perverted of them all had been this short, fat guy from California, a local hero who went to Hollywood and made good and now came home to visit his mother for Christmas.

Sherri could tell right away that DeSalvo didn't really like women; he liked watching them have sex, usually in submissive, subservient positions, as if being taken advantage of by men and, oddly, by "tougher" women. He would have objected violently to the phrase *more masculine women,* but there it was, regardless. Billy DeSalvo was not a homosexual, but he wasn't quite heterosexual, either. He had been cursed with a tiny dick, and that was a lifelong source of embarrassment and humiliation to him, and so he got aroused watching beautiful girls "naked and in heat," as he called it.

He zeroed in on Sherri, and because he was the visiting celebrity, an old friend who might soon be able to help the others take a few more steps up the ladder, anything he wanted was the way things were going to be. Sherri found herself making love to one of the other girls while one of DeSalvo's friends was anally fucking her. DeSalvo filmed the whole scene with his camcorder.

Sherri found herself naked and on her knees in front of a row of five of these cheap hoods, Billy holding a stopwatch to determine which one came the quickest. The winner got another blow job, courtesy of Sherri.

Of course it was demeaning. But it wasn't any different from blowing her brother or his friends, or that fat, smelly truck driver, and this was a grand for the night. She had long ago learned to block out her feelings and her objections to almost anything. Hell, there were times when she wasn't even aware of where she was, whom she was with, and, most critically, what she was doing.

DeSalvo liked her. He liked her looks and her sexuality and her resignation to his orders. "Best piece of ass I've ever seen," he cackled most of the night, running a tongue around her nipple or slipping a finger into her vagina to watch her squirm, shift her weight from one foot to the other while she smiled, to make him think she was enjoying herself. "If you want to come to California, you look me up," he said when the night was finally finished. "I can set you up with some guys and a job and you'll do all right. With that body and that mouth, you can own the fucking world."

He liked that. He laughed. So did the rest of the morons, because he did. And Sherri smiled through her hatred, because this fat piece of shit was, indeed, going to be her ticket to moving up.

From there she went to Vegas, tried going legit for a while, working as a waitress in one of the casino coffee shops, but soon discovered that six bucks an hour and tips couldn't even bring her what one night in bed with a high roller pulled in, and not a penny of that was anybody's business.

So she began hooking, and it was easy. She was a knockout, and the more money she made the more she had for the right clothing, the right grooming. The people with whom she had sex were nameless, faceless men and women who represented nothing more than an income, a way to make a living that escaped 99 percent of the rest of the world, mostly because she had the looks that no one else had, sometimes because she didn't have the conscience others possessed. And that was something she simply couldn't understand. Why was sex so important to men? Why were her breasts enough to drive guys crazy? Why were they all so absolutely crazed by the thought of making love to her? What was it that made them drool when she slowly licked her lips while looking directly in their eyes, or at their groin? What was there about men, and about women, that made this all so ridiculously easy?

Love? She never loved anyone. She was without emotion, except for that most basic sensation of exquisitely good sex, those rare times when a man found her secret spot and actually enabled her to feel.

Like Adam Benson had done.

And the men she knew never understood what that secret was. It had nothing to do with sex or physical appearance. She had enjoyed sex more with men who had small penises than with those whose organs were so gigantic it was a struggle just to get them to fit someplace.

One night she was involved in a party in a penthouse suite at the MGM Grand, one of the top-floor extravaganzas that cost $2,500 a night and came complete with, well, with everything.

Including women.

Or men, if the occupants so desired.

Or boys and girls.

This group was the party of a successful, and therefore wealthy, Hollywood movie producer, celebrating the premiere of his latest box office smash, a stereotypical collection of shootings, explosions, sex, drugs, lots of near-naked women, and the

all-around all-American violence that played successfully before 80 percent of the public.

He brought his girlfriend, Harmony Hunter, a starlet hoping
to fuck her way even higher; the supporting actor Bobby Moska,
whose legendary sexual exploits almost always involved men;
the studio's publicity head, Judy Brett, an ordinary-looking
shrew with an acid tongue and a liking for beautiful women,
which she had in common with her boss; and a sloppy little
gambler, a converted New Yorker who had helped the producer
make additional hundreds of thousands of dollars through the
judicious use of information allowing him to bet on the right
Los Angeles Hoops games and only the right games.

Billy DeSalvo.

They were, in a strange way, glad to see each other again.

Billy laughed at the recollection of the Christmas party in
Brooklyn eight months earlier, then turned to Teddy Corr, the
producer, and said, "Hey, this broad is the best cocksucker I
have ever seen, anywhere. She's a fucking artist."

Corr had to see for himself, and Billy DeSalvo proved to be
accurate. "There are people you have to get to know in Hollywood," he breathed, "important people who can help you. A
talent like yours should never go to waste."

It didn't go to waste that night, for certain. While Billy
watched, which was his favorite thing of all, Teddy Corr availed
himself of the talent three times; Bobby Moska once, although
against his wishes; and Judy Brett most of the rest of the time,
much to her delight. In fact, it was she who suggested that Sherri
come to Hollywood soon and stay with her at the beach house
in Malibu "for as long as you need before you find your own
place." At the same time she made it clear to Corr that finding
work for Sherri would be a great idea.

But DeSalvo put a stop to that instantly. He knew the value
Sherri Novak would have in his particular world and wasn't
about to allow an empty suit from Hollywood to stand in the
way.

"I have already arranged for Sherri to work for my people,"
he said, growing suddenly and strangely quiet and formal. None
of those present misunderstood the change in persona, not even

Sherri, who recognized that an offer, a lucrative one, had just been made and that her silence was acceptance.

"Hey, great," chirped the ever-alert Corr. "That way, we can get to see a lot of Miss Novak anyway."

It was left at that. She never saw any of those people again, although Judy Brett tried several times to find her in the next few months.

Sherri did go to Los Angeles, about two months later. She called a number DeSalvo had left her and in two days had an apartment, a job as a special escort to select individuals, and a thousand dollars a week, plus whatever she could raise on her own. But she was to never, absolutely never, try to get any money out of DeSalvo's special friends. For them, she was bought and paid for.

She understood perfectly.

Three weeks after going to work for DeSalvo, she also picked up a cocaine habit, courtesy of her employer. For her, life was much, much better than it had ever been before. Now she wanted to look into the possibility of an acting career, and when she mentioned it to DeSalvo he readily promised to help her. "We have friends in the business, more important than that asshole Corr," he said, cackling at the memory of that night in Vegas. "We can arrange that. You do what we ask, and one day you won't need us. You'll be a star."

For a smart girl like Sherri, she was unbelievably stupid to believe the little fat man.

FOURTEEN

THEY decided to go through with the funeral first and spare Andy Benson the anguish of knowing about the dark, ugly side of his son's life. It would be better, they decided, if he could remember Adam as a golden, somehow blessed athlete, a quarterback with ethereal skills and magnetism who was better and cleaner and more close to perfect.

But Ed did call Gerry Keegan late that night to tell him what he had learned and that they wanted to put everything else aside until the funeral was done and the man was buried. Keegan, understanding that no one had an inkling of what had been uncovered, agreed to wait. But when he hung up he did make one call, and when he got Laskey he told him to look extra carefully.

"The man died from being healthy," the doctor said. "Of course I'll be careful—"

Keegan cut him short. "No, he didn't die naturally. Find out how they killed him, and don't say anything to anybody until I talk to you again. Nothing, to nobody. Oh, and, George? He was a hard cocaine user. You should be able to find that with a blood screen procedure, right?"

George Laskey nodded, then realized Keegan couldn't see that reaction. "Right, Gerry, I understand. I'm still holding the body; this may take time. Tell his family not to make any strong commitments yet for a funeral and burial."

Keegan put the receiver down and stared into space. Laskey put his receiver down and stared at his hands. He owed Gerry Keegan big-time, and this might be his only chance to square the debt. No matter how Keegan shrugged it off, covering for Scott had been an incredible piece of work. The kid was going to be a doctor. Almost there. And he was still a fag. Well, sure. These days it was acceptable. But you have to call them gays, not fags. George Laskey would have to remember that.

FIFTEEN

BILLY DeSalvo wasn't exactly nervous, but he had enjoyed better days and he knew there had been many times when his mind was more clear and relaxed. He hadn't heard from Sherri in three days. He knew she got there. He knew she was staying with the sportswriter's girlfriend. Buck had played with Benson in college. They had stayed friends; Benson gave him some stories, nothing much. Big fucking deal.

DeSalvo also knew, through the scores of pipelines he had in New York and could never, would never, lose, that the Buck guy was handling the burial arrangements, that he had met with Benson the Friday night and the Saturday night before the game, that they had gone to his apartment and kind of in a hurry, the waiter said to Tony the Freak, who felt he had to call one of the bookies he knew, who in turn told his boss, and, eventually, that guy thought it was important enough to tell Billy. Not that he knew anything about any of the plans, just that Billy was a major player in pro football gambling and would probably appreciate the information.

"The waiter said that they didn't even order dinner, just had a drink, talked for a while, and then got up and raced out," said the guy from the right-hand side of the country. Billy thanked him, told him to thank Tony the Freak, and said he'd take a look at the line when it got close to kickoff and if he learned anything he'd get back in time for the guy to take advantage.

Done. A favor given, unbidden. Now a favor owed.

But Billy was a little nervous about the thing. The killing had gone perfectly. The rat was dead, before he could fuck up a major money deal. Before he could run to the cops. Before he could bring ruin and, more seriously, shame and ridicule to the Assante family. But before he could tell the fucking sportswriter? Nobody knew. Billy had to have somebody close, somebody watching. Sportswriters in New York know a lot of people. Cops and politicians could be bought, and cheap. But the people in the NFL office, which had a better security crew for investigating gambling than the fucking FBI, they were the dangerous ones. They still believed in honesty and straight games, and the dumb bastards wouldn't even let the casino owners build a $300 million stadium in Vegas to hold the Super Bowl every year. For free. Why? Because you could bet on organized sports in Nevada, on the NFL games. It was a fucking joke. Didn't they think people all around the country bet on NFL games every week? Didn't they know that the Super Bowl was the greatest single-game betting action in history, that more people bet on the sixteen-game NFL season than they did on the eight-fucking-million-game major-league baseball season?

Of course they knew, and when it was "the right time" Billy was sure the NFL would suddenly recognize "its friends" in Las Vegas and among certain of the politicians, but it wasn't the right time and that was that.

Big fucking deal.

More important, did Benson and this sportswriter just talk about old times, the games they played and the broads they fucked, or did he spill his guts to his buddy just before he got ready to suit up and die? This bothered Billy DeSalvo, this not knowing, and it was important that he find out. Critically important. After all, Mr. Assante had put him in charge of this operation. The last thing in the world he wanted was for it to get fucked up. Getting whacked would be a blessing compared to things Billy had heard happened when Mr. Assante really got angry.

So someone had to go to New York, to be there, be aware. Billy couldn't send Rico Scalzi, even though the big man was the perfect choice, because the broad knew him—and blew him, wasn't that an old punch line to an old joke?—and the second she saw him she'd flip out. Whoever went had to be able to hang around, just on the edge, someone who, if Sherri noticed him, wouldn't matter, wouldn't set off any bells and sirens.

Also, Billy would prefer not to have Mr. Assante know that the situation was cloudy. The man would probably find out anyway. He had a way of knowing everything. But Billy had to make every effort to keep it a secret. And if Assante learned? Well, not a real problem, Billy felt. "Just making sure, Mr. Assante. Just making sure we were covered everywhere. Nobody likes surprises, right, Mr. Assante?"

Hell, Billy might even earn points for being extra careful, and that couldn't hurt him when it came time for another big job, another slow but definite move up the ladder. Billy DeSalvo was ambitious, but it was ambition mixed with caution and animal street cunning. He knew when to bow and scrape, and he felt the big shots who suddenly woke up dead, almost every one of them, had never learned how to do that. It was important, to his way of thinking, a critical part of the overall intelligence with which a guy had to approach his goals. If people thought you were sucking up to them, they might not respect you a hell of a lot, but guys like Billy never expected respect. What he wanted was success, money, recognition in that small circle in which he wanted to travel.

If it was ass kissing, then he was an ass kisser, and he had refined it to an art form.

He needed someone he could trust, or someone who was afraid of him, which would be even better. Because while Billy knew he was relatively low on the list of important people in his world, he also knew he had climbed out of the muck at the bottom and there were lots of people he could step on. And he enjoyed that, possessing a knack for zeroing in on people who had something to lose, something that would be catastrophic if it was made public or if it was suddenly snatched away. If Billy DeSalvo was a bottom feeder, he had learned to be a very skilled one.

In his particular business, finding someone he could trust was not a goal easily achieved. He trusted no one and didn't expect anyone to trust him. Such a man would be marked as a fool, and fools were not to be easily suffered. No one really trusted anyone in this life, not even at the top. They all worked together because of the common goal of substantial profits and the other common bond, fear of the bigger and more powerful bottom feeders.

So Billy DeSalvo had to be smart. He had to find somebody to act as his eyes and ears. A reporter, sort of, and he giggled when he thought of that. A reporter to spy on the reporter and the new widow piece of ass.

First he had to get some information, and this was incredibly easy; all he had to do was work through the good old NYPD.

He dialed a number. On the third ring a voice said, "Detective Quinn."

"Hey, jerkoff. You still peepin' through keyholes?"

A half-second of silence, followed by a high cackle. "Billy, you fat fuck, how are things in California?"

"Shit, it's easy out here, Patty. These LA cops couldn't find their dicks if they were in their hands. You guys are the real goods back home."

"Yeah, yeah. You fucked us pretty good, too, Billy. You know somethin'? I miss you. I do."

Now it was Billy's turn to laugh. "Yeah, bullshit. You miss the money I used to lay on you to leave my bookies alone. Can't find another source these days?"

"Nah. Shit, it's all dried up, Billy. Hey, I know you didn't call to say hello. What do you need?"

"Nuthin' much. I'm interested in that quarterback who bought it during the game the other day. Benson? I'm just curious. What happened? That cost me a bundle out here, and now I think everybody in the country is gonna be bettin' down on whoever the Bears play the rest of the season. I may take Chicago right off the board."

"Yeah. Makes sense. They don't have anybody even close to bein' a suspect. They don't even think it was anything but the poor bastard getting wiped out by a heart attack. Strange, the guy just dropped dead, just like that, during the game. Medical examiner couldn't find shit. Said the guy was too fucking healthy, that's what killed him. Some shit, huh? Hey, he went out a hero. Ball in his hands, just scored a touchdown. Perfect for him. Me? I wanna go in the saddle, but not with my old lady. Those new saddles are a lot better, you know?"

Billy laughed, a hearty laugh only he knew was forced. "Yeah. New saddles are the best, especially the ones that suck, too. So what I want to know is what his friend has been writing. You know, the guy he played with in college? The sports-writer."

"Oh, Eddie Buck? Shit, he's like shattered. He hasn't been in the paper since it happened. Damned good writer, too. I miss his stuff. He's takin' care of the arrangements, you know? Benson's wife came in from Hollywood. Man, what a looker that one is. I'd give a month's pay to get her in the sack."

Billy laughed. "A month's pay for you doesn't even buy her a good vibrator, Patty. But yeah, I know what you mean. Super good-lookin' cunt. Best I ever saw. Met her once at a party." He giggled silently at his private joke.

"Yeah, you're livin' the life, Billy. So this guy is handling the funeral as soon as they release the body. The broad is stayin' with his girlfriend, some chick named . . . hold on. I'll look at Keegan's book . . . named Leigh Janice Crespino. Lives on East 72d. Works for some major big-hitter advertising agency, DD Ads. That's about all I know, Billy. Hey, when you come home to visit your mother stop up and say hello. You left a lotta empty pockets in this precinct."

"Yeah, right, Patty. Right. I'll do that. Hey, thanks. Keep it hard."

It wasn't often you hit a home run the first time up, you know? DD Ads? The guy who owned that . . . what the fuck was his name? Oh, right. Drexler. David Drexler. In the hole for over four hundred thousand to Tony the Freak's boss, Philly Gags. Favor for favor, right. Now he was going to call in an old one.

He dialed Philip Gagliardi's number.

One ring.

"Yeah?"

"Put Gags on the phone," he said.

"Who the fuck is this?" A gruff, deep voice. Probably Louie Donato.

"It's DeSalvo, Louie, you piece of shit."

"Oh, hey, Billy. How's it hangin'? Gotta be careful, you know?"

"Yeah. I know. Put him on."

"Right away."

A few minutes, duly noted.

Then, "Billy? Hey. What's up?"

"I need something, Gags. It's important."

"Sure, Billy. What I got, you got."

"I want you to put that asshole Drexler's tab on me. And I want you to have him call me today. Tell him if he thought bein' in a deep fuckin' hole with you was trouble, now he's got so much grief he won't be able to sleep even if I let him off the hook. But first fax me everything you got on him. Do it now."

"Can I ask why?"

"You know better."

"Yeah, I do. Where should he call you?"

Billy spoke a phone number, his private number. Then he gave Gagliardi the fax machine number. Then Billy hung up, without saying a good-bye or thanks, and waited for his newest pigeon to fly into the coop.

Philly Gags was prompt, probably because he was nervous. He had asked DeSalvo for information and was offhandedly dismissed, shrugged off like some piece of garbage. That always made him nervous. DeSalvo was moving up, and Philly seemed to be headed in the other direction.

Two minutes later the fax started beeping, then sheets of paper spewed out. In all, eight of them, and it showed a guy up to his balls in money trouble, wife trouble, and business trouble.

David Drexler was forty-seven, a pushy Jew from the Bronx who had made it on nerve and lies. He had moved up through three different advertising agencies, taking clients with him whenever he got a better offer. In fact, those better offers came after he had sworn he could get the clients. But there wasn't much integrity in any of the advertising agencies in New York City anyway, so nobody thought he was necessarily a bad guy, just another asshole with some money, a few contacts, and the nerve to pull the trigger when a chance came along. The major difference, Drexler always felt, between him and hundreds of others was that they thought too much about which way to go, what was right, who would they hurt, should they, shouldn't they? Fuck it. Just do it. If it was wrong, you could always fix it later.

Finally, armed with other agencies' accounts, money from his parents' estate, which was considerable, a gift for lying and fixing things, and a long list of the absolutely most gorgeous call girls in New York from which he selected those to use as party favors, Drexler opened his own agency. DD Ads flew right from the start, with such accounts as Hertz, Burger King, Ford, Panasonic, Merrill Lynch, and those less impressive in terms of name recognition but just as lucrative when it came to billing, like automobile parts manufacturers, airline caterers, the people who made the fabric for the clothes but you never saw their name on the labels.

Drexler hired more than fifty staff members, stealing the best account execs from the other top agencies, including his vice president in charge of dirty deeds, Andrew Mosca, one of the world's true creeps and backbiters, from Johnson, Gaskill, Henderson and Ziebart, the second-biggest agency in the world.

Drexler found a gem named Leigh Janice Crespino working as the executive secretary to Harry Olsen, the president of Smith, Slocum and Jensen, where Drexler had started as a junior account executive right out of Syracuse University.

Right now, DD Ads was moving up in the marketplace, moving up fast. But like all these guys, Drexler had a bunch of weaknesses, the kind that people like Billy DeSalvo lived to find out about, then lived off the knowledge. Billy was going to be the salt on an open wound, a whole fucking bag of salt for a long list of gaping wounds that were so easily exposed.

For instance, Drexler kept a penthouse apartment on East 86th Street for a broad named Jennifer Robinoff, a cosmetics model whose face was on almost as many covers as her body was under them. She latched onto Drexler, and he to her, and they fed off each other in a vicious symbiotic relationship. It was his money and prestige and her body and class. It was Drexler at all the major events that New York City could muster and this five-foot, ten-inch former model draped on his arm like the world's most expensive hood ornament. She would drop him in a New York heartbeat—it was inevitable and they both knew that—but as long as the money kept rolling in, his money, because while she earned upward of a million bucks a year that was hers, all hers, she would indulge every one of the little Jew's sexual fantasies.

Drexler's wife, the former Karen Schneider, lived on Long Island with their three children. She had long since abandoned all hope of their marriage working. Resigned to living in empty luxury, she spent all the money she could spend, fucked people like her tennis instructor and her personal fitness trainer and half the semiretired stockbroker millionaires in Sands Point, and took three or four very expensive vacations a year. She and her husband barely spoke. He seldom slept home, preferring the surroundings of the East 86th Street apartment and the erotic embraces of Jennifer Robinoff—Jenny Bird to an adoring public as well as the ultimate wet dream of every straight male under fifty. Make that eighty.

Drexler's high-living finances had begun to put a crimp even in such a cash-flow fortune as he had established. Trips to Las Vegas, Reno, and the Caribbean almost always turned into financial nightmares. The cars, the clothes, the estate on the Island, and the penthouse on the Upper East Side, everything together, wound up putting Drexler in a position of needing slightly more than five million bucks a year, from profits or expenses or his overblown salary and every other way he could find to take it out of the company.

He usually found the way by simply writing checks, leaving it to his comptroller and accountants and lawyers to find a way to explain it or, short of that, cover it up and make it go away. His perception of that money was that it was all his anyway, and let other people explain it or make it right with the government. He always smiled at a slogan on a sticky pad he once had: "I can't be overdrawn; I still have checks left."

But expenditures like that weren't easily covered and did not easily disappear. There were records. Some people knew how to get them. Philly Gags was one of them, especially since the cocksucker was into Drexler for almost half a million bucks.

Gags didn't want to cut Drexler off, because he brought with him lots of other high rollers who didn't know a football from a dildo but managed to fuck themselves pretty good anyway. They all seemed to lose nine out of ten bets. Big bets. But Gags couldn't let the guy skate, so he was really happy when Billy DeSalvo called to broker the debt. Thrilled. Off the hook. He would reduce the nut by half for DeSalvo. It's good luck to do favors for guys on their way up.

Good riddance. Wash the hands and get rid of the prick.

Billy picked up his telephone and placed a call to a man named Eugene Medici, another kid from the streets of Brooklyn who turned up as vice president of advertising at the Skeezixs Candy Company, not as big as some of the other accounts tied to DD Ads but enough to put a hurting on Drexler should he lose it. Skeezixs Candy billed $25 million a year.

Past tense.

"Gino, it's Billy DeSalvo," he said when he had finished being passed off from one secretary to another. "How the hell are you, goombah?"

"Great, Billy. This isn't a social call. I know that. What do you need, ten tons of Milky Way bars? Tell me."

DeSalvo laughed. "Gino, I would like you to find another advertising agency. Today."

"Why?

"Because the Boss would like you to do him this favor, Gino."

"Done. The kike got himself in deep shit, didn't he?"

"Yeah. The deepest kind, Gino. Hey, thanks. Regards to Angela."

End of phone call.

Beginning of the end for David Drexler.

Almost as DeSalvo put the receiver back in the cradle, the phone rang again. He smiled. Damn, it was a rush to have this kind of power. It always got him a hard-on.

"Hello?"

"Who the hell is this?" asked a man trying to keep strength and authority in his voice and losing the battle every second.

"My name is not important," Billy said. "But what I am about to tell you is very important."

"Fuck you."

"If you hang up, there is nothing in this world that can stop what will happen next," DeSalvo said. "You will stay on the line and listen to me. I am the man who just assumed the debt you have run up with Philip Gagliardi. By my reckoning, you now owe me almost half a million dollars. Let's make it seven hundred thousand, which includes interest and the fact that you intended to fuck my friend Philly Gags and for the inconvenience of me having to spend this time with you on the telephone."

"What?"

"There is no way for you to get out of this debt, and I want the money tomorrow. All of it. In cash. I am aware of the fact that your son, Michael, attends the Adams-Osborne Day School. I know that your two girls, Michele and Amy, attend the Harriet Douglass School. I know your wife, Karen, goes to the tennis club for lessons almost every day and that four mornings a week somebody named Joseph comes to your house to act as her personal trainer. I have photographs of Karen giving each of these men blow jobs.

"Oh, and more bad news, Mr. Drexler. You will receive a call later this afternoon from Gene Medici. You know him, don't you? He will tell you that the Skeezixs Candy Company advertising will no longer be handled by DD Ads. And I am totally confident that with one more telephone call I can convince Revlon that Jenny Bird is no longer their ideal model, now that she has AIDS and all.

"Mr. Drexler, do I have your attention now?"

"Yes. What can I do for you?" There was no bravado in his voice now, no power and no influence, just the whining of a desperate man waiting to be told exactly what to do.

Billy smiled. God, he loved it. "I want to arrange a meeting with Leigh Janice Crespino of your office. I want it to be . . . let's see, this is Tuesday? Friday. In New York. At a place I will decide on later. You will tell her it is about a possible advertising account. You can say whatever the hell you want about the kind of advertising. It doesn't matter. I don't care and it isn't important. I just want to talk to her and I want her to meet me, which is probably more important. It may take the entire day. We are to be alone. Is all this perfectly understandable to you?"

"Yes."

"Thank you. Arrange this meeting, you will have bought yourself another week to come up with the money. And at bargain rates. Six hundred thousand. Cash."

"Yes. I understand. I will do everything you asked. But what about the Skeezixs account? Is that still gone?"

Billy almost burst out laughing. "Don't sweat it, Mr. Drexler. Sugar is bad for you anyway."

SIXTEEN

THE funeral was scheduled for Thursday or Friday at St. Matthew's Roman Catholic Church in Oliphant, depending on when Dr. Laskey was able to complete the second autopsy. Sherri had agreed to allow anything Ed and Gerry Keegan advised. She was still staying with Leigh and had decided not to call Billy DeSalvo. She knew he'd be looking for her because she hadn't called yet and making a call now would only open up several questions that she did not want to have to answer. Besides, she was done with him, with all of them. It was time to take another route, time to care about herself just a little. She had met some nice people here. She wanted to be one of them.

She was going to work with the police, tell them what she knew, and if it was discovered that Adam had indeed been murdered—with enough clarity that the police would be able to call it that—then she would agree to become an informant and go into hiding until the case was made and arrests had been completed.

But for now, while Dr. Laskey worked on her husband's corpse, while she took comfort from the newness of having friends like Ed and Gerry and Leigh, there was nothing to do but wait.

And talk. It was Tuesday night they had met at Leigh's apartment for a quick, light dinner. Gerry Keegan had agreed to work on an anonymous basis for now. Nothing Sherri, or any of them, said would be written or recorded. Or remembered. So Sherri began to talk, and she talked for hours, chronicling the beginnings in Buffalo, the move to New York, then to Las Vegas, finally to Billy DeSalvo and the Hollywood scene.

She told them everything and with each word grew more and more convinced that she was killing any chance of forming real friendships with these three people, but they reacted with sympathy and understanding for her and contempt for the people who had combined to turn her life into the hell it had been, and for one of the rare times in her life she knew what it felt like to have the genuine support of people who really didn't want anything from her, only for her. Leigh reached out and touched Sherri's hand, taking it and gently squeezing it, smiling at her with what looked almost like tears in her eyes.

"Sherri, the first major problem we have to deal with," Gerry Keegan was saying, "is that we have to prove it was murder. There is just no way we can do that. The autopsy shows a perfectly normal man, healthy and fit, who just happens to be dead. The doctor has no idea why Adam is lying there and not getting ready for next week's game. There is no explanation for his death, other than that he simply stopped living.

"We know what you've told us. We have no reason not to believe you. So Adam was involved in some crooked games. Well, that's more of a National Football League problem than it is ours now. If he was alive and we found out, we'd have to arrest him. But he's not, and we only have your word that DeSalvo actually arranged for Adam to be killed. There is no way on earth to figure out how he did it. If it was done."

"They did it. I know they did it. DeSalvo arranged it, with the help of this guy Assante and the scary one, McDonald. They told me they did it. I told you all that. There is no question, no doubt. Adam was murdered."

Keegan held up his hand to calm her and quiet her. "Stop. I'm talking like a cop now. I said I believed you. When the little slime said he had your husband killed I believed he did it, and I believe he told you he did it. I knew that little bastard when he was here, a nickel-and-dime crook, and telling you about it and forcing you to do what you told us the day after Adam was killed was just up his alley. He probably got off telling you, too, and I don't think he gets off doing anything else except watching."

Sherri's startled glance and reaction told Keegan he had touched a nerve.

"So all I have to do now is learn how it was done. But until then, we don't have a damned thing. Not a damned thing. And I want to get something on this piece of shit. Anything. I want to make this case airtight and get you off the hook and away from these people once and for all. And get that little bastard on murder one. But frankly, right now I don't know how to proceed."

Leigh, who had been listening quietly, suggested that Dr. Laskey be called again. Gerry Keegan shook his head. "No, he knows where I am. If he finds something, he'll call."

Ed turned to his friend. "Have you been able to turn anything up? Anything at all, Gerry? Did you question the guys who were on the field when Adam was killed? Did you find out about the doctors on the sidelines, the food the team ate that morning? Anything look suspicious? Different?"

Keegan shook his head. "Ed, that's been done, or it's in the process of being done. That and a lot more. You know I'm not going to be able to sit here and tell you step-by-step what's been taking place, how we've been working. Can't do that. I'm not even sure who I can talk to in my precinct anymore. There are so many dirty cops I think they make up the majority now, at least here in New York. Too much money, too many bad guys walking because of too many scumbag lawyers and a legal system that is a hundred years outdated, with more holes and escape hatches than ever before. The good guys are losing ground every day, and I don't see how it's going to get better anytime soon. Cops don't get paid what they need for the risks they take. And more than anybody else in this society, they see how easy it is to make staggering amounts of money. And you know something else? Nobody really gives a shit. Drug dealers, if they do it with class, are like American heroes, for God's sake."

Leigh shook her head violently, angrier than Ed had ever seen her before. "No, that's not true. They're scum. They're killers. They sell that shit to kids and they are killing an entire generation. It's in the rock music and the rap music and that hip-hop shit and it's in the schools and it's in the fact that the middle and upper classes don't want to know. They've got what they wanted and now they don't want to hear about the problems. And when those problems reach out and touch them, they buy their way out of it. Except, of course, for all those well-to-do kids who wind up dead because of drugs. Then the idiot parents blame the cops."

Gerry Keegan looked at her with something approaching reverence. "Well said, lady," he whispered. "Now if you were the police commissioner or the mayor or somebody who could make something happen, we'd all be a hell of a lot better off."

But Leigh wasn't finished. "Gerry, look, when I was in high school, the boy I was dating, maybe someone I could have had a life with, decided to try to be 'cool' and use drugs. He got some bad stuff. He had a violent reaction to it. And he died. Poor, sweet Howard Irving died because of one mistake."

She took a deep breath, lips flecked with spittle, eyes wide, cheeks flushed. "It's important to me, more than just important. It's critical. The stuff's pervasive. It's all over. Look at those commercials, the ones that preach, 'Just say no'? That's bullshit. The ones the kids are listening to are the Nike things, the ones that say, 'Just do it.' And they do. They put shit in their noses and they shoot it into their veins and they kill themselves with dirty needles and they think it's cool. There are gangs of kids on the streets in this city, and in lots of other cities, that 'initiate' their girls by making them shoot heroin into their bodies or have sex with guys who already have AIDS. To prove that they want to belong, you see? Belong? They're proving they want to die, and for being that fucking stupid they deserve to."

Suddenly, as if touched with a hot electric wire, Leigh realized that Sherri was silently sobbing. "I'm sorry; I'm sorry; I didn't mean that. It wasn't about you, Sherri."

"No, you're right. It was stupid and I was stupid and I liked it too much to stop. I didn't have anything except my body, and that helped me get where I thought I wanted to be. Trouble is, once I got there I couldn't think of anything except getting out. But I can't. And now I wound up killing Adam, or getting him killed, because I couldn't say no to the same kind of people you are talking about, Leigh. Except you have no idea just how vicious Billy DeSalvo can be, and he isn't even in charge of much. He works for men who would just as soon kill someone as say good morning to them."

Keegan said, "We know the chain. We know which animal is higher than the last. We know it moves all the way up to Anthony Assante, and there has never been a thing we've learned that could directly tie him to anything. But we know it's him. He knows that we know, and he knows we can't do anything about it. He laughs at us, and it drives me crazy. If this can lead to him, if we can tie him to this thing, then whatever we do to get there is worth the ride, don't you see? If we can stop him, we stop hundreds of people underneath him, at least for a while. If we can cut off the head, it will take a while until the snake can grow another one."

Sherri nodded. "I'll tell you everything I know," she said, "and I know a hell of a lot more than they think I do."

SEVENTEEN

WEDNESDAY morning, midweek except for the fact that it was Leigh's first day at work since the previous Friday. She planned to finish the week and then drive with Ed to Oliphant for Adam Benson's funeral Saturday morning.

There was a note taped to her computer screen: "See me when you get in. DD."

From the boss. Maybe it was good news. Maybe they had just landed that Donna Karan account. Maybe even the PSI Network billing. Or maybe he just wanted to say he was sorry, knowing that Adam Benson was Ed's best friend.

So she carried her coffee mug with her to David's door, knocked once, and entered.

He was seated behind his desk, one of those ornate old mahogany monsters his wife had found years ago in an antique shop in Cos Cob and had repaired, restained, recoated, and shipped down to his office. He thought he hated it until one day, quite accidentally, he discovered three secret compartments opened only by pressing a hidden button underneath the desktop, inside the top drawer. For a man like David Drexler, something like that, under lock and key, was an invaluable security blanket.

"Leigh," he said, getting to his feet and stepping around the desk. "I'm sorry about what happened. I know what a difficult time it must be for Ed, and naturally for you. Is there anything I can do?"

"No, David, but thank you for asking. Yes, it was a shock, a terrible thing that will take him a long time to get over. But thank you for your concern. Is there anything else? I'm two days behind, and with the funeral this weekend I hope I can be back on Monday and try to get into the normal routine again."

Drexler sat back behind his desk. "Yes, an assignment. We are trying to get a major account managed out of Southern California by a company called Interim Basis. It controls a large portion of tourism advertising in California, Washington, Oregon, Alaska, and Hawaii. We're looking at upwards of $30 million in initial annual billing. The guy is coming in to meet with Barnes, Ralph, and Barry on Thursday and then with us Friday. I want to you to handle the negotiations. You'll meet a man named Edward Small. I'll have more details for you tomorrow. It's very important, Leigh. A major responsibility, and it will mean a huge bonus if we get the account."

Leigh was at first flattered and surprised—flattered that David would hand her such a plum, surprised that she had not known of any preliminary contact or ongoing, if premature, negotiations. But he had always been straight with her, so there was no reason to suspect that he had wanted to give it to someone else first, as well as no reason to be annoyed that he hadn't seen fit to fill her, his chief assistant, in on the project from the start. In addition to being terminally unpredictable, David was often secretive. He didn't trust anybody in the advertising or communications world, and there was probably great validity in subscribing to such a theory.

"Well, thank you, thank you very much," she managed, unusually flustered. "I'm excited about this. If you can fill me in on some of the details, I'll prepare the next few nights at home. There are so many things cooking here . . . I don't suppose you want me to hand off anything to Robert or to Kimberly, do you?"

Drexler smiled. "If it's important stuff, why would you want either of those two to handle it? They're fine as assistants, but I don't think they'll ever be really qualified to manage their own major billing accounts, do you?"

"No, I guess not. Anyway, get me something to study, and maybe I can talk to this guy Small before he flies in. All right?"

"No. He doesn't want telephone contact. He's a little eccentric, I suppose. He wants to walk in and find prepared proposals.

He has culled about six agencies from his short list, leaving just the two of us. And we kind of have to guess at what he wants to see."

Leigh bridled. "David, that's insane. How can I prepare a major advertising proposal when I don't know what the client wants, what the client is looking to spend, where the client wants the message aimed, or any of about another hundred or so things? Are you sure this Interim group isn't just jerking you off?"

Drexler smiled. "Leigh, please. Who jerks me off is my business."

She smiled, a bit tightly. "OK, then. I have two days, you're telling me. Not even. To come up with a major proposal for a major advertiser and I don't even know what he wants. Any chance we can postpone the meeting?"

"None."

"David, this is crazy."

"I know, Leigh. But we meet all kinds. Who knows? He might just want to see how you work under pressure. How we work, I should say. Let's meet later and I'll throw a few ideas at you and we'll brainstorm for a while. Tell Ed you're going to be late tonight."

Bad timing, Eddie, but I have to do this.

"All right. I'll talk with you later today. I'm going to try to clear everything off my desk in record time."

She left the office and Drexler leaned back in the rich leather chair, put his feet up on the desk, and looked out the glass wall/window. *What the fuck am I going to tell her?* he wondered. *I don't know what this guy DeSalvo wants, but it ain't advertising and I don't think it's pussy. All I know is I made a hundred grand by arranging this meeting between them. Great. Now all I have to do is find 600 more big ones for this Mafia ginny prick who sounds like he'd just as soon kill me as take my money. Maybe both. Shit. Shit. Shit.*

EIGHTEEN

GERRY Keegan figured that Sherri Novak Benson would be better off in a safe house somewhere, managed by the New York Police, not in Leigh Crespino's apartment on the Upper West Side. She hadn't made contact with DeSalvo in three days, and it was too late for her to suddenly call now. It was done. He had to be beyond suspicious by now, had to be wondering where she was and whom she was with, who was talking to her. And what she was saying.

Keegan made the arrangements, and he hadn't been just scaring the general public when he told Ed, Leigh, and Sherri that the crooked cops outnumbered the honest ones these days. He got in touch with Homicide Detective Mike Herbert, a gold shield who had been on the force longer than anyone and still drove a ten-year-old Ford. "Mike, I need a safe place," Keegan said when he called Herbert at his home in Queens. It was near midnight, but he decided he would rather wake him than risk the usual office listeners' snooping on this kind of call.

Herbert didn't have to guess at the voice. He viewed Keegan as one of the few untouched and uncorrupted members of the force. "Where and who?" was all he said.

"I don't care where. For the widow of the football player."

"Drugs?"

"Right again, Mike. I think we can get a line on DeSalvo and through him we can hook that Assante asshole, maybe for good."

A deep intake of breath, followed by the calm, methodical planning of a veteran policeman.

"We are not supposed to have this place, and nobody knows we do, and if anybody asks we don't know a fucking thing about it, Gerry. It's in an apartment building right across the fucking street from Gracie Mansion that only a few of us know about. Nobody from city hall even has a clue. The damned police commissioner doesn't know about it, either. All told, I think maybe twenty guys are aware of it. You want to use that?"

"Yes. I'm going to have to tell two other people where she is, though. Is that all right?"

"You trust them?"

"You know I do."

"Then it's OK. It's the Venture Arms, sixteenth floor, Apartment 323. You'll find the keys in your top left-hand drawer tomorrow morning. It's stocked. The telephone is on and it can't be tapped. No bugs. We sweep it once a week. Use it as long as you need. There's recording equipment built right into the entertainment center in the living room. The button to start recording is on the floor at the edge of carpet in front of the fireplace. Just walk to it and step hard. You'll feel it. And it won't make a sound when it clicks on. It's self-loading, self-rewinding, and you can't record over it. You can't erase anything, in other words."

"Thanks, Mike. Owe you one."

"Just get that fucker and we're even," Herbert said, and then he placed the receiver back on its cradle, picked it up again, and arranged for the keys to find their way into Keegan's desk before morning.

And then Herbert made one more call—to Anthony Assante in the posh suburb of Bedford Hills, in Westchester County.

NINETEEN

PAUL Boland got a phone call from Detective Joseph Gerard Keegan asking for an appointment later that day, two days before the funeral would be held for Adam Benson.

Of course, Boland complied.

Three hours later he was answering questions about the previous Sunday, what had happened that was different, who was hanging around the locker room who didn't usually make an appearance, something that was said or overheard. Anything.

Paul couldn't really be of much help. He generally had no idea what went on during the hours before a game, except for the numbers of friends and/or business associates he was drinking with in the upstairs and very private Stadium Club. His brother, Peter, would not have been any more help, even if he had been available and had not taken the company jet to the Bahamas for the week, from where he would fly to Dallas in time for the Giants' next game and the Boland brothers' next staggering party.

Keegan quickly realized he was talking with an empty suit of Hall of Fame proportions, so he politely exited from the conversation by offering his thanks for the cooperation and for permission to speak with Duane Charles, the Giants' head coach.

To Paul Boland's mind, he couldn't have cared less if the detective spoke with Charles or had him electrocuted. Boland didn't like the coach very much. It was probably a combination of two things: he had to pay him too much money and he resented that deeply, and he didn't understand Charles's speech, had always harbored a deep distrust of the southern drawl, and was disappointed that Charles treated him much the same as everyone else did—that is to say, with no respect and an all too obvious superior attitude, which Paul Boland interpreted as "he's the boss and he owns the team so we might as well be nice to him, but he's a fucking moron and who gives a shit about him anyway?"

He reached over and pushed the intercom button. His secretary, a good-looking unmarried woman in her late thirties, answered immediately. "Yes, Mr. Boland."

"Jacqui, call Coach Charles downstairs. Tell him Detective Keegan needs some time. Now. And tell him to drop everything else."

Jacqueline Appleton, who enjoyed the relatively easy job she had taking care of these two idiot brothers, would have gladly fucked either or both of them had they asked, which they never had. She thought Peter Boland was gay, and while nobody had ever seen him in such a situation, women sometimes sensed that better than men. She hung up, depressed the intercom button, and pressed another, punching in the numbers that caused the phone to ring on Coach Charles's desk.

"Hey, Duane, it's Jacqui," she said.

"Hey, baby, what's it like upstairs?"

Jacqueline Appleton had fucked Coach Charles, many times. Lately, in fact, on a weekly schedule. She liked him and thought his gifts were cute, mostly coming in the form of checks. And unlike many other men she had known, his checks never bounced.

"A detective is coming downstairs to talk with you," she said. "Pretty Paul said to tell you it's important, you have to do it, and no arguments. The guy's name is Keegan. I guess it has something to do with the terrible thing that happened last Sunday."

"Shit. Damn. Fuckin' waste of time. All right. Tell him to come down. Tell him I'll meet him at the basement elevator. Damned stupid mule-fucking New York City detective might get himself lost between there and the damned locker room. I knew a cop whose hand used to get lost between thinking about jerking off and reaching for his pecker."

Jacqueline smiled. She also loved the down-home kind of cussing Duane did, creating almost another language of the profane. She was waiting for the right Thursday night to tell him how it turned her on.

Keegan emerged from Pretty Paul Boland's office. "Follow me, Detective Keegan," Jacqui said, swaying just enough to let him examine the terrain as she led him to the interstadium elevator. "Coach is waiting for you. He'll show you into his locker-room office."

She flashed him a bright smile and swayed her way back to the executive offices, knowing that he was watching her.

He was. *Silly-looking broad,* Gerry Keegan thought. *Kind of a fat ass, too.*

When the elevator doors slid open in the basement, there stood head coach Duane Charles, once an All-American middle linebacker at the University of Nebraska who broke the University of Alabama's heart by leaving his home state. He then embarked on an All-Pro career at the same position for the Atlanta Falcons. Generally considered to be a horse's ass with a wide mean streak, he didn't make many friends during his career, but he was recognized for having a down-home football-smarts intelligence that boded well for a career in coaching just as long as he didn't ask for too much money.

And he didn't. Charles thought money wasn't nearly as important as winning, and as long as he had enough to pay the bills, afford the nice house in Connecticut and the one he called home on the panhandle of Alabama—the Redneck Riviera he loved so much—he was not going to worry about which new young coach had signed a contract for how many millions of dollars.

Charles had made $400,000 for the last six years, never thought about asking for more, and felt strongly that football players made a hell of a lot more money than they should. He was violently against contracts that ran more than one year in duration. "Kid gets three years not to worry about his money, he sure as hell won't worry about football, neither," he moaned. "Pay 'em all the same and pay 'em all for one year. Then fire the ones who didn't play well and double the salaries of the ones who did."

The old school, of course, would not be listened to in these days of megadollars and the television networks running the league. But it was what Duane Charles was all about, and he had no problem telling people exactly how he felt, whether the people were his players, other coaches, the press, the electronic interviewers, or the various women he enjoyed.

Coach Charles shook hands with Gerry Keegan and led him into his office, which was a neat but not overly large room cut off the main locker room. The door closed, which was good, but it couldn't possibly shut out Duane's deep booming voice when he had to explain things to a player who had played badly or not taken well to on-the-field criticism.

But now voices were modulated and the door was closed and those players straggling in early for afternoon practice had no way to know if the coach was in or not, which led more than a few of them to flip the finger at the closed door.

"Coach, I'm investigating the death of Adam Benson," Keegan began. "It happened right here on the field and it happened in a pileup involving players on your team, and that's about the only reason I have for being here today at all. This is mostly background, I guess. Was there anything unusual that day? Did any of the players or your assistant coaches say anything or see anything different? Do you remember anything out of the ordinary?"

Charles thought. "No, sir. Can't say that anything sits up and bites me about Sunday. Just the usual nerves and guys pukin' in the john and punchin' lockers and so forth. The game? I thought the game was well played, close. That Adam Benson, my God, when he had it workin' there just wasn't anybody better. Never. Nobody, not even Joe Willie Namath, who beat us in the Orange Bowl. But unusual? Nothin' really. We let them move pretty well down the field, which is not something teams usually do against us. And he fooled us a couple of times really good, especially on that touchdown. Nobody knew he was going to keep it, not even his own guys. That's what makes it work. When nobody knows it's coming."

Keegan had heard that several times. But it was better to just let Charles keep talking. Most people, Keegan had found, don't know when they're saying something that might be important to an experienced interrogator, and whether it was gentle or harsh, when a detective talks to a civilian about a crime it isn't an interview; it's an interrogation.

"So that play, nothing unusual? Except, of course, that Benson didn't do what you expected."

"Nope. We had a three-fill defense. That's a coverage that concentrates on the run but allows some of our faster guys to be there just in case the quarterback decides to throw. The three-fill is, well, a defense we use a lot."

"Same people?"

The coach looked up, just for a second, but it was a reaction that could be read. Not many civilians knew that certain defenses used different players, that the same eleven starters don't play all the time, the way most fans think. "Yeah, I think so. No, wait. Robbie Banks twisted an ankle in warm-ups. He didn't play. We used Parks, the kid from Florida State, pretty good draft choice for the third round. Kid likes to hit. Mean bastard. But he wasn't in on that play. No, sir. That would have been ... let's see; Benson ran right, then cut back, so he finally wound up being hit by the left end. That would be Marshall. The left tackle, Johnson. The left outside linebacker, Simpson. The left cornerback, St. John. And the free safety, Harrison. No. Not Harrison. That dumb bastard missed the assignment. He was back on the right side of the end zone playing with his dick. So those were the guys. Marshall, Johnson, Simpson, St. John. Those four. You want them in here?"

"No, coach. That won't be necessary. Nobody was hurt on that play? Nobody on the Giants?"

"No, sir. I don't think so. I'll check with Sid Marr. He's the trainer. He'd know for sure. But nothing was serious, or I'd know that."

Marshall. Johnson. Simpson. St. John. They were the four Giants closest to the scene of the murder, however unlikely that word seemed when applied to the death of Adam Benson. Larry Marshall, Melvin Johnson, Jackie Simpson, Eldon St. John. Buck would help him build preliminary profiles on these four, background information, anything that might lead to a suspicion, a doubt, a connection to anything that had to do with Billy DeSalvo, Anthony Assante, or the organization that hid and protected them.

Marshall, Johnson, Simpson, St. John. Could one of them be not only a professional football player but also a murderer?

Keegan drove back to his precinct office, sat at the desk, and dialed the number he had previously obtained for the Bears office. He dialed, asked the switchboard operator for Rick Odoms, the public relations director, and when he answered introduced himself.

"Yes, sir," said Odoms. "How can I help?"

"I would like to know if anybody can provide me with the names of the players who were closest to Benson on that play," Keegan responded. "We have the videotape shot. We have played it back and forth, over and over, but some of the players are hidden. There's an arm we can't identify. Somebody's ass. You know."

"Right. I have that. The coaches broke it down as soon as they got back Sunday night. God, I don't know how they're going to manage this next game or two. The players are in shock. One of the team doctors called in a psychiatrist to treat them for the posttrauma disorientation. The coaches are just wandering back and forth. Nobody wants to go near Adam's locker. What a nightmare."

"Yeah," said Keegan.

"Oh, OK. Hold on. I'll get the list." Keegan could hear the receiver being put down on the desk, not on hold. He heard a muffled voice. "Anita, where's that damned list of players who were on the ground with Benson?" then heard Odoms pick up the phone again.

"Detective Keegan? The players closest to Adam when he ran that play were the right tackle, Bill Jillian, the tight end, Mark Tucker, the wide receiver, Thomas McNeely, and the fullback, Harlan Ellsworth. But none of them were absolutely next to him, you know? It was a surprise. He didn't tell anybody he was keeping the ball. So he ran into the end zone kind of on his own. That's why they call it a naked reverse."

"Yeah, or a bootleg," Keegan said, remembering a little bit more from his college football days and his long conversations with Ed Buck each day he spent tracking down this mystery. "I understand just enough to know what you're saying. But what about when your players realized he had scored? Didn't somebody jump on him? That always seems to happen."

"Yeah. Tucker did. The fullback, Harlan Ellsworth, he did, too. And the center, Michael Lee Reasons. Then everybody else joined the pile. It was an electric sort of moment."

Yeah, right. What crap. All public relations people must be cut from the same flawed cloth.

Great. Mark Tucker. Bill Jillian. Thomas McNeely. Harlan Ellsworth. Michael Lee Reasons. Five more to add to the list of those players who were near or underneath or on top of Adam Benson when he drew his last breath.

Keegan needed to talk to George Laskey, so he picked up the phone and dialed the interoffice system exchange that put him in touch with the medical examiner's office. He asked for Laskey, heard the connection being made, and then heard his friend's voice.

"Keegan here, George," he said. "What's up? Anything?"

There was a lift, a lilt, to Laskey's voice. "You must have ESP, Gerry. I just finished dictating a report to you. We got it. We found what killed Adam Benson, and I'll be double damned if it isn't the smartest piece of murder I've seen in years."

"Tell me."

"Well, if you just stay with me," Laskey said, "I'll try to explain it in layman's terms."

"Damn it, George. I've been doing this for twenty-something fucking years. I have heard enough medical examiners give me their findings. I am not a fucking idiot. Now tell me what happened."

"Somebody poked a long, very thin needlelike object into Adam Benson's heart," he said. "Like an old-fashioned hat pin, maybe six inches long, but thinner. It was a direct hit, but if administered properly, or just through blind luck, that's all the heart needs to have a momentary seizure. It's exactly like a muscle cramp, like when you wake up at night with your calf muscle all knotted and it hurts like hell. Except this produces a heart attack with no signs, no warning, no symptoms, no traceable evidence unless you really look hard for a puncture mark. We found it. That's how he died, and it most definitely was murder. Intentional, clever, and absolutely premeditated. And the guy was lucky, too, because he could have hit a rib with the thing and nothing would have happened. Or he could have missed the heart and just given Benson a bruise. But it went in exactly the right place and at the right angle. He was either very lucky or well coached."

Keegan paused, carefully measuring what he knew and what he had to do.

"Don't say a word," he finally told the doctor. "Fill out the report. File it. But take your time. And don't get yourself in any trouble. And keep quiet about it. Don't say anything. Can you tell me anything else about the murder weapon, George? Anything at all?"

"Not really. Just a long, very thin instrument. Easily hidden, just as easily disposed of. I mean, whoever did it could have simply pushed it into the ground. Maybe a hundred pairs of feet have stomped over it since then, with shoes, cleats, boots, whatever. That's if it's there, Gerry."

"Yeah. The guy could have stuck it in, made sure it worked, then pulled it back and hid it in his uniform. If he did that, it's long gone by now. And forever."

Dr. Laskey interrupted the conversation, which was really Gerry Keegan talking to himself out loud. "Gerry, I've got to go. I have to fill out this report. I've got to put the guy back together again. I've got to tell the funeral parlor the body is ready to be claimed. I'll talk to you tomorrow."

"OK, George. Thanks. I'll be in touch."

Keegan put the telephone down and stared at the wall in the precinct house. He didn't really see anything. He was just staring.

One of the players on the field last Sunday was a murderer. One of the players killed Adam Benson. But who? And why? And exactly how?

TWENTY

THE call Billy DeSalvo didn't want to get, not now and not ever, came that night. DeSalvo was home in his Bel Air mansion. The bodyguards were there, of course, positioned intelligently and unobtrusively, but they didn't count. They weren't supposed to be seen, and certainly they weren't supposed to bother Mr. DeSalvo. To his mind, they were just vicious two-legged Dobermans used to patrol the grounds and the house and trained to kill on command. Nothing more.

Rico Scalzi was there, too. Naturally. The big man didn't live with DeSalvo, but he spent enough time there so that he might as well get his mail delivered to the Harlene Hill Road address. He was there that night, near midnight, to go over with DeSalvo the impending trip to New York and the meeting with the broad from the advertising agency who was close to the sportswriter, Benson's closest friend.

The agency guy was clever. He told the girl, Leigh Crespino, that she was going to meet a businessman from the West Coast who had control over more than 30 million bucks in advertising for tourism to the Coast and Hawaii.

Good. Fine. Who the fuck cared? She agreed to meet with him Friday, and that's when she'd know who he really was and what this really was all about. She'd find out just how important it was for her boyfriend to back off, to drop the questions, and to get the detective, Keegan, to do the same.

Billy had told Scalzi to stay in Los Angeles. There were things to do, things to oversee. Rico was becoming increasingly more crucial to the daily operation of DeSalvo's little empire, one that existed with the blessing of Anthony Assante, and only because of that.

And the telephone call was from Assante.

"Boss, it's him, Mr. Assante," said Rico, and DeSalvo wasn't comfortable with how long and how apparently friendly the preliminary conversation between Assante and Rico had been.

"Yes sir, Mr. Assante," DeSalvo said. "How can I help you?"

The voice, disembodied as it was, three thousand miles away, still carried with it a threatening, ominous tone all the more frightening because it was never raised.

"You are coming home this week, Billy?"

"Yes, sir. I am flying in Thursday night. I am going to meet with a woman who lives with the sportswriter. He is the one who was friendly with Adam Benson and he is the one who called in the detective. We don't know yet if they know how Benson died—"

"They do," Assante interrupted. "They know exactly how it was done. Billy, it wasn't that clever. It was too easy to discern."

Beads of perspiration began to line up in little rows of buttons up and down the back of Billy DeSalvo's neck.

"The fix in the National Football League was brilliant, Billy, and I gave you much credit for arranging it. Bringing in the Novak girl, getting her to marry Benson, addicting her, and thereby putting a hook up his ass, that was all brilliant, Billy."

"Thank you, sir," DeSalvo said, although at the same time wondering where the conversation was going.

"But, Billy, Benson decided to back out of his deal. I understand that. So he had to be killed. I understand that, too. A man should live or die by his word."

"Yes, sir."

"The detective, Keegan, is not going to change his mind and go looking for something else to keep him busy, Billy. The sportswriter is too close. His girlfriend knows too much. You have created a dangerous situation for me, Billy. I hope you can find a way out of it quickly and cleanly. I cannot have things like this going on in my business."

"I understand that, Mr. Assante," Billy murmured, and now the droplets of perspiration had turned into rivulets down his back. "I am going to take care of it all. I promise that to you. I guarantee it, Mr. Assante. No one will ever know what really happened."

A silence.

"Billy, that is not entirely correct. In truth, you are never going to know how this comes out. Do you understand?"

Billy DeSalvo began to formulate an answer, which was really a question, but the words never got out. They were blocked, as was his oxygen supply, by the tightly wound silk scarf wrapped around his neck, held there by Rico Scalzi's powerful, hammerlike hands. Oddly, the most interesting part of dying an agonizing, asphyxiating death was watching the veins pop in Rico's massive forearms as he tightened his grip and pulled the scarf ever tighter. Billy was fighting for breath now, struggling for air. There was a buzzing in his ears growing louder, the room was spinning, and then it went all black, and all he had left to see was Rico's forearms and one of the corners of the Fendi scarf.

Billy still didn't believe he was going to die. Hey, he had been in worse spots before. Surely Rico would relent. They were friends. It was a joke. Mr. Assante would change his mind. Mr. Assante had told Rico to almost kill him, just to show how angry he was at the way Billy had fucked this thing up.

But die? No, not him. There was too much left on his plate.

Then, suddenly, one last light. It turned from bright to opaque and then quickly to a swirling black fog. A final, frantic gasp for air died hopelessly in his throat. And then he died, and the last flash of awareness he had was one of great surprise.

Billy DeSalvo was no longer a player in the world of Anthony Assante.

Rico, hardly exerted, stepped over the body, mildly offended by the stench of feces that had been released when all muscle control left DeSalvo, and he picked up the telephone.

Assante was waiting.

"It is done," Rico said.

"Good, come home," said Assante.

Rico smiled. He had never liked Los Angeles.

The next call he placed was to a number he had been given

just two days ago. He did not know who would answer, and it really didn't matter.

"I am calling for a friend from New York," he said. "There is a house here in Bel Air that needs cleaning."

"We'll be right there," said a woman on the other end. "Leave the front door unlocked but not open. Go now. Touch nothing. Have a pleasant trip."

Once again Rico smiled. Assante had everything covered. By morning the house would be empty and the two bodyguards would have been sent elsewhere. Nothing was ever left to chance. Billy DeSalvo would simply have disappeared, and the house, which had been purchased by a man named Arthur McDonald, who did not exist, would be sold through a real estate company owned by Assante.

The money from the sale would be deposited in a bank in the Cayman Islands, in the name of Maria Scalzi, Rico's mother. Even as a bargain, priced to move cheaply for the sake of a quick sale, it would net slightly more than $2.5 million, which was more than a fair price to be paid for three minutes' work, to rid the world of another animal dirtying the name of Anthony Assante.

Rico made his exit, returned to his beachfront home in Malibu, and threw his few personal items into a small duffel bag. He was going to miss the place, with its privacy and the nymphomaniac woman next door whose husband was never there, but New York was better. It was home. And maybe, if it looked like he'd be staying long enough, he'd bring his mother back, at least for the spring and summer months when it wasn't so cold.

Rico climbed back into the new Buick Park Avenue black four-door, exactly the same kind of car that had been left for him each year since he had been told to move to Los Angeles three years ago. He would leave it at the airport, and it would disappear, just like Billy DeSalvo. If Rico couldn't get a red-eye flight to New York or Newark, he'd sleep at the airport Marriott and get the first one out in the morning. He was going to be needed to brief the man who would be keeping DeSalvo's appointment with Leigh Crespino.

TWENTY ONE

THE four of them sat in Ed's living room. Adam's father had made the lonely trip back to Oliphant to handle funeral arrangements for Saturday. Ed and Leigh and Sherri, who wanted to go to Oliphant but was convinced to stay and help, listened as Gerry Keegan outlined the cause of death and the probable method of its infliction.

"I don't understand," Ed said. "A long needlelike thing just slipping into the heart and he's dead? The heart is a muscle. I can stab my bicep with a needle and it won't stop working. I can puncture my pecs, damned near put a needle into any muscle, and not have it stop. I don't understand."

Gerry nodded. "Right, except for the fact that the heart is more or less electronically regulated. It needs to keep its beat, its rhythm. That's why hearts can be started again with electrical impulses. Inserting the needle, even twisting it around some, caused the heart muscle to contract. When it contracted, it stopped. But it would have been simple to get it going again— if Adam had been in a hospital or even near any kind of paramedic treatment. But he wasn't. So it contracted, stopped for a second, and . . . well, it stayed that way. Stopped.

"According to George Laskey, he suffered a heart attack, but it was more like a trauma to the heart. There have been fighters killed by a direct, powerful punch to the heart area. It stops that muscle for a second, and when nothing comes along to revive it the heart stops pumping. That stops the blood flow and that's it. Dead."

Leigh shook her head. "So what you're saying is that one of

the players involved in that particular play, in that pileup, was carrying a needlelike instrument, that he had the chance to use it and so he did, under orders from somebody. Wouldn't all that gear players use have prevented it from getting through? Shoulder pads, something?"

"No, only if he had been wearing something for bruised or cracked ribs, and then a kind of corset would have been in place. But Adam wasn't hurt. He wore his shoulder pads, and they come down only to a point just below the front of the shoulders, like halfway down to the sternum. And the pads are longer on each side than in the middle of the chest. The guy didn't even have to be very educated in the human body. He would have needed one lesson, someone to show him just once approximately where to jab it in, and the length of it would have taken care of the rest. Laskey said it could even have been more sophisticated, somewhat thicker around on the handle to contain a small chip that emitted a charge of electricity when the tip met some resistance. A small electrical charge, he said, would have made sure the heart would stop."

"Well, so now we know how," Ed said. "But we don't know why and we don't know who. I suppose we know why, come to think of it. Bad break for the bad guys, sure, but then he said he would blow the whistle. And I guess even if he never said it, they would have had to do this just in case he ever decided it would be a good idea. So we need to know who did it. Do you have any idea, Gerry?"

Keegan shook his head. "Nope, but we're working on it. Sherri, I got you into a safe place. I'd like to move you in tonight. It's a great apartment, right across from Gracie Mansion, the mayor's official residence. There are more cops around there than at a rally for Louis Farrakhan. We know Billy DeSalvo engineered this thing, but we don't know who directed him. I know him. He isn't smart enough to get this NFL-fixing thing into operation. He's a soldier. He gets told what to do and then he does it. I have my suspicions, but I doubt that I'll ever be able to make anything stick."

She nodded and got up from her seat. "I have to go to the bathroom for a minute," she said. "Be right back."

Keegan shook his head. "Sherri. Don't go. I know why you're going and what you're going to do. Let us help you beat it. You can, you know. Let me see what's in your purse."

She barely resisted but handed him the small purse and watched as he pulled from it a cellophane packet of white powder. Cocaine. Watched as he opened it, emptied it into the ashtray, and poured some of his drink on it. She nodded. "I'll go where you say, Gerry, and I'll do whatever you say. I want to be off this. I want to get the people who killed Adam. I don't want to live the kind of life I've been living." Her eyes watered over, and she sat down again, putting her face in her hands.

"I don't know if I told you everything I know, but I keep thinking of new things," she said, after drawing a few deep breaths. "Billy had a lieutenant. Rico. Rico Scalzi. Big, mean, does anything he says. Mostly his dirty work. And you're right. Billy didn't put this football deal together, but he was in charge of it. I don't know who was his boss. I only met one other guy, some older man everyone was afraid of. And I met him just once, with Billy, in some office building in downtown Los Angeles."

Keegan's eyebrows raised ever so slightly. "You remember his name?"

"Yes. McDonald. Arthur McDonald. Maybe seventy, seventy-five. Could have been even older. Silver-gray hair. Good shape. Not too tall, but he looked taller. And lean. He slapped me when I said something he didn't like. Just reached over the desk and slapped me in the face. Hard. I could feel his power. And Billy never moved a muscle. I know he was scared to death of him. It was this guy, McDonald, who laid it all out for Billy. Told him to use me to get to Adam, told him to keep me supplied with coke, told him to cut me off if I didn't cooperate.

"Gerry, he promised me a movie role. It was all set. And you know what? I'm a good actress. I really can do this work. But it's like, well, you don't get a chance unless you know somebody. Once you have the work, it's easy to get more. I'm not stupid, not some dumb blonde, but I didn't have anything when I got out there and I had to do all the demeaning, garbage things to get closer to some of the important people. This guy Mc-

Donald, he was as important as I ever met, and I think maybe one of the most important men in Hollywood."

Keegan nodded. "Or New York," he said softly. "The man I think you met was Anthony Assante, who almost never goes anywhere. This must have been very important to him, or somebody out there was."

Keegan was right. And Keegan was wrong.

TWENTY TWO

THERE were probably no more than half a dozen people in the world who knew the man called McDonald, and they lived with this burden uncomfortably. Several others had met strange and mysterious ends, and although McDonald was clearly the reason and none of the people with whom he did business found it mysterious at all, not once was he ever even suspected.

One time, just disappoint him one time, and there was no second chance. He was reluctant to the point of intractable to add anyone to the list of those who knew who he was and those to whom he might extend a small bit of friendship. Once someone was accepted, McDonald expected total and complete loyalty, unswerving, unquestioned. There was no other choice, not family and not friendship, not business, and not even religion. McDonald was the most important person in their lives, their most crucial consideration, and the fount of incredible sources of nontaxable income in the lives of those few who knew him; he was almost as critical in the lives of hundreds of thousands who did not and never would know him.

Arthur McDonald was eighty-three years old, officially. Actually, he was almost eighty-six, except only he knew that and there was no one left who could provide similar information. Those with whom he did business did not know his real name, although they thought they did.

They thought he was Salvatore Posilipo.

He wasn't. Salvatore Posilipo was the first man McDonald

had murdered, on a battlefield in Europe in 1944. It was a necessary action. He needed a new identity.

It was the perfect time. The confusion was chaotic. The visibility was almost zero because of smoke and flames and black, sucking fire. The guttural bark of machine guns and the sharp cracking sound of rifles and the almost incessant rocking of exploding hand grenades and the sickly yellow-green fumes produced by the bombs that fell from the air and dismembered friend and foe alike combined to create a nightmarish, surreal setting in which nothing anyone did could be seen or chronicled or even remembered. Too many men were fighting for their lives, and it was a fight most of them would lose.

So Salvatore Posilipo became a sacrifice. He was a twenty-six-year-old man with a young wife and a son waiting and praying for him at home in Philadelphia. He was fighting because they told him he had to. He didn't mind, of course. He was a first-generation American citizen, and he was inordinately proud of that. He would have willingly laid down his life to protect those things that his father, also Salvatore, had told him were the most important in life.

But no one ever would know that he hadn't been killed by a German bullet or run down by a German tank or blown up by a German land mine. It would have been incomprehensible to learn that he had been shot in the back by his own kind, a man named Giovanni Impelliteri, who was the same age, who had no family, who had listened to the news of the Japanese attack on Pearl Harbor with a grim smile on his face. This would be a war that lasted for a long time, he thought, and it would provide a chance for those who saw it to become rich and powerful and, most important of all, to become invisible.

So Giovanni Impelliteri had enlisted at the Church Street recruiting center in lower Manhattan three days after the bombing. He requested immediate action, on the front, so that he might help defeat the enemy. He was a natural, a fighter with no fear, a killer with a flair and absolutely no remorse or hesitation. He would do whatever needed to be done.

Six months later, when he boarded a ship and set sail with fifteen hundred others for the European continent, he had gone through basic training at Fort Dix in New Jersey and earned grudging respect from the instructors and officers. He was totally ruthless, hard to know, but not a single man at Dix would hesitate to go into battle with Giovanni Impelliteri.

They had started to call him Johnny Imp, but he glared the first time someone said it to his face, eyes boring painful holes in the guilty party, and after that they never called him Johnny Imp to his face. As his legend grew, most never even used it behind his back, certain somehow that he would know and be angry.

Giovanni was not a big man, perhaps five-feet-nine. Hard as metal, lean as bone, he weighed 155 pounds and never moved an ounce from that number. He was handsome in a hard way, like a stone replica of a human being, and as far as anyone knew he never went out with the others to drink, to search for women, to use the increasingly available whores who set up shop just outside Dix.

He had no friends. He had no vices. He had no hobbies or interests.

He simply wanted to be taught to kill.

He learned quickly and well.

But in his mind, where he had formulated his plan, one that would have made a chess master proud for its far-reaching and incredibly logical thought processes, he could not remain Giovanni Impelliteri. Not for long, anyway. He had to start a new life, create a new identity, and he was going to use the war, this unexpected and welcome opportunity, to set his career in motion.

So the ship disgorged yet another load of American boys in England, and Impelliteri's group, the Eighty-first, was dispatched almost immediately to Poland. In the spring of 1944 slow, painful advances were being made that brought the Americans to the German border. That assault stalled for six months or more, a holding action that was nevertheless deadly. And then the breakthrough. It was in early November of 1944. Impelliteri and his platoon were part of a massive charge through the Rhine Valley and finally, inexorably, found themselves on German soil.

They watered that soil with German blood. They left German bodies to become fertilizer for that German soil. They swept through the countryside with the violence and effectiveness of a new strain of uncontrollable airborne sickness. Impelliteri's group—he had already received a battle promotion to sergeant—was particularly forceful, which is the way the higher-ranking officers put it. They were, in truth, frightened of this man, this cold and ruthless man who seemed to derive more pleasure than any man should from taking the lives of others, although those who had "liberated" the concentration camps silently and sometimes even vocally praised Impelliteri's intensity and dedication.

And then it was time for him to disappear. He had looked long and hard before he found Salvatore Posilipo. They were the same size, had the same general features, exhibited bravery and determination that would see them successfully through life-threatening situations. Giovanni cultivated Salvatore, "Sally," he called him, "the toughest girl I ever knew." Posilipo, who had grown to admire Impelliteri for his courage and had come to respect him, was pleased at the friendship and the good-natured teasing. No one else ever got close to Johnny Imp. No one.

It was a gray, cold, and bitter day. Approximately fifty U.S. soldiers had broken through a shoulder-high stone wall outside Munich and were greeted, from the other side of the field, by intense fire. Everyone began shooting in the general direction of the attack. Men on radios frantically screamed for air cover, shrieked out locations, and then fell. Giovanni Impelliteri kept his eye on Posilipo and, when the carnage was at its peak, calmly shot him in the back, between and slightly above the shoulder blades. Sally Posilipo fell, dead instantly. No one noticed.

Impelliteri crawled to the body, swapped dog tags, said a brusque farewell to his friend, and then planted a hand grenade under Posilipo's face, rolling out of the way just as the explosion ripped off Sally's head, rendering him totally and forever unidentifiable.

But, of course, once Impelliteri had assumed the identity of Salvatore Posilipo, there would be those who would know him. Those who would meet him, do business with him, and therefore know his name. That could not be, for Sally Posilipo was dead and, as his personal sacrifice, so was Giovanni Impelliteri.

He would never be Giovanni Impelliteri, and he could not be Salvatore Posilipo.

It was another two steps removed from his real identity. Men like Giovanni/Salvatore need to distance themselves from whatever it was they planned to do, as well as from reality.

Impelliteri had made one more switch of dog tags, later that night, and had "traded identities" with another young man, lying dead on the side of the road, his face blown away by a mortar round. His name had been Arthur R. McDonald.

Impelliteri became Arthur R. McDonald.

The war ended.

The body bearing the dog tags of Giovanni Impelliteri, the body that had once been christened Salvatore Posilipo, was buried, unmourned, in a cemetery in France. The grave was unmarked save for a small white cross. The name scratched into the cross in rudimentary lettering was Impelliteri's.

The body of Arthur R. McDonald, which had been identified as that of Salvatore Posilipo, was buried with honor and ceremony in St. Vincent's Reform Catholic Cemetery outside Philadelphia, by the proud and grieving Posilipo family.

Arthur R. McDonald's parents never understood why their son stopped writing to them and never came home. They mourned his loss as surely as if he had died.

Impelliteri was safe.

TWENTY THREE

ONE of the few men in the world who knew this story, and therefore knew that McDonald was Posilipo and that Posilipo was Impelliteri, was Anthony Assante. They had been doing business since the early 1950s. It was Assante, a high-ranking member of one of the most feared organized crime families, who made the introductions that brought McDonald/Impelliteri into the same inner circle. Since McDonald wasn't Italian, at least to the outside world, he could never become a "made man," could never be as close as the others. That was fine. He never wanted that kind of association. It meant giving away too much personal information, and that was what he guarded most zealously.

But McDonald showed the powerful families how to make more money than they had ever thought possible, and they responded with respect and information of their own. It was a magnificent association: McDonald was a perfect front man, white-haired and genteel, educated, and impossibly wealthy. The families needed someone like him and never expected he would be so productive for them. What they didn't know until it was far too late was the sinister danger he represented.

Success came faster and more successfully than anyone could have imagined, and it was the kind of business—banking, stocks, legitimate—that became increasingly more difficult for the authorities to trace, to chart. McDonald's genius, coupled with a predator's ruthlessness, was made to reflect off Assante. He was impregnable, untouchable, directing business deals and takeovers, administering life lessons and death with the impunity of a man protected by layers and layers of alibis and shell corporations and, as well, by the absence of anyone who knew more than a small part of the overall operation.

It was safe and foolproof, Assante realizing early on that any investigation could be squashed by money, that any group of law-and-order civil servants could be bought, at a price so ridiculously low it inspired only disdain in the minds of those who wielded the power.

Police were nothing, politicians even less, and the more important the politician, the easier it was to buy him. Construction and corporate swindles were almost too easy. Brokering for state- and federal-level lobbyists became simple. Millions upon millions of dollars were flowing into the carefully structured cobwebs of revenue depositories, but the action was gone. If it can be imagined that generating more than a billion dollars over a four-year period was boring, then that is exactly how Assante felt.

McDonald did not feel the same. He was content. He had done all that he had started out to do, in the streets as a child and on the battlefields of Europe as a young man. Every conquest, every success, was a powerful incentive to do more, to make more, to bring another man to his knees.

He had little need for the money, and he had shunned public displays of recognition and power all his life. His desires were simple and mostly revolved around privacy and comforts. He had no family, no children. He was not a charitable man. The money simply accumulated and had reached a point where no one could count it, not McDonald and not any of his accountants and financial advisers and attorneys.

McDonald had no close friends, save for Anthony Assante, and when Assante came to him with the idea of "arranging" NFL games he gave his reluctant approval because it was something everyone knew about, something glamorous and romantic, and it sparked just a touch of excitement in this old man's dull life.

"Get me the best," he told Assante, "and make it foolproof."

So Assante arranged for Adam Benson, clearly the best and most visible. It was as if some earlier McDonald had turned Joe

DiMaggio or Mickey Mantle. It was impossible, so much so that no one would even dream that it might happen.

But Assante knew the lure of sex, drugs, and money and the effect of the implied threat of power and force. Once in, the hook was forever. No exit. And Adam Benson had become another example.

McDonald was angry, for a short while, because of the resultant media frenzy, even when the fools didn't know the truth but thought the quarterback had simply died of heart failure on the field. But he had seen enough of this television/advertising/season-ticket bonanza to realize that there might be something huge, financially speaking, in getting the game under the control of one of the "organizations" he headed. So he forgave Assante for his indiscretion, counted the small amount of money the project produced as a bonus instead of a liability, and forgot the entire nuisance.

So did all his people, those who knew, and there had been that termination of the one who had managed it.

The project was over, as dead as Adam Benson.

But one of the most dangerous men in the world had made one small mistake. He had underestimated the power of genuine friendships.

TWENTY FOUR

GERRY Keegan sat alone in a small office the day after Adam Benson's funeral. It was a circus in the little town of Oliphant, with dignitaries from the various sports worlds present, not to mention headline-famous athletes and coaches. In all, more than five hundred people tried to jam into the small Miller & Sons Mortuary on Front Street, which of course didn't work.

Keegan was bothered by the funeral at several levels. Sherri Novak, for instance, and there was no hiding the fact, at least to himself, that he was attracted to her.

He was also disturbed by the inescapable fact of the murder. Benson had been killed, with intent, on the football field in Yankee Stadium. The murderer was more than clever; he was diabolically gifted. But there were only football players as suspects, and none of them had any serious hook to Benson or to the organized crime animals who had clearly orchestrated this killing.

So how to get more from Sherri, and how to get a lead on which one of the players might have actually done the deed? There would never be a murder weapon found. Keegan was as sure as he was about anything in the world that the needle, the hat pin, whatever it was, had been secreted back into the player's uniform and taken away, and if it had been disposed of later on somewhere in Manhattan or the Bronx this indeed would be a case of searching for a needle in a haystack.

But the basic rule of any crime still applied. Somebody did it. Somebody was out there waiting to be discovered, then arrested, then prosecuted. It was merely a case of finding the guilty party, and almost never did a crime of this magnitude simply disappear. Someone did it because someone else had ordered it done, and in between there had to be another handful of culpable enablers.

Keegan was convinced that the actual murderer was the least important person in the chain and would bet that the incentive there was money or drugs or both.

Who ordered it done and why were of far greater importance.

But detectives began at the beginning, at the point of the crime, and then worked out from there in ever-widening circles of involvement.

So once again Keegan went over the names of the players not only on the field but also in the pileup in the end zone.

The players for the Bears were Bill Jillian, the right tackle; Mark Tucker, the tight end; Thomas McNeely, the wide receiver; Harlan Ellsworth, the fullback; and Michael Lee Reasons, the center.

The Giants were Larry Marshall, the defensive left end; Melvin Johnson, the defensive left tackle; Jackie Simpson, the left outside linebacker; and Eldon St. John, the left cornerback.

Nine men.

One of them was a murderer.

But who? And how to find the answer?

As in any investigation, Keegan had to start with the experts. He had already visited with the Giants' head coach. He would do that again, almost certainly. But this particular man was a Cro-Magnon type. If he couldn't talk about football, he had nothing to talk about. Duane Charles reminded Keegan of the joke about the scientist at Rice who built the first interactive computer and wanted to show it off to his colleagues. So he called in the head of the math department and said, "Hey, Harold, ask him a question."

Humoring his friend, the mathematician asked, "What is the obverse of the triple gain of a quantum equation moved to unidentifiable sectors?"

Whirr. Buzz. "It would have to be six trillion minus the unidentifiable portion of the sector, sir, but probably no greater than a plus-minus of twenty nanoseconds.''

Harold was amazed.

Now the professor called in the head of the English department and said, "Hey, Ralph, ask him a question.''

Another case of humoring a friend. "Machine,'' said Ralph, "when one combines the best parts of the structural verse of Russian sonnets and the influence of the early Moorish poets, how does that combination best reflect in modern poetry?''

Bells and whistles. One minute, tops. "Most opinions offered to date identify e. e. cummings, but the stronger case can be made for Ezra Pound.''

Ralph was amazed.

And now the professor spotted the football coach walking down the hall. "Billy Joe, come in here; ask my machine a question.''

The coach looked warily at the computer. "I'm the football coach; what do you know about defense?''

Less than five seconds passed, and the computer said, in a high-pitched, nasal twang-drawl, "How 'bout them Cowboys?''

That joke always made Keegan laugh.

Ed Buck had first told it to him.

So now Ed was going to do profiles on the four Giant players involved. He was home when Keegan called.

After listening to the request, Ed readily accepted but asked his friend if he could bring someone else in on the investigation.

"Who would that be?'' Keegan wondered.

"The Giants' psychological profile guy, a really good guy named David Silverman. He sits on about six different boards of directors, does all the employment profiles for most of the major corporations in the area, and works with the Giants on an almost daily basis, especially when it's time for the college player draft. They won't take a kid unless Dr. Silverman has passed on him, and he interviews about two hundred of them at the tryouts and workouts. The coaches hate him because they'll take anybody who can play, but David won't approve certain guys. Why? I don't know for sure. That's why he does what he does."

Keegan had no problem with the involvement of Dr. Silverman. The more experts the better, and this was absolutely on the money in terms of the man fitting the job.

"Call him. Give him Marshall, Johnson, Simpson, and St. John. I guess you'll have to tell him why we're interested, too. Fill him in."

"Why these four?"

"Because they were the four Giants in the pileup," Keegan said. "I have five Bears I need to get work-ups on. Do you know if anybody like this Silverman guy does the same job for them?"

"Yeah. David Silverman."

A break, if even the smallest kind. "Call him," Keegan said. "Who are the Bears?"

"Jillian, Tucker, McNeely, Ellsworth, and Reasons."

Buck put the telephone down. Something was starting to happen, and it was encouraging enough to lift him slightly out of the depression that lingered from the funeral the day before.

Most of Adam's high school friends, now prematurely pot-bellied, wore on their faces the look of the loss of a very close friend. Many of the NFL players had tears on their cheeks. The idiot Boland brothers, in an uncharacteristic fit of generosity, had chartered a bus to bring the entire team and all the front office personnel to Oliphant. Most of the Bears were there, too.

Services were short. The local priest, who had seen Adam through all his religious passages as a boy, officiated. "We miss him mostly because of who he was here in Oliphant," intoned the Reverend Louis Asher, "and we were proud of who he was after he left us. Adam Benson will be missed by those who knew him then and by those who knew him after he left."

Done. Benson's father shook hands, tears streaming silently down his cheeks. Sherri stayed at his arm, black dress and black veil only adding to her unintentional sexuality. Ed and Leigh were with the official mourning party, too. A short stop at a local restaurant, too quiet and too sad, finished the day. Andy Benson went home to be alone, while Sherri accompanied Ed, Leigh, and Gerry Keegan to the limousine that would take them back to New York.

Adam Benson was dead and buried.

Now Keegan wanted to be able to say the same about whoever killed him.

TWENTY FIVE

DR. David Silverman sat at his desk in his office on Park Avenue, intentionally selected to be near both the NFL and the Giants' offices—walking distance, actually. He was sketching abstract designs around the list of nine names, drawing circles around a few of them, squares around others. That he was shocked to hear that players were being investigated, that one of them almost certainly had to be implicated in the murder of Adam Benson, was a gross understatement. But shock was not surprise. Nothing much surprised Dr. Silverman anymore. Professional football players, as well at athletes in other pro sports, had been allowed for way too long to live in their own world, with their own rules and too much money and virtually no supervision. The teams "arranged" to get them out of trouble. All they needed was a jump shot or the ability to hit a baseball or pitch it.

And in the case of football, with which he was mainly involved, any of the world-class skills that could be translated into winning and, therefore, profits for the team were worth preserving, even if it meant breaking a few silly laws along the way.

Three of the names earned a circle or a square as well as an asterisk. Dr. Silverman knew all the players, of course. They hadn't been in the league that long. It seemed as though no players stayed around too long in these days of salary caps and ever-increasing demands to be faster and bigger and stronger. He had run through all nine during the various free-agent tryouts held each February in Indianapolis, where upward of three hundred college athletes were poked, prodded, timed, asked to lift weights and jump vertically as well as horizontally, and measured and, in more recent years, tested psychologically.

"We do not expect to find any potential rocket scientists," David had said once, over a long dinner with Ed at LeCirque 2000 (Silverman paid), "but we don't want to draft any psychotics, either. We understand the football aspect of colleges in this country. It's as though they have two groups of student bodies, the ones who have to earn passable grades to stay in school and the athletes, who can do anything they damned well please short of murdering someone as long as they can help the team win games."

Silverman's track record had been nearly flawless over the years. He didn't reject too many potential draft choices, but those he did had turned out to justify his negative feelings. Three were already out of the league because of drug abuse, uncontrollable drug abuse. Another was serving time in jail for operating a ring that sold cocaine in the streets of Miami. Two others were currently under suspension.

Yet another had been signed by the Giants after being released by two other teams because of allegations of sexual and physical abuse of women and an alcohol problem out of control.

"If we can get him off the booze, we can keep him away from the women," Silverman had told the Giants' personnel director, an intelligent, thoughtful man named Henry Olden. "He is an intelligent, relatively decent young man who cannot be allowed to go anywhere near alcohol. I think he's worth the cost of rehabilitation."

That was four years ago. He had played well for the Giants, once being voted to the Pro Bowl, and had never again been involved in anything seamy. Nor, for that matter, had he ever again touched a drop of alcohol. On the other hand, Silverman's wife, Roberta, had refused to soften her view of this gargantuan kid and refused to discuss it in public or even quietly with friends. She was offended that her husband could have acted in such a "feminine unfriendly" manner, all in the interest of providing a football team with another good player.

Of course, Silverman's recommendations were just that.

Opinions. He had no real control over which players the teams' personnel and coaching staffs finally isolated as their draft picks. But more and more, his input was being considered as a necessary ingredient in making an intelligent decision.

So there he sat, nine names scrawled on paper, being asked by a good friend, on behalf of an official police investigation of homicide, to decide which one, or more, of the nine could have actually agreed to commit murder.

Silverman knew, from his years of study and experience with infinitely more dangerous men than football players, that anyone could commit a murder. "If the right buttons are pushed," he had written in a University of Pennsylvania doctoral thesis, "then the basest emotions and instincts are released. Most people have found ways to guard against those buttons being pushed. Some don't have the necessary protective devices, and so we must all hope they don't find themselves in those specific situations."

Football, especially on the professional level, strips away layers of social behavior and does, in a real and valid sense, expose the basest emotions and instincts. It would be easier, Silverman had always felt, to turn a pro football player, rather than an ordinary man, into a murderer. And defensive players were more likely to slip into that role. Their game was far less controlled and far more vicious. Just go get the ball, and the man with the ball, and do whatever you can, even going beyond the scope of the far too lenient rules, to get the job done.

He started with the four Giants. Marshall was a three-year veteran; Johnson and Simpson had been in the NFL five years; St. John was playing in his sixth season. Perhaps as a partial testimony to Silverman's input, all four had been drafted by the Giants and had remained with them. None of them had been a problem, although Silverman had been slightly less than absolutely confident in the futures of Marshall and St. John. Both of them had been in trouble in high school and college. Nothing serious, just the antics of young blue-chip athletes exercising their strength and superiority. Silverman had passed both of them because the infractions were physical, no drugs involved, no criminal mentality noticeable. Marshall was simply a bully with a mean streak, which is almost mandatory for one who would play defensive end at this world-class level. St. John was quiet, moody, extremely intelligent, and just slightly unbalanced. Again, for those who play cornerback that is recommended.

The cornerback is out there all alone. The receiver knows where he's going, knows the route he's going to run, while the cornerback has to guess. And if he makes one mistake, one false step, one split-second stumble, the receiver is downfield with the football in his arms, blurring his way into the end zone, while the cornerback is trudging off, head down, kicking at the ground, totally and completely embarrassed and exposed.

"You have to have the mentality of an assassin to play cornerback," an earlier team psychologist, Dr. Arnold Mandell in San Diego, then doing a profile of the Chargers, had written. "Cornerbacks get no help and never get much credit, but they get all the blame, and it's there for millions of people to see."

Dr. Mandell had provided the definitive profile of linebackers, too, calling them "the ideal soldiers in war, the ones who have enough cunning to slip behind enemy lines and enough innate violence to coolly murder the enemy."

But he had identified the cornerbacks as the latently psychotic, the ones most likely to murder, to take a life in a premeditated and cold-blooded fashion. Silverman remembered interviewing St. John at the Indianapolis tryouts, looking into his dark, deep stare, noticing, almost surprised, the high level of intelligence. And he remembered the critical response to what he highlighted as the most important question he would ask this young man.

"How would you feel about playing offense, if the Giants were to try to make you a wide receiver?" Silverman had asked.

St. John had looked him hard in the face. "No, man. No offense," he had replied. "I like hitting too much to play offense."

"Like it? Why?"

"I get excited, man. Like aroused. You know, like when I'm with a girl."

David Silverman knew this kid was highly rated. He knew

the Giants liked St. John a lot. He knew that they needed a cornerback. And here he was, six-two and 210 pounds, ran the forty in 4.35 seconds, had a forty-one-inch vertical jump, went off the charts on the watered-down intelligence test generally administered to football players.

And yet Silverman recommended that they pass him up in the draft, let another team take him.

"Why?" asked Tom Royster, the assistant personnel director.

"I don't know," Dr. Silverman had answered, for the first time in all the years he had been judging the personalities and psyches of prospective draft choices. "I don't know, but he frightens me."

Rooney and the team had taken this into consideration, but without specific points of discontent they chose to pass on the negative evaluation. They drafted St. John in that year's first round, and he had played with exceptional skill.

Silverman still wasn't sure why he had felt uneasy. Now, perhaps, he would come closer to fingering his source of concern.

He had been slightly upset by Marshall, too, but never suggested avoiding him. Marshall was simply a bully, strong and quick, agile, and without conscience. He could be controlled, managed, manipulated, and, in all, coerced into playing well for three or four years, maybe more, until his inability to discipline himself led to obesity and eventual early retirement.

But St. John made Silverman nervous, then and now.

Could he murder? Absolutely. Was he clever enough to pull it off? Definitely. Given the proper circumstances, would he be a viable suspect? Certainly.

But why? How? And what did he have to gain? Maybe more to the point, what did he stand to lose if he refused to do this?

Well, the entire list Buck had given Silverman would have to be checked. Never leave a job undone; never do a job less than completely. He had all his files at hand, nine folders, one of which may have held an answer.

Of the nine, Silverman was absolutely convinced that Jillian, Tucker, Reasons, Johnson, and Simpson could not have been involved. Not possibly. He would stake his reputation, not to mention his high six-figure salary based on that reputation with teams and major corporations, on that feeling.

That left four. McNeely, Ellsworth, Marshall, and St. John.

He would get to work immediately.

TWENTY SIX

THOMAS McNeely, who had attended but did not graduate from Clemson University, had been evaluated by Dr. Silverman as a nondangerous, nonpsychotic, not overly intelligent person. His work ethic soared in direct proportion to the amount of incentive placed just ahead of him, within his reach but only with great effort.

He was perfect as a wide receiver, stretching that extra foot, finding one more burst of speed, not so much in celebration of his athletic skills but for the inherent glory in making a big play. He liked that such things called attention to himself.

There had been only one incident at Clemson, when McNeely and three other men, two of whom had been football players, were arrested on rather common charges of drunk and disorderly one Saturday night following an unexpected victory over heated rival Auburn. McNeely had punched one of the policemen, which in turn got him a billy club on the side of his head, but he and the school agreed not to prolong the incident. For their part, the Clemson police (the town, not the campus, cops) dropped the matter. No record, no problem.

McNeely was genuinely contrite. His fear of authority had kept him clean until then, and he was not going to become a chronic offender. He was not a problem, but reports at the scene indicated that he had lost control when the police officer struck him with the club and was consumed by his rage, threatening to kill the man, promising to return with a gun. It was the alcohol, nothing more. But there was a tendency toward violence.

David Silverman studied his notes carefully and then rejected McNeely as a possible suspect.

Harlan Ellsworth, possibly the best blocking fullback in the NFL, had been a linebacker at Penn State, one of those players moved by legendary head Joe Paterno into a position he needed and not necessarily what was in the best interests of the player. Paterno recruited several quarterbacks and tailbacks each year, arguably getting the pick of the nation's high school kids because of his reputation and Penn State's decades-long history as a contender for the national championship. Each one was promised that the starting job would be his. The mothers and the fathers urged their sons to take kindly old Joe's offer and, of course, the free, full-ride scholarship.

Then the boys would show up for summer practice and find eight quarterbacks and ten tailbacks, discover they were in a competition for the job among the best the nation's high schools could produce. The losers became second-and third-teamers. Some were told to "look elsewhere," because there wasn't much chance of any change in their immediate futures.

Others were offered the chance to change positions, to compete at a new position that might take advantage of their skills and athleticism. One example was quarterback Jim Kelly, recently retired after a certain Hall of Fame career with the Buffalo Bills. He attended Penn State, was told he would not, after all, win the quarterback job, and was offered the chance to move to linebacker.

Kelly told Paterno to stuff it, transferred to the University of Miami, and became an All-American player and a first-round draft choice.

Well, Ellsworth had been given that choice, one of moving from linebacker (where Paterno was well stocked) to fullback, where he needed someone to make way for his next custom-tailored All-American, Brian Wharton (who, in fact, did become an All-American, largely due to the ferocity of Ellsworth's blocking).

So here was Ellsworth, with the temperament of a defensive player, having been switched to perhaps the only offensive position that allowed, condoned, and encouraged a player's ability to generate that kind of unbridled defensive fury.

Ellsworth had to be kept in school by some complex manipulations on the part of the office of the dean of students, activities that the NCAA, the colleges' governing body of all things athletic, would have found not only reprehensible but also illegal and in direct and blatant violation of its often-sanctimonious rules. Ellsworth was not much of a scholar. He did not believe in attending many classes. But he was so good, so valuable, that certain allowances were made, with season tickets to the Nittany Lions' home games (ranging from hard-to-find to absolutely rare) offered to various professors for a minimally passing grade. Such tickets in the hands of such underpaid men of academe could produce up to five hundred dollars a pair for each home game. Certainly, it was a reward well worth the incidental action of changing a grade of 68 to 70; even 58 to 70 was not out of the question.

Ellsworth was a bully and a braggart. He had been in numerous fights while in school, had been picked up once in a scheme to use stolen telephone calling cards, but all of his indiscretions were without that seething rage that Silverman looked for as one of the basic symptoms of possible psychosis. It was probably all he looked for, since the young man wasn't mentally or emotionally capable of suppressing those feelings and then successfully hiding them from society.

But Silverman could not arbitrarily discount Ellsworth as one of the suspects. He put that file aside.

As for the two Giants remaining on his list, he, frankly, did not like either one of them very much. He had told the scouting department as much, although failing to absolutely reject Marshall. So far, the big lineman had been kept under control. There had been a few incidents—he had been ejected three times from games for palpably unfair acts of violence—but he had stayed away from the real trouble, the career-ending kind of trouble.

St. John was a different matter. He had become articulate, poised in public, popular with his teammates and the public, and three times a Pro Bowl nominee. He now earned more than $750,000 a year, with built-in performance clauses that provided another $100,000 or so. He was successful, in both football and his social adjustment. Maybe he'd been wrong about him.

But not so fast. St. John wasn't off the list of candidates, not yet and perhaps not ever. Something lurked there, just under the surface. His new face, his new image, his new persona didn't ring true. In Silverman's considered opinion, the same bad seed still lay dormant, but far from dead.

Eldon St. John, one of nine children produced by four different fathers, had been raised by his mother, Jessie, and his three older sisters. It was a meager existence, punctuated by trips to the welfare office in Chicago, highlighted by gang fights and dead friends and drugs being sold rampant on the streets. But Eldon could play sports. He was a quality basketball player, the fastest sprinter on the high school's track team, but he really excelled in football.

From the minute he learned the game, he knew it was what he wanted. It was the only way he could imagine being able to hit other people and not be hauled off to the local police station, where the white cops would take him and others like him into a back room and play tattoo on his back with rubberized crowd control clubs. It all came to him naturally, the ability to see where the receiver was going while at the same time keep his eye on the ball, the gift of running backward almost as fast as others ran forward, the boiling, roiling sensation of pure pleasure when he crashed into a receiver, especially when the unfortunate player had just jumped for the ball and was coming down.

The scout from Ohio State saw St. John play four times in his senior year at James Polk High School, and that was enough. He told the head coach, Jake Maddock, that "Eldon St. John is the best high school cornerback in the country, and right now he may be the best cornerback in college football, too." So all the stops were pulled for this six-two, 200-pound blue-chipper. His mother got a job that paid her three times what it was worth. His oldest sister got one, too. One of his younger brothers was guaranteed a scholarship to Ohio State when he got out of high school. Eldon got so much undisclosed, untraceable money from Ohio State alumni groups that he never even considered other offers, many of them equally illegal, from the other thirty or forty colleges that wanted him to play for them.

While in college, Eldon got one girl pregnant, and when she asked if he would marry her or at least take his share of the responsibility he beat her so badly that she lost the child. But only a handful of people knew that happened: her story, once she deposited the $25,000 in cash handed to her in an envelope by a used car dealer in Columbus, was that she fell down a long flight of metal steps in the girls' dorm.

One major problem had been handled, but not with sufficient secrecy to prevent Dr. Silverman from finding out.

There were other incidents, all of them stemming from a violent nature, uncontrollable in its fury and unpredictable in its emergence, but they were all handled, dealt with in such a way that the career of Eldon St. John would not be interrupted, nor would the winning tradition he helped instill in the Buckeyes' football program.

Without being able to prove the girl-falling-down-the-flight-of-steps incident was a heinous fabrication, Dr. Silverman could not, ethically would not, present that as a matter of truth to the Giants. He alluded to it, referred to the questionable situation that had occurred with the girl who had been St. John's close acquaintance, but had to disavow any claim of absolute knowledge. Silverman did, however, mention it to St. John one day, long after the Giants had drafted the athlete.

He got, in return, a cold, hard stare.

"I felt real bad for Darika," St. John said. "She really got hurt, I understand, and I was sorry. I really liked her for a while, you know? You know what she's doing these days?"

St. John's folder went on top of the pile.

TWENTY SEVEN

DAVID Drexler got a phone call the day before Billy De-Salvo was to arrive for his meeting with Leigh Crespino, from someone he didn't know, to whom he had never spoken, but who knew the number to his private telephone, the single unit that sat on his desk.

"The meeting with DeSalvo and the broad is off," said the man, in a hard, clipped voice. "Someone else will be there tomorrow."

"Why?" Drexler asked.

"Billy's dead, that's why."

Click.

Drexler found himself wondering, just for a fleeting second, if this meant he could get the candy account back. Then he picked up his interoffice phone and dialed Leigh's number.

"Yes?"

"It's David. The meeting with the guy from California is still on tomorrow, but not with the guy you were going to see. That shouldn't make any difference to you."

"No, it doesn't. What happened to the first guy?"

"He died suddenly. Tough to keep appointments after that happens."

Leigh thought this new development was interesting, and that night at home, over dinner with Ed, she mentioned it. He thought it was a little odd, too, and phoned Gerry Keegan to tell him.

"Just to keep everything on the record," Ed said to Leigh.

Keegan, too, thought the news had some peripheral interest, that it might somehow pertain to the case under investigation, so he called one of the Madison Avenue guys he knew and asked if the name David Drexler was familiar.

"Sure, owns a big ad agency. Kind of a prick but gets some major billing. Why?"

"He had a meeting, with some guy who represents the tourist Boards of California and Hawaii, scheduled for tomorrow. Wanted to give Drexler a major account. Now the meeting is still on but not with this guy. He's dead."

Aside from wondering whether this could allow his firm to steal the account not yet awarded, Ralph Johnson had little interest. Guys died every day, especially in this business.

"Yeah. Shit happens. So what, Gerry?"

"Find out who the dead guy was, Ralph? OK? I'll owe you one."

Johnson placed a call to one of David Drexler's private secretaries, a girl he had fucked a few years ago and one of the few such past-tense lovers with whom he still had a friendly relationship.

"Hi, Kathy, it's Ralph Johnson. Sorry for calling so late."

Kathy Layton's interest flickered. Johnson was only a fair fuck but made a lot of money. "Don't worry about it, baby. What's up?"

"I've been thinking about you, Kath," Johnson said, absolutely unable to stop himself. "Thought we might get together for a drink Friday night."

"You still married, Ralph?"

"No, but my wife thinks I am," he said.

She smiled. Same old Johnson. But why not? "Sure, the Crown, maybe seven?"

"Done. I'm excited. Oh, by the way, how's business at DD Ads?"

"Good, as far as I know."

"Kathy, I know Drexler had a meeting scheduled tomorrow with some California and Hawaii tourist board guy with a bunch of money to spend and he's dead. The meeting is still on, and

I'm interested in the account, too, you know? And with the guy dead, maybe they need more time to work it out? You know? Do you know who the dead guy was, or his company?"

"Hold on, Ralph. Let me get my book."

A pause. One minute. Two. Then she returned.

"A man named DeSalvo," she said. "William DeSalvo. That's all I have, Ralph. I don't know the company."

"Thanks, love. I'll see you Friday night."

He put the receiver down, aware he had built half a hard-on and realizing he'd get the rest of the way there, and then some, Friday night. It was a good thing Keegan had called.

Johnson returned the favor. Keegan picked up on the second ring.

"Gerry, Ralph Johnson. The dead guy was named William DeSalvo."

Bingo, thought Keegan. "Thanks," he said to Johnson. "Doesn't mean a thing to me. But thanks anyway."

A mistake, Keegan thought. The big guy, and Keegan had a feeling who it was, had made a mistake. He had had DeSalvo killed without canceling the meeting with Drexler's company first. Now someone else would have to show up. And Keegan was absolutely convinced that it had nothing to do with advertising; it was to get somebody close to Leigh, to frighten her, to pump her for information, or, conceivably but not likely, to kill her right there as a warning to Ed Buck.

But something tickled in the back of Keegan's mind. If everybody was crooked, and as a good cop you learned to make that assumption early in your career, then how could he absolutely, positively trust Mike Herbert, the guy who had arranged for Sherri to stay in the Venture Arms apartment? She had been there for a few days now and nothing had gone wrong, but it was time to move her. Especially with DeSalvo dead, somebody was going to have to clean up his mess, tie together all his loose strings, and certainly getting Sherri to stop breathing had to be high on every agenda and every list of priorities. She knew too much, had clearly demonstrated that she no longer wanted to be a part of the situation, and had become dangerous. Hazardous material.

So both women were in danger, to one extent or another. Keegan had to tell Ed about Leigh's jeopardy; he knew that. He did consider not doing so but got past that immediately. Ed had to know, and Gerry had to tell him. The situation with Sherri was more delicate. If Gerry was right and someone had found out where she was staying, even if it wasn't Herbert but someone else in that office, then there was no safe place in New York. And the scumbags had things tied up in Jersey, too.

But who could possibly guess that Sherri Novak would move in with Gerry Keegan's mother in Brooklyn, right under their noses?

He would see to that right now, not wait for morning, and the cover story would be that Novak had left to go back to California. Or something, somewhere, some other place. After all, she was not a suspect, simply a grieving widow. And personally, he would deal with what he thought was totally out of the question for him at this stage of his life, a budding emotional feeling for a woman.

Even though it was late, he called Sherri. She answered on the second ring, and her voice did not sound as though he had awakened her.

"Hello?"

Remember the tape, he reminded himself. *It's always running. Don't say anything stupid.* There was a woman officer living with Sherri, and if you don't trust one, you don't trust any.

"Hello?" she asked again.

"Hi, Mrs. Benson. It's Detective Keegan. I know it's late, but I have a few things to talk to you about. I'll pick you up in an hour, if you don't mind going out this late. It's kind of important."

She had been around subterfuge and mystery long enough to know he was speaking in code. He had stopped calling her Mrs. Benson a long time ago.

"Sure, Detective Keegan, if you think it's important. I'll be ready." She paused and decided to make it even easier. "I'll wait for you at the front door," she added. "No reason for you to come up."

Good girl, he thought, smiling. "That's fine. In half an hour. Put Officer Pearson on the phone. I'll get her off the hook."

He cleared it with the woman cop; then he called Ed.

"It's late," Gerry said, "but it's important. Leigh has a meeting tomorrow and we aren't sure who it's going to be with. It was supposed to be with a guy named DeSalvo, who has as much to do with advertising as Mother Cabrini. He's a mob guy. Or was. He's dead. I think it was somebody who wanted to get a message to you. To shut you up. To make you think about sports and not dead quarterbacks. Is she there?"

"Yes, I'll get her. How serious is this, Gerry?"

"I won't bullshit you with fairy stories, Ed. It's about as serious as it gets. I would rather not have her keep the meeting, but it would be the best thing to do, to solve this, to nail the guys who did it."

"Gerry, I can't tell her what to do. I'll put her on. Just be careful. You know how important she is."

Leigh came to the phone, wasting no time. "What's going on, Gerry? Ed looks a little scared."

He told her. Almost everything.

"Of course I'll go to the meeting," she said. "You want me wired?"

He laughed. "You've been reading too many mystery novels," he said. "We don't really do that anymore. It's primitive. In twenty minutes, someone will leave a newspaper wrapped in a plastic bag at your door. He'll rap on the door a few times just to let you know he was there. You won't see him. Don't even try. Take the newspaper out of the plastic bag and feel along the center fold. You'll find a small coin-shaped item, like a quarter, no thicker. And it will look like a quarter, just like one. When you have your meeting tomorrow, just keep it in your pocket. Just make sure it's with you. Body heat activates it. When you get back home, leave the coin in the same place you found it. Just put it in a newspaper, then ring my private desk number three times. No one will answer, but the third ring will trigger a message and the device will be picked up within an hour."

"I'll put it in my bra," she said.

Keegan smiled. "I don't need to know that, and I'll never tell the tech who works with it later where it was."

He would call no one, assign no one to this job. On his way to pick up Sherri, he'd make the drop himself. If you do it yourself, you know it gets done, and you know nobody else gets involved.

He retrieved a recording wafer from the supply he kept in the small steel box under his bed. It was safe there. He had the only key. He kept two other handguns in there (one registered, one a mystery guest), along with the recording devices, three passports (one of which was his), and other assorted items of interest and use to him.

He dressed, took his copy of the *New York Times,* which he had not had time to open, inserted the wafer recorder exactly at the center-fold crease, and slid it back into the plastic sleeve. One long strip of clear sealing tape ensured that the disk would stay where it was.

He drove over to Ed's apartment, dropped the paper so that it leaned against the door, and rapped a few times, to let them know something had been delivered. Then he ducked into a small alcove down the hall and waited until Ed came out, picked up the paper, and looked around, and Gerry Keegan was on his way when the apartment door closed again.

He drove toward Gracie Mansion, turned left at the next corner, and found himself in front of the Venture Arms. He didn't have to tap the horn. Sherri was there, waiting, and quickly slid in. He smiled when he noticed that she had her small overnight bag with her.

"Good thinking," he said.

"I didn't think you'd be picking me up to ask questions," she replied. "Am I in trouble?"

"Yes, you probably were, but no, you aren't now. We're moving you to another location."

"Where, Gerry?"

"I'm taking you home to see Mother," he said.

She smiled.

TWENTY EIGHT

ED handed the coin recorder to Leigh, who smiled thinly, put it in her pocketbook, and went back to bed. So did he, and neither of them slept. Nor did either of them feel any magic. No sex on this night. No contact, at least physically, but Ed never felt closer to Leigh than he did right now. She was going to risk a great deal, perhaps even her life, in order to help get the people who had had Adam Benson killed.

Ed could never tell her how much it meant to him, nor, he feared, could he ever tell her how much she did, either.

They were quiet for most of the rest of the night, except to occasionally blurt out, unsolicited and almost unexpected, things like, "I love you, Leigh," and, "Just hold me, Eddie; make me feel safe."

At six in the morning, as she was leaving the bed to shower and prepare for the day, he asked, "What are you doing next weekend?"

"Why?"

"Well, if you aren't busy and don't have anything planned, how about we drive down to . . . oh, I don't know, someplace like Long Beach Island in Jersey and get married?"

"I'll let you know," she said, voice cracking and catching, and then she began to cry.

They held each other for another thirty minutes, which caused her to rush the rest of the morning until she was ready to leave the apartment. "I decided," she said as she left. "The answer is yes, and the question is why did you wait so damned long?"

A huge grin plastered itself across his face. "Hey, you know that old line about why buy the cow—"

"Pig!" she exploded, and he laughed even after she kicked him in the shins.

TWENTY NINE

DR. Silverman had put out all his lines, left the appropriately disguised messages to colleagues around the league, spoken to those who had already called back, and gathered as much information as possible by telephone. He found himself wanting the guilty party to be St. John but found, as well, more and more evidence that Eldon was not a monster, even if he was someone Silverman would fight to the death to keep away from his family and friends.

Dr. Aaron Pierce, under whom Silverman had studied for two doctoral semesters at Northwestern, offered another insight. "Someone who has already disguised himself is likely to do it more effectively the next time, and the time after that, and the time after that."

St. John had disguised himself, certainly, in the cloak of a respectable citizen. But he wasn't attempting to prove to be something else. He still was an arrogant, ego-centered man, flashy and garish.

But whole.

At least on the surface.

What about Harlan Ellsworth, who had once played defense, who had once borne the label of "probable assassin profile" that psychologists affix to a segment of the professional football population? The High School All-American linebacker had latent violence ingrained in his football persona. It was what enabled him to excel at both positions, as an All-American fullback/ blocking back at Penn State (who stepped in for three games in his senior year when the middle linebacker was injured and played both ways) and now as a budding Pro Bowl fullback with the Bears. He was huge and powerful, his six-foot-two body layered with 240 pounds of muscle, but there were hundreds of players that size and bigger. The difference, which always amazed Dr. Silverman, was the emotional output generated when a few of them, a sparse handful, were placed in a highly competitive situation.

"Some players refuse to fail," he once told Ed, "and others are simply satisfied with doing well, reveling in their own physical gifts, if you will. That represents a huge difference. It can take a player, or a businessman or anybody else who deals with competition, well past what his normal physical barriers would be."

Was Ellsworth a possibility, somewhat overlooked because of the garishness and visibility of St. John? It was worth some investigating.

Dr. Silverman called the Bears' offices and asked for Louis Jerome, the team's head trainer and an old friend.

"David, what's up?" Jerome asked, clearly pleased to hear from his mentor.

"Terrible thing about Benson," Silverman answered. "Just a nightmare."

"Yes, and shocking. I mean, he was a little older, but I worked with him every day. The guy was in great shape. His annual physical showed no heart problem at all. Nothing except normal range everywhere."

"Lou, I have to ask you something that I'd like to see doesn't go any further. Is that acceptable?"

Pause. "Sure, David. We go back too many years for me not to trust you now."

"Lou, what's going on with Ellsworth? Anything different? Anything strange?"

"You mean is he on anything?"

"Yes, that, too. Is he?"

Pause. "David, I thought he was last off-season, but we can't just spot-check for substance abuse unless there's a reason, you know? Once they reported to camp, we gave him the standard blood screen and urinalysis and nothing showed. I don't think the bad guys have come up with a better, super masking drug yet, so no, I can't say he's on anything."

"Does he hang with that type?"

"David, he's a thug, not a nice man, nobody you'd want to have dinner with. I think there are some psychological warts on him, too, things that don't look good in sunlight, if you know what I mean."

"Yeah, so what makes him different from three-quarters of the players in this league, Lou? This isn't a game for sane people."

Jerome took a long time before answering.

"I think Harlan Ellsworth is dangerous. I think he can really hurt somebody. And he has no fuse at all when it comes to temper. He explodes, instantly. I guess that's what makes him such a great blocker, that plus the fact that he actually, literally hates the people he's playing against. He's a frightening man, David. He scares the shit out of me."

Was that a tingle?

"Lou, find out what you can about what he does off the field, in the off-season. I can't tell you why. Not yet. But it's important."

"Does it have anything to do with poor Adam?"

"I can't tell you anything, Lou. Trust me for now."

"Done. I'll call tomorrow. Maybe tonight. Still have the same home number?"

"Yep."

"Good. And say hello to Bobbi."

St. John could have done it. So, too, could Ellsworth. Silverman figured he had the final two candidates for the grand prize.

THIRTY

LEIGH was scared, really, truly scared, and she was not the type of woman to get that way very easily, without considerable prodding. Ed and Gerry both insisted this meeting had nothing to do with advertising, that whatever it was, with whomever she met, it was about Adam Benson's murder and she was going to be far more of a focal point than she could ever have dreamed. To say it made her nervous, frightened, and fearful would have been to seriously understate her situation.

But she was going to do it, and walking the ten blocks to the office she ran it over and over in her mind. What to say? How to react? How to respond? Was she in actual physical danger? Would the little recorder work? Did David Drexler know what was going on or was he just an innocent pawn in all of this? Was Ed in danger? Was something going to happen to her?

The recorder felt heavy in her bra, as though everyone on the street could see it, although she knew that was ridiculous. She clutched her handbag tightly, tighter than usual, and the click of her heels on the sidewalks of Manhattan sounded loud, ominous, louder than the noise of the other pedestrians, louder than the blaring of the horns and the shouts of the cabdrivers and the roaring of the trucks and buses streaming up and down Madison Avenue.

At the same time, David Drexler sat in his office, having arrived far earlier than he usually made his appearance. He was talking to someone he didn't know, someone with whom he had never spoken before.

His hands were filmy with perspiration. He heard the words,

spoken in a soft, unhurried, cultured tone. He got the meaning, which was as direct as the voice was soft, and the insinuations were subtle. But all he could think of was that his business, his little empire, was about to crumble, that all he had worked for, at first, and then enjoyed to the fullest was about to explode in his face.

"Yes, sir. I understand," he said. "I will speak with Miss Crespino as soon as she gets in. I will make it clear what it is you want, Mr. McDonald. Absolutely clear. No question. And thank you for this opportunity to help."

There was no response. For a few seconds, which seemed like long minutes, there was just silence. Then he heard, soft but distinct, the click of someone breaking the connection. Hanging up.

He put his receiver back in its cradle, took a deep breath, and reached for his handkerchief to wipe his forehead. He didn't know the man who had been on the other end of the conversation, and was sure he didn't want to, either. A voice so soft that it sent daggers of fear piercing through him. Whatever this man wanted to know he learned. Whomever he wanted to hurt he did so easily, by lifting a telephone, perhaps, just as he had done this morning. Drexler's hands were still shaking, although less noticeably, when he rang for his secretary and asked if Leigh had arrived yet.

"No, not yet, but she should be in any minute," Kathy Layton said. "She usually gets in around nine-thirty."

"Tell her to see me first thing," he said.

"Sure, Mr. Drexler."

He sounded nervous, she thought, and wondered whether it had anything to do with that call from Ralph Johnson last night and this guy DeSalvo.

Fifteen minutes later, Leigh Crespino walked in and passed Kathy's desk. "Oh, Leigh, Drexler wants to see you. First thing, he said!" she called out.

"Thanks, Kath. Just going to put my stuff down. Tell him I'll be right in."

Leigh sat in the soft chair opposite David Drexler's desk, notepad in her hands, assuming he wanted to see her to some-

how prep her for this meeting. Instead, she sat in stunned silence as he stammered and stuttered his way through the
delivery of this cryptic but absolutely real message.

"Leigh, the man you were going to meet with this morning—
the guy who died—I don't know who he was, only that he was
on the phone last week and insisted on seeing you. He controlled a lot of people, some of them very important to DD Ads.
Just to prove to me how important he was and how much he
could do to hurt us, he caused us to lose the Skeezixs candy
account.

"Nobody knows this yet. But we have lost it, just because this
guy DeSalvo called somebody and asked for this favor."

He paused.

"The word *favor* should imply what I think is going on here.
He asked for a favor, and somebody else important readily
agreed. So we lost an account, for no good reason. In fact, I heard
yesterday that it's already been picked up by Huff and DeCicco.
But that's not important. It's gone and we have no choice but to
accept that."

Another long pause, as he played with his ballpoint pen.

"What I am going to tell you now has nothing to do with
advertising or business or accounts or any of that, but it has a
lot to do with this business and you, personally. Me, too, I think.
I received a call earlier this morning from a man named Mc-
Donald. That's all I was told. McDonald. How he got my private
phone number I don't know, but honestly, I wasn't surprised.
This DeSalvo had it, too. These people get whatever they want.

"Leigh, DeSalvo was coming in today to warn you, in no un-
certain terms, that any more probing into the death of that football player—what was his name, Benson?—will result in your
boyfriend getting hurt, possibly you getting hurt, maybe the
both of you winding up dead. This was a very scary man, Leigh.
It was made very clear to me that you are to tell Ed that he
should stop the investigation. That he should tell the detective,
and I was told the guy's name is Keegan, that he is no longer
interested in pursuing this. That he is in fear for his life, and
yours, and that no one can protect the two of you should you
ignore this warning.

"And this McDonald said that if the detective stops, nothing will ever happen to any of you, that it will be forgotten, and, most important, that it will be considered a favor done for him by the both of you. Those kinds of favors to these kind of people are often repaid handsomely."

Drexler didn't bother to add that should the police be called off and the matter dropped, DD Ads would receive a replacement account for the lost candy billing, one that would be far larger and more profitable. Which account he didn't know, nor the extent of the dollar value, but he realized that the favor he had done for this man would be repaid and the parameters for the payback had already been established.

He simply had to see to it that Leigh Crespino did as she had been told: actually, that she did as he had been told.

Leigh thought carefully as to her response, her first response. It would be critical, because Gerry had instructed her to see if she could extract more information from the man sent to interview her.

"David, let me see if I understand this. Somebody is in effect claiming responsibility for the death of Adam Benson, and that somebody doesn't want any police investigation to go forward. That's murder, isn't it? Are you telling me to ignore a murder, to just forget it, make believe it just didn't happen, and then to tell Ed and Detective Keegan that it doesn't matter, just go on with something else?"

Drexler stirred uncomfortably in his chair. "Yes, I guess that's it. The guy's dead; wouldn't make sense for other people to wind up the same way, would it?"

"Who was this guy? Who called you? Who was supposed to be here today and what happened to him?"

"Leigh, the guy who called me this morning said his name was McDonald. Arthur McDonald. A businessman out in California with offices and interests here in New York and many other places. He said the guy who was supposed to be here, William DeSalvo, had been killed. I don't know how. I don't know what happened. But he was going to deliver this same message in person. I think this way was a lot safer for you, you know?"

She nodded. "I guess so. Look, David; I'll give this message to Ed. What he decides to do about Detective Keegan is up to him. I know what a strain this has been for you, and losing Skeezixs is going to hurt. I'll do what I can. Do you mind if I take the rest of the day? I'm a little shaken by all this. OK?"

Relieved, Drexler nodded. He stood, offered Leigh his hand. "Sure, go home. Go shopping. Just remember, these guys mean business and I hope we can not only do what they want but keep it quiet. Just us, OK?"

She nodded, turned, and left, hoping beyond hope that the coin-sized tape recorder had captured it all.

As it turned out, it had.

Gerry Keegan was delighted.

Now there were two major assignments remaining, one for him, one for Ed Buck.

Keegan had to find out who Arthur McDonald was, who he really was. Buck, with the help of Dr. Silverman, had to come up with the player who had committed the murder.

THIRTY ONE

ELDON St. John was concerned. It was not something he could put a finger on, nothing specific, no reason for this silent alarm. He was just stricken by a feeling of unrest, nerves and malaise. It felt like something undone, unsaid, seen but not remembered. Kind of strange, kind of odd, and definitely unsettling.

Did it have something to do with Sunday's game, with the death of Adam Benson? St. John was sure it did, certain beyond question that whatever was bothering him had something to do with the game, had everything to do with the death.

How could Adam Benson be dead? How could a guy like that just die? He was a pro football player, man, in top condition. He had passed his team's physical that summer; he had played in every game, done all the running, gone through all the practices. Why would he suddenly fall down and be dead, man?

St. John remembered the play, of course. Strong-side right, power sweep. Except Benson had fooled even his own guys, faked the handoff to the halfback and kept the ball, wheeling to his left. He had a lineman there, maybe two. He had the fullback. The Giants were fooled, even though four or five of the defensive guys made a strong adjustment and came back to the ball, himself included.

He got in on the hit, but Benson was already in the end zone. Eldon was pretty sure of that. And he heard the usual noises you'd hear in that kind of a pileup. The groans, the screaming, the cussing. Normal stuff you don't even really register, just part of the game.

Except he thought he heard a little something else. Not a scream, not exactly. More like a sharp intake of breath, like from a quick pain, like when you had the wind knocked out of you and couldn't catch your breath, like maybe when you fell on the ball and somebody piled hard on top of you.

Just that one sound, man, a kind of deep breath. But in reverse. Like it was all going out. And he heard the fullback, Ellsworth, yelling, "Man, what's the matter? Benson? Hey, Adam, what is it, man?"

Except that was what Eldon had heard first.

Then he had heard that funny noise.

Ah, shit. Must be in his head.

You know?

But nobody has asked him anything. Beside, what did it matter? The cat was dead, man. Cold. And that noise, that sound, it was just in his mind anyway, right?

THIRTY TWO

FOR the first time in his life, Anthony Assante was terrified. Absolutely, positively terrified.

He had made the decision to have DeSalvo killed, and to him it was entirely logical, devoid of any emotion at all. It was a business decision, and he had made many in the years since he had ascended to second in power. This was no different. There were many credible reasons for the act. It was important that this thing take place. It would serve the best interests of many people. And so it was done.

Rico Scalzi was the perfect choice. He was more than just loyal. An order from Assante was tantamount to a commandment from heaven, and Rico was a very religious man. He was also ready to die for Assante should that be requested, for favors long owed on behalf of his parents and for providing him with an income and a job and a feeling of importance and respect.

But for some reason, which Assante could not fathom, Arthur McDonald was furious. Seldom, if ever, had Assante known him to be this angry, and it was obvious in the icy response he received when he told him that the decision had been made, the execution carried out.

"Who told you to do that?"

Short, staccato bursts of barely restrained anger, delivered in a cold fury, followed by the telephone connection being broken.

That had never happened before. Assante was terrified.

But because he had not survived these many years by allowing himself the luxury of acting foolishly or rashly, he tried to understand the anger. McDonald was overreacting. That much was obvious to Assante, who knew McDonald perhaps not well but better than any other living human being, and he never overreacted. Never.

So what was it that suddenly made him act this way? Did DeSalvo mean anything to him? No. Assante was sure of that. Was it the meeting with the advertising agency woman that McDonald did not want to cancel? Perhaps, but why? It didn't mean anything, not really. It was a front, a scam.

The fact that Assante had used Rico was of no consequence. Rico belonged to Assante. There was nothing personal there.

The quarterback? He couldn't possibly have mattered. He was simply the tool through which a small inroad to the NFL had been made, and that it turned out badly didn't change the fact that there had been a lot of money made with no way of tracing the fixes back to the key parties.

No, it was something else. Fear of the media? Never. Something personal? McDonald had no personal attachments, not to anyone or anything, and every indication through all these years was that he feared no one.

So what could have happened? Did Assante overstep his authority? Did he go beyond what was within his area of responsibility? It had never come up before. Assante made decisions as if he had to answer only to himself, which was almost always the case.

So what had happened?

Why was the killing of Billy DeSalvo such a mistake? Why did Assante have the growing feeling that he had committed a grievous error? He had to know. He had to solve the puzzle, because it was not out of the question that his life could depend on it.

Was it something to do with Rico? He couldn't see how, because Scalzi belonged to him, to Assante. Rico's whole family did, and he was indebted to the point of giving up his life if that was requested.

Was it DeSalvo? How could it be? DeSalvo was a piece of garbage, an insect who got as far as he did with a few lucky breaks and the time-honored trick of being in the right place at the right time, of being in possession of a professional athlete at a time when they wanted to move into that market.

But DeSalvo didn't count. He was more trouble than he was worth. He was nothing. Why would anyone be so upset that it was done? That he was whacked? Why?

Getting the answer was more important than anyone else could realize.

THIRTY THREE

A lot of otherwise secretive people, many of them members of New York's Finest, were looking for Sherri Novak. To no avail. She had vanished from her "safe house" in the middle of the night and hadn't returned.

Detective Keegan said he had no idea where she had gone, and he expressed great indignation and concern at her unexplained absence. Several telephone calls had been placed to those who were paid to know the answers to otherwise unanswerable questions, and there was no positive response to be found. Assante was livid. He had received a telephone call, and the tone in the old man's voice was at least as ominous as it had been when he inquired as to why DeSalvo was killed.

Mike Herbert got a telephone call from a man he had never spoken to but knew only too well. By reputation.

"This is Anthony Assante," said the voice. "I am interested in a person who is no longer living where we were told she was living. I understand it was you who made the arrangements. I would consider it a personal favor if you could help me find her."

Herbert felt that cold, chilling know in his gut. "Mr. Assante, I didn't know until this minute that she was no longer where we had placed her—for her own safety, of course. I don't know how she could have disappeared, but I'll find her. I'm sure there's nothing to it."

A long pause.

Then the connection was broken.

Mike Herbert had good reason to be in fear.

Keegan called Ed Buck, told him where Sherri was, told him why she had been moved, told him that the guy who had been scheduled to visit Leigh was not an advertising client and, in fact, had no connection with advertising at all. He was a known member of organized crime, and he obviously had been told to come in to scare Leigh.

Or worse.

"You're in more danger than you can imagine," Keegan said. "I would like to know you're going away somewhere. Like today."

"Gerry, I can't. What about my job?"

"What about your life?"

"OK. I get it."

"Go away, Eddie. Just take Leigh and go someplace. I'll leave a message on your answering machine. Check once a day. From a pay phone."

Buck put down the receiver, then picked it up again and dialed New Jersey Information. "Police department, Ship Bottom," he asked.

He wrote down the number, dialed.

"Do you know of a place in town where a guy could get married without a big fuss?" he asked the desk sergeant who answered.

"Yes, sir. The courthouse. It's in the police department building."

"What do I need to get it done fast?"

The sergeant chuckled. "Well, you need a license. You can get that here. You need the blood tests. You can get them here. You need to find out if they'll be open when you want them to be, and if you're thinking about any time between nine in the morning and four in the afternoon they're open."

It was Ed's turn to chuckle. "See you tomorrow," he said.

He called Leigh's office.

"Come home," he said.

"I was just leaving," she said, a catch in her voice. "I just had a frightening conversation with Drexler. I'm taking the rest of the day off."

"No, you're taking a few days off. I'll pack. I'll rent a car. We're going away."

"Where?

"Ship Bottom, New Jersey, I'm going to make an honest woman out of you, remember?"

"I'll be right there."

By four, they hit the New Jersey Turnpike, then switched to the Garden State Parkway, followed directions from the toll booth guy, and left the picturesque highway at Exit 63. Down the causeway, heading east, until greater Long Beach Island was reached.

"The man said to turn right," Leigh said.

They did, and about half an hour down the ocean road they found the St. Rita Hotel, which was actually more of a boarding house, once recommended by old friends, Mindy and Scott Rittenhouse.

They checked in. Dinner was acquired at a neat little "Jersey Shore" place called the Hook and Sinker, all seafood, heavy plastic dishes and fresh salt air supplied with every breath at no extra cost.

It was, indeed, a special pre-wedding dinner, followed by their first restful night in weeks, and at nine o'clock the next morning they showed up at the police station/courthouse/volunteer fire department.

"Oh, you must be the man who called yesterday," said Sgt. Andrew Rollo, blond and young, red-faced, and friendly. "Doc Adams will take the blood. He'll run it through the screening in an hour. We aren't real busy right now, looks like. Soon as you're cleared, Fred Hanson in the Hall of Records will issue the marriage license. Fifty bucks. Fred will also perform the ceremony. Fifty bucks more. You got a witness?"

They shook their heads.

"I'll stand up for you, sir, no charge," Andrew Rollo said, and Leigh had a feeling he actually blushed.

Leigh Crespino and Edward Buck were married at one o'clock in the afternoon. Ship Bottom police sergeant Andrew Rollo served as the best man. Fred Hanson performed the civil ceremony.

But the best thing about it was that no one knew where they were, and there were a lot of people looking.

THIRTY FOUR

AFTER talking to his coach, Eldon St. John called Gerry Keegan.

"This is Eldon St. John," he said. "I play for the Giants and I think I have something that might help you."

"Regarding?"

"That Adam Benson thing."

"I'll meet you at the stadium."

"No, man, no good. Too many people here. You know the Grand Concourse?"

"Near the stadium?"

"Right, that's it. There's a restaurant, Livingston's, corner 161st Street and Lenox Hill Avenue. An hour."

Keegan found it, seamy and dark, with its own particular odor wafting from floor to ceiling, and then he found St. John in a booth in the back. There were three patrons at the bar, all of them telling very important secrets to their glasses of beer.

"Hi, I'm Keegan," he said, sliding in and shaking hands. "I admire your skills."

St. John shook Keegan's hand, then shook his head. "Fuck that," he said. "This isn't about football and fan shit. You ain't gettin' my autograph. This is about something I know that I know you want to know. Need to know. About the play when Benson came up dead. I just don't want anybody to know I'm talkin' to you. I ain't spent much time in my life being sociable with the police. You understand?"

"Done."

So Eldon St. John told Keegan about the funny noise, about the sharp release of breath, about Harlan Ellsworth, the Chicago fullback, asking Benson if he was all right seconds before St. John heard that strange breathing sound.

"I won't release your name," Keegan said, "but you're going to have to sign a statement, and you may have to testify in court."

St. John nodded. "I know, I know. And I don't like it. But, man, I'll do what I have to do. But I don't want you to use my name unless we can't help it."

Again Gerry Keegan nodded. "We'll find a way to do this without you being seen. I'll prepare the statement. I'll get it ready for you to sign. Then we'll get it to you somehow. You want a lawyer to be there with you?"

"No, man. I like lawyers even less then I like cops. But how do you know what I said? How do you remember everything?"

Keegan smiled. "One of the reasons you don't like cops, Eldon. I just taped you."

Gears were meshing. The pace was picking up. Keegan could feel it. He returned to the precinct, told his superior officer, Capt. Nelson Edwards, that he had to issue an arrest warrant to hold Harlan Ellsworth of the Chicago Bears until someone from New York could get out there and question him. Keegan said that Ellsworth was the newly identified suspect in the murder of Adam Benson.

Edwards picked up the phone immediately and got the Chicago police, and the necessary steps were taken. "Go," he said, and Keegan left the office to return home, pack a bag, and get on the next flight to Chicago.

He had one stop to make. His mother's apartment in Brooklyn. He wanted to see Sherri, not only because there were some questions he had to ask but also simply because he wanted to see her.

It would be nice to see his mom, too.

They both smiled when he opened the door, although he scowled at his mother because it had been left unlocked.

"Hi, Mom. Is Sherri being a good girl?"

Mrs. Keegan beamed. It was enough of an answer, and it implied a question, too, one that he didn't feel like addressing even to himself yet, much less his mother.

"Mom, I have to talk to Sherri. It's police business. I don't want to take her out, so could we have a little privacy?"

She beamed again. "Why don't you go into your old room?" Mrs. Keegan suggested sweetly, and that caused both Gerry and Sherri to blush, just a little.

Gerry closed the door. Sherri sat on the leather recliner, and he plopped down on the bed. She looked around and took in the old-fashioned bookcase, from which was hanging a New York Yankees banner, a baseball glove with a baseball tucked into the pocket and held forever in perfect position by a wide, thick rubber band, a trophy with the figure of an athlete leaping high and straight into nowhere.

"What's the award for, Gerry?" she asked, her voice taking on just a slightly teasing edge.

She was right. The tough guy actually blushed.

"High school basketball team," he said softly. "We won the city championship."

"But you have the trophy?"

"Well, no, the school has that trophy. I have this one."

"Why?"

"I was named the tournament's Most Valuable Player," he said, now beet red.

He had to get away from the personal questioning, so he put on his most stern face and said, "Sherri, do you know the name Harlan Ellsworth?"

"Yes. He's a football player, isn't he?"

"He is. Do you remember his name ever coming up with DeSalvo or Scalzi or McDonald? Have you ever heard it before?"

"Adam talked about him, how he really didn't like him or trust him, but how good a player he was and how much the team needed him. I don't think he trusted him much."

"How do you mean?"

"He said that Billy told him if he didn't keep cooperating, they'd get Ellsworth to do it, because he knew what was happening and he was interested in the money."

"You'll sign this? Testify to it?"

"Of course, Gerry. You don't have to ask."

Closer, closer.

"Sherri, I'm flying to Chicago in about an hour. I just have time to get to La Guardia. You stay here. Please, please stay here. Don't go anywhere; don't take any phone calls, don't do a damned thing. Just stay here. This thing might be over soon, and we'll move on from there. Do you know what I'm trying to say?"

She smiled. "Yes, I do, Gerry. I'll be here. It might be a long time before you can get rid of me."

The pace, he thought happily, was definitely picking up.

"Sergeant Keegan, I'm Randy Miller, I'm to take you directly to the precinct. I don't think it's a secret that you have set off a shit storm down there, sir."

Keegan smiled. "I take it, then, that Ellsworth has been placed under arrest?"

"Oh, yes, sir. And the owner of the team is about to have a stroke. The newspapers are all over us. The radio station, QYK, is calling everywhere, the players, the coaches, the police, even the mayor's office. Just what is going on, Sergeant, if I'm allowed to know?"

"Son, you are not allowed to know. Not yet. So why don't we just get to the house and maybe this will all get unwrapped."

"Yes, sir," he said, and Officer Miller didn't say another word during the drive from the airport to the downtown police headquarters building.

Capt. Amos Logan, a big, burly man with a weathered, wrinkled face browned by years of sun and heat, was waiting for Keegan.

"Sergeant, I've done everything your captain asked. I have had Harlan Ellsworth arrested. At the Bears' practice field, no less. I have him isolated. I have read him his rights, but he has not yet had the opportunity to seek counsel, and that's going to happen in just a short while, because we simply can't hold him like this. I'm sure you know all this."

"I do, Captain, and I appreciate the cooperation. Where is he? I have to talk to him immediately, and if it goes well then this is all over quickly."

Logan nodded and motioned for Keegan to follow.

They went to the elevator, took it down three floors, walked along a well-lighted corridor to a sign that read: LOCK UP. A guard at a gate nodded at Logan and pushed a button from inside, and the gates swung open electronically. There was a row of cells. They stopped at one that had no residents on either side of it, and there was Harlan Ellsworth, still in jeans and a Chicago Bears T-shirt, glaring at his visitors.

Logan unlocked the cell door with a key hanging from his belt loop and motioned Ellsworth outside, and the three of them walked down to another room, empty but for a long table, which was bolted to the floor, and four chairs. There were metal rings affixed to the floor and the table, to handle handcuffs or leg irons, but Ellsworth wasn't cuffed, nor was there any evidence of resistance.

Ellsworth was smoldering, a huge, muscular man with an easy athletic gait and eyes burning like black coals. "I want my lawyer," he said.

"In a minute, Harlan," said Captain Logan. "This is Sergeant Gerard Keegan from the New York City Police Department. He'd like to ask you a few questions."

"Go ahead," Ellsworth mumbled.

Logan held up his hand. "You're willing to answer questions, even without your lawyer being here?"

Ellsworth nodded.

Keegan looked at Logan, who raised an eyebrow and mouthed, "Mirandized."

"Harlan, do you know a man named Billy DeSalvo?"

"Yes."

"Do you know a man named Rico Scalzi?"

"Yes."

"Have you ever met a man named Anthony Assante?"

"Yes."

"Were you involved in a plan to fix the scores of games?"

"Yes."

"Did you kill Adam Benson?"

A pause. A last flight from hope.

Then, "Yes, I had to."

Keegan turned to Logan. "Captain, this man is to be arraigned on charges of first-degree murder in the death of Adam Benson last Sunday in New York City. He is allowed to seek legal advice, and I will ask if I can use your telephone so that we can begin extradition proceedings. The murder took place in New York. It's ours."

Logan nodded, clearly shaken.

Keegan turned back to Ellsworth, who was staring at the ground. "Harlan, you don't have to answer me, but I'd like to ask one more question for now. Why did you do it?"

Ellsworth looked up, and now his eyes weren't blazing; they were damp. Fear and realization had sunk in.

"I had to," he murmured, "or they would have killed me. I was in too deep. So was Adam; so are a dozen other guys. It was my way out, and they told me I would never get caught. Never."

Keegan nodded. "What did you kill him with, Harlan?"

"It was a long sticker thing, like an ice pick. Steel. I slipped it into my jersey, in my shoulder pads, and when we had the pileup I just reached in and slipped it out and stuck him in the chest. Somebody showed me where and how. Some big dude. Mean. Good shape. I didn't know if it would work, but it was a chance I had to take. You don't know those people, what they do, what they can do."

"Who showed you how to do it, Harlan?"

"The big guy. Rico."

"Where is the murder weapon, Harlan?"

"Man, I don't know. I threw it in the trash in the locker room when we came in. Long gone, I guess."

Indeed, long gone. But a confession in the presence of Logan as well as a detective sergeant of the New York City Police would almost certainly suffice.

Logan stared at the man. "I'll have a statement prepared, Harlan. Then you'll sign it. Right?"

"I will. I need this to be over. I didn't mind killin' the white dude. It was me or him. But these people, man, I won't be worth an hour on the street now."

Keegan wondered how long Harlan would live in jail but kept that question to himself.

THIRTY FIVE

WHEN Keegan got to his hotel, he called Ed's apartment, waited for the recorder to pick up, and then said, "It's half-over. We arrested and charged Harlan Ellsworth with Adam's murder. He was ordered to do it, frightened into doing it, and we don't yet know who made the decision. He knew all the names we knew, met them and talked to them, but he doesn't know who's over them. Stay wherever you are. Don't come home."

It took less than twenty-four hours for the courts to clear the way for Ellsworth's transportation to New York, and Keegan was pleasantly surprised that Ellsworth's attorney, appointed by the team, was absolutely no trouble. Though Keegan had to remain in Chicago overnight, he turned down Captain Logan's invitation to take in a Bulls game. Keegan would have loved to see Michael Jordan once more, with the great athlete's retirement so close and so certain, but didn't much feel like enjoying a basketball game. He did, however, accept a dinner invitation at Eli's, one of the grand old stockyard-style steak houses in Chicago.

The next morning Ellsworth was escorted, handcuffed to a local detective, to the airport. There, officially, he was handed over, and cuffed, to Keegan and they boarded the plane for the trip east. The flight went uneventfully, without much conversation.

At one point, Ellsworth looked up and said, "I didn't want to do it, you know? I didn't care much about Benson, not either way, but I didn't want to kill him. Or anyone else. But when they told me it was going to be me if it wasn't him, man, what choice did I have?''

"You could have gone to the police. You could have done a lot of things.''

"Yeah, but me and the police . . . well, no, that couldn't happen.''

Keegan stared at him for a long minute. "So what do you have now, Harlan? You've got a murder rap. You knew what you were doing. You planned it. You carried it through. You are going away for life, if you're lucky, maybe even execution. You know how they do it these days, Harlan? They strap you to a cold metal table, they inject a poison so strong you're dead in three minutes, and you don't even have much time to think about how fucking sorry you were and what kind of a fucking moron you were to do it at all. You like that, Harlan? Sounds good to you? So was it worth it? Did those people scare you more than this?''

"The old guy did,'' he said. "I never met anybody like that. I never talked to anybody like that. Man, he, like, looked inside me and turned my shit into soup, you know?''

Carefully, slowly, Keegan asked, "What old guy? You didn't mention an old guy.''

"Hey, you didn't ask me. You just asked me names, if I knew those people. This dude, that dude. And I said I did. They all . . . like . . . seemed to work for this old guy. In Los Angeles, end of last season, when we played the Rams.''

"Where?''

"I don't know. Some big office building. All white, lots of glass. Near the top floor, maybe the top floor. I don't remember. I got picked up by a limo at the hotel Saturday morning, met with this guy and DeSalvo and Rico, made our deal, and the limo took me back.''

"This old guy, Harlan. What was his name?''

"McDonald. They called him Mr. McDonald.''

McDonald. The guy Leigh said her boss had talked to on the phone, the one who said DeSalvo was dead and couldn't make the trip, the meeting. The guy who told Drexler what to say. McDonald. Who the hell was McDonald?

"What do you remember about him, Harlan? This is important. If you give him to us, we could do something for you. Anything is better than execution. You know what I'm saying?" A flicker of interest. "What do I remember? Just that he was cold. I never met a man with such cold eyes. Like nobody mattered, like everybody he saw was a piece of shit. He scared me, man, and I haven't been scared since I was little and one of my mother's boyfriends used to beat on me just for fun."

The arrest of Ellsworth had become a media sensation. Keegan's name had been linked to the arrest, so he, too, was suddenly much in demand. He hated it, chose not to answer questions put to him as he left the airport, his prisoner in tow, and later when he entered and then exited the courthouse. He pleaded with his captain to assume all such duties "so that I have the time I need to work."

Ellsworth's attorney, H. Elliott Brechner, one of several on retainer to the team, came in on a later flight and checked into a midtown hotel. He was licensed to practice in the state of New York and so would remain as the player's counsel. Brechner was more than agreeable to Keegan's request that he be given all the time he needed to speak with Ellsworth, the obvious assumption being that all the help Harlan could provide would probably work in his favor at the end.

For the next two days Keegan spent most of his time with Ellsworth and Brechner. He began to see an intricately woven web of corruption that led to several players and several teams. Ellsworth incriminated eight athletes, most of them well-known, not only on the Bears, but also the Dallas Cowboys, Oakland Raiders, Arizona Cardinals, Miami Dolphins, and New York Jets. He knew most of them, and they spoke about their situation on occasion. To the best of Ellsworth's knowledge, all the players were receiving between fifty thousand and two hundred thousand a game. All were offensive players. All had met with DeSalvo and Scalzi and, only once each, had been brought to a meeting with McDonald.

"Will you identify them for the record?" Keegan asked.

Ellsworth looked at his attorney.

"Harlan, you are facing a murder rap," Brechner said. "They could decide to execute you. I'll give you the best defense I can, if that's what you want. I will plead not guilty for you. But my best advice is to take whatever deal you can get; you won't get squat without cooperating. Do you owe these other players your life?"

"No. It's just me now. I'll identify them. I'll swear to all of it."

THIRTY SIX

GIOVANNI Impelliteri was busy on the telephone. He had lots of people to find, including Ed Buck, Leigh Crespino, the detective Keegan, Assante, Sherri Novak, and the cop Michael Herbert, who had let her slip away.

Impelliteri was in his home in Pound Ridge, New York, one of the most elegant of the posh Westchester County area. It was a ten-acre estate, guarded beyond all remote chances of an intruder getting through. The home itself, more than twenty rooms with a four-car garage, was more than one hundred years old, but everything was new, the wiring and the plumbing and the security system and even the protected telephone lines. No one got in or out physically, and no one got in or out electronically without Impelliteri knowing.

Few people lived there. The cook, the driver, the three who cleaned and kept things arranged carefully, because Impelliteri was a meticulous man whose compulsion for neatness bordered on the obsessive. He had been married, but Maria, the only woman he had ever loved, had died eighteen years ago, the cancer eating her up, it seemed, even as he watched it happen. From one day to the next she was thinner, more drawn, in greater pain. She pleaded to be set free. One day she stared up at him from her bed, from her pain, and said, "Nanni, please let it happen; please let me go."

He nodded, cold because that's what he had trained himself to be, but not dispassionate, not uncaring, at least not for this one woman, and he smothered her. She had closed her eyes as he bent over her, and when he lifted the pillow from her face he saw peace in her expression, an almost invisible hint of a smile gently curving her mouth. She had gone off to wait for him, who knew where? He was convinced she was waiting, just as he was convinced there was something next, something beyond this adventure, and he wondered, from time to time, if his independence and strength would be rewarded in the next place or if the cruelty he had had to inflict would be punished.

No matter, there was no longer any time to think about changing, no time at all.

Maria had borne him one son. He was a handsome, strapping, strong young man now. But Maria had never known the boy had lived. While she was carrying the child, Giovanni Impelliteri decided he could not be burdened with family. He could not allow himself to be weakened by the presence of a child. It was a difficult, hard, and cold decision, but one he had to make. So much was at stake; so much else remained to be done. No strings, no hold on him. A child would be a weapon to use against him.

So he arranged for the child to be taken the night he was born. Impelliteri told the doctor to tell Maria that it had been stillborn. He paid handsomely for the favor. The doctor knew who he was, what he was, only partially, but it was sufficient knowledge to frighten him. He did as he was told. Maria wept, because she knew Giovanni hadn't wanted a child in the first place and that this was to be her only chance at motherhood. An accident, carefully planned, had taken root, taken hold. Except now the child was dead, was born dead, and that vital part of her life was gone. There had been a funeral, incredibly well attended, and that had been the end of it.

Giovanni would not speak of it with her, forbade her from speaking of it at all, and after a while she stopped mentioning it. But she never stopped grieving, and often she sobbed herself to sleep. It became her cross, her sorrow.

The boy was taken to the family of an old friend and raised there, with two other young sons who never realized he was not their own flesh and blood.

His name was Enrico. The family name was Scalzi. Rico had

never known his father. No strings, no attachments, no danger. But Giovanni had made sure, beyond all normal considerations and cautions, that Rico would be cared for and taken care of and looked after by his friend Scalzi. There was enough money in secret accounts around the world to keep Rico a rich man if he lived to be 1000. There was real estate, jewelry, stocks, and bonds. Rico Scalzi didn't know it, but he was worth in excess of $100 million. He thought old Scalzi was his father, and that was fine. Rico worshiped Assante, and that was as Impelliteri had managed things.

He watched with joy and pride as Rico grew to manhood, became part of the organization, showed courage and bravery and cunning. There were times when Impelliteri had almost told him about his history, times when he wanted Rico to know just who he was and just how proud of him his real father had grown.

But the life, the duties, the obligations . . . it all prevented such disclosure.

Until now. Rico had been summoned. He had to be told everything. Giovanni Impelliteri was furious that Assante had involved Rico in the murder of that piece of slime named DeSalvo. Impelliteri knew that Rico had murdered before, but those were absolutely and totally untraceable killings. This one was too close to the police, to the newspapers. This one had to do with nonfamily matters. This one was too public. Giovanni had learned long ago that when another gangster gets himself killed nobody really cares. But when this football player had to go, when the murder was done, it caused a public outrage. Bad enough. But now DeSalvo, who had already been tied to it, had been killed by Rico. That was too close.

Impelliteri was furious. He would now be forced to do what he had never wanted to do, acknowledge to Rico that he was more than a member of the extended family, more than the son of an old and trusted friend.

That he, himself, was next in line.

Where to start? How to tell him? Should he be told? What were the options? How should they be implemented? How could they be implemented at such a late date, with so much to be explained, with a fortune rivaling those of the most powerful men in the world soon to be at the disposal of this simple man?

Impelliteri loved his son, the son he had never publicly embraced or privately acknowledged. But he also realized the enormity of his responsibilities to his colleagues and to the thousands of those who worked for him, without really knowing who he was, and to the vast sums of money and property he had assembled through the years.

The detective and the newspaperman were going to continue the investigation. There would be no way to stop them, and even killing them, which would be a normal reaction in this situation, would not serve Impelliteri's cause. It had already become too public, too notorious, and there was no way to stop it unless the authorities were given a guilty party.

There was only one solution, painful and final. But there was much to protect, much to preserve.

Impelliteri picked up the telephone, the one that was a single, direct-dial line and as clean as a connection could ever be, and dialed a number known only to him.

"Yes?"

It was Anthony Assante.

"You have created a situation that is unacceptable. You must now provide the solution."

"I understand."

"Who is your best man?"

"Rico."

"No."

A pause.

"Nicholas Conti."

"For certain?"

"Yes."

"Contact him. I have a contract. Immediate."

"Who?"

"Rico Scalzi."

The sharp intake of breath gave away the shock.

"It is your fault, Anthony. I will not forget it."

"I understand."

From the moment Giovanni Impelliteri put the telephone back on its cradle, Rico Scalzi was a dead man. So, too, was Anthony Assante.

But there was a difference. Assante knew it.

THIRTY SEVEN

ASSANTE picked up the phone, hands shaking. He had been pushed to the brink of terror more than a few times. He had cried out in abject horror on three separate occasions, fortunately not in anyone's presence. Only to himself would he admit he had wet his pants once from fear, as a grown man, and he held onto that memory as a sign that never again would he allow himself to lose control.

But Impelliteri's calm, his detachment in the face of the unthinkable assignment he had just issued, the contract he had just ordered, was as cold a piece of business as this cold, cruel man had ever experienced.

He knew in his heart that when he arranged to complete this contract he, too, would be somebody's target. Nick Conti himself, perhaps. Conti, assuredly the most heartless of all the killers Assante had ever known, would have no more compunction at killing him than he would at killing Rico Scalzi or an old woman in a wheelchair or a small child skipping home from grade school. Conti was one of those rare people born without a conscience, a man who neither enjoyed nor detested the killing of another person. It was a job. His job. And he did it with remarkable and terrifying efficiency. Scalzi had killed, and killed efficiently and cleverly, but he did it out of loyalty and love for the man he viewed as his patron and protector. He probably did have a conscience. Some of the deaths he administered certainly must have caused him remorse.

Assante dialed a number known only to a few. There were the usual four rings, then a click, then a recorded message.

"Try your party at the fifth number," it said.

Assante knew all eight numbers by heart. He redialed a number that, like all the others, was totally untraceable. It rang once.

"Yes?"

"This is Assante."

"Yes?"

"I have a contract for you."

"How much?"

Assante noted that the first question was not "who?" but "how much?"

"One hundred thousand."

"Acceptable. Who is it?"

"Rico Scalzi."

"When?"

"Now."

"It's done. And, Anthony, are you sure he would approve?"

Assante knew what Conti meant. "Nick, he is the one who issued the contract."

"It's done. Payment in the usual manner?"

"Yes. It will be done today."

Both ends of the connection went dead.

Assante would wire the money to the Cayman National Bank in Grand Cayman Island, to a numbered account accessible only by one person. Nick Conti. When Assante received confirmation that it had been done, by calling a man at the bank, J. C. Calhoun, who was the best he had ever known at keeping secrets, he would fulfill his part of the bargain—neatly, cleanly, and ruthlessly.

Now Anthony Assante had to see about his own safety.

He picked up the telephone again and dialed another number plucked from memory. All his life he had been able to remember telephone numbers, bank account numbers, anything to do with numbers, and if he had ever dialed a number even once it was somehow recorded in his mind's Rolodex.

"Who is it?"

"Rico, this is Anthony Assante."

"It is my pleasure to hear from you. How may I help you?"

"Leave. Leave now. Go away. Do not return. Do you still have that bank account in Grand Cayman?"

"Yes."

"I will put money in it. Go away. It is important that no one knows where you are. Even me. Contact me in a month."

"This is all right with the don?"

"It is his instruction."

"Then I am gone."

Assante rang off, to pick up the receiver a moment later and dial yet another number.

"Yeah?"

"This is Assante. I want to talk to the commissioner."

"Yes, sir. Hold on, please."

If Nick Conti found Rico Scalzi before Rico got away, so be it. There was nothing further Assante could do. More to the point, he had just sealed his own fate. But by bartering everything he knew about the transactions and businesses run by this one particular subject, Assante would become a most important person and would, as such, be protected, hidden, made comfortable for the rest of his life, and, most important, taken out of the spotlight.

He had just arranged for whatever remained of his life to be spent in hiding or under constant surveillance, but it would provide a far longer life than had he done nothing. He was among the walking dead.

"Mr. Assante? This is James Fox."

"Commissioner, I would like to arrange a meeting. I have some information you have wanted for years."

"At your convenience."

"Today. Your office. Three o'clock. I know there is a side door to the building. I will enter that way."

"We'll be waiting, and you will be safe."

"I would expect nothing less, Commissioner. I am about to make you a famous man."

It was done.

THIRTY EIGHT

CAPT. Nelson Edwards got a call moments later. "It's from Commissioner Fox," said the desk sergeant.

"I'll take it in my office." Edwards snapped, striding to his glassed-in cubicle, closing the door, and sitting down before picking up the phone. The rare occasions when Fox had called him directly always required him to be sitting.

"Yes, Commissioner. This is Nelson Edwards. How can I help?"

"Good afternoon, Captain. I would like you here, at my office, at two-thirty today. With Detective Keegan."

"Yes, sir. May I ask why?

"No."

"We'll be there, sir."

Keegan was somewhat disturbed at the command performance. "I had an interview set up for today," he said.

"It's the commissioner; he wants us there and we'll be there," Edwards replied. "There is absolutely no question in my mind that we will be there. And we will go there together, so I won't worry that one of us might forget to attend."

"Damn it, Captain, I just—"

"Forget it, Gerry. It's not up for discussion."

Keegan went back to his desk and phoned his mother's house. "Hi, Mom; is Sherri there?"

"Yes, Joseph," she said. "Hold on. She's right here. We were talking."

He smiled.

"Hi, Joseph," she said, brightly.

Her, too? He smiled.

"Sherri, I can't see you later. I have to be at the police commissioner's, and I don't know how long it's going to take."

"Sounds important."

"These things are usually the opposite. He's going to tell us just how important it is that we get a quick solution to this case, that the newspapers and television stations are all over his back, that the whole country is making fun of New York City because we lost a player on the field during the game and we don't even know how or why it happened. He is going to, as they say, read us the riot act and we will look ashamed and nod politely and tell him we'll try to do better and that we have several promising leads."

"Do you?"

"Well, the player, Ellsworth, has admitted to the killing. That we have. But he doesn't know who ordered it. We have no record of a guy named McDonald. The office building Ellsworth said he was taken to in Los Angeles is owned by the Fuji Corporation, for God's sake, and the suite rented to McDonald Enterprises is paid for the full year, every year, with a check from Holiday Business, Inc., which has no individual owners or officers, as far as we can determine, and which in turn leases it to McDonald Enterprises. It's a shell corporation, impossible to trace."

"So you don't know who McDonald is?"

"No, we don't. You're probably one of only two or three people who have ever met him, and you don't have a clue, either, do you?"

"No."

"So we have the guy who admits murdering Adam. He told us how. It fits. He said he threw the weapon in the trash in the locker room and it went out with the garbage that night, lost forever. That fits. Why did he do it? Because he was being threatened with exposure for fixing games, because they told him if he didn't do it he'd stop getting all that extra money, because he's a bad guy to start with and I hope they find him hanging in his cell someday after he's convicted. But who ordered it? Why? How the scheme was implemented? We don't know shit."

"You'll find it, Gerry. I know you will."

"Yeah. I hope so. Listen; I'll talk to you as soon as I get finished."

"I'll be here." She paused, and it seemed like a long time. "Honey," she added.

Then Keegan dialed his own apartment, accessed the answering machine, and listened to the newly married Ed Buck.

"Gerry, damn it, I need to come home. My office is on my ass about taking this sudden honeymoon vacation. I'm losing my fucking mind out here and I can't eat any more fish. Leigh is being brave, but she is going nuts, too. She hasn't called her office, like you said, but she would like to get back to work.

"I heard about Ellsworth. He admitted it, right? So it's over, right? Damn it, Gerry, get us out of here."

Keegan smiled. He called the Bucks' answering machine.

"Not yet, children," he said. "But soon. Meanwhile, enjoy."

Then he went off to the meeting that he had no choice but to attend.

He arrived with Captain Nelson at two-thirty, as ordered. Commissioner Fox was seated behind his desk when the uniformed cop, a guy Keegan knew named Halloran, ushered them in.

"Leave us, Tommy," Fox said.

Halloran disappeared.

Fox looked at them, then began speaking. "In about twenty-five minutes, an old man will be joining us," he said. "He is almost seventy-five years old and, to our knowledge, he is the most influential and important man in organized crime. His name is Anthony Assante."

"Jesus Christ," Nelson murmured, totally unaware that he had spoken. "Assante? Jesus Christ. What's he doing here? And why is he showing up? Is he under arrest? Am I losing my mind?"

Commissioner Fox managed a wan smile. "He says he has information we have wanted for a long time. He says he is ready to give it to us."

"Damned right he has information," Nelson said. "It could take weeks to get everything out of that old son of a bitch. He has his fingers on everything. Everything. We can tie a dozen murders to that cocksucker alone. Drugs, gambling, prostitution, bank fraud, money laundering . . . should I go on? He's got it all, probably in his head. What the hell has scared him this much?"

Keegan, who had remained silent, spoke one word: "McDonald."

"Who?" Both men asked it at once.

"Arthur McDonald. The man Sherri Novak said she was taken to meet once. The same guy Harlan Ellsworth said he was taken to see. Except he's not McDonald. There is no record of this guy named McDonald. Nowhere. Not in any of our case files. None of our sources know him or anything about him. There is an office in Los Angeles called McDonald Enterprises. Doesn't exist. Rent is paid by the year, 200 grand a year, from the checkbook of a dummy corporation. For all we know, Arthur McDonald could be the president of the United States or the pope or Leonardo DiCaprio. But he sure has scared the shit out of Anthony Assante, hasn't he?"

There was a quiet rap on the door. "Come," said Fox. Tommy Halloran, pale, led a small old man into the room.

He looked at the three men present.

"Good afternoon, gentlemen," he said. "I am Anthony Assante."

He sat.

"I have come without an attorney and without a driver. I am alone. I am totally and completely in your control and under your protection. Have I made myself clear?"

"Yes, Mr. Assante," said Fox. "What is it you want to share with us?"

"Everything. Fifty years of everything I have ever been involved with, but there is a price."

"Of course there is. What did you have in mind?"

Assante smiled, and it was a sad, old man's smile. "I want complete privacy. I want an identity, all the money I can free up without a single question being asked. I want to leave the country, and I do not intend to tell anyone where I am going. I will ask that you arrange my departure and that, when this is all finished, all the records and transcriptions and tapes are erased or destroyed. I will give you everything."

"We accept," the commissioner said. "Where would you like to start?"

A pause. Assante took a deep breath and stared at the three men, each in turn, hard, cold eyes reading their thoughts.

"I will start with a man named Arthur McDonald," he said. "His real name is Giovanni Impelliteri, and he is one thousand times more important in this world of organized crime than anyone else."

THIRTY NINE

ED put the phone down, looked at Leigh, and shook his head. "Not yet," he said. "It sounds like it's getting closer, but not yet. I don't know how much more I can take, babe. What about you?"

"I think we should do what Gerry says," she said, tan because of their almost-constant walks along the deserted beaches despite the fact that it was November, albeit a mild, warm November. "I'm afraid of these people. Eddie, and I don't want to risk what we have. Not now. Not ever."

"Yeah, I know. But, Leigh, what do I do about my job? I can't be on a honeymoon forever, especially since it was such an unexpected thing to do. I have responsibilities. I have to do something."

"Tomorrow. Let's talk tomorrow. Not tonight. Let's go to that Italian place for dinner tonight, OK? Down the road, on the corner. What's it called? Raymond's? Let's, Ed. It might be our last night here. I know you want to go back, and I don't think there's going to be a way I can stop you."

He smiled. Relaxed. Reached for her.

"Let's don't get dressed just yet," he said as they tumbled on the bed in the suite of the St. Rita. "There are a few things I haven't shown you yet."

She smiled. "And just imagine how many things there are I still have to show you, darling."

He feigned anger but couldn't hold it and broke into laughter instead. "Yeah, right. Well, here's your chance."

There was very little speaking for a long time after that, just the whispers and murmured words that two people dramati-

cally in love share with each other and no one else, never anyone else. And then they were in each other's arms, nearly
asleep, just drowsing in that warm, insulated feeling that comes
only sometimes, even with people so in love.

"Pretty good," he said. "I think you have a lot of potential."

"Mmmmmm, and I'm glad of it, you know?"

They dressed and walked the six blocks or so in the fading
daylight, the weather chilly but not cold, to the little restaurant
they had grown to like a lot more than the all-seafood joint with
the plastic plates and the greasy fries.

They had stopped at the liquor store a block before the restaurant. Raymond's was a BYOB place, and for less than ten
bucks they got bottle of a superb Pinot Noir. It was a special
night, a special meal, and they both knew it was their last one
on this island, in this comfortable place that had served as a
honeymoon and a retreat and, more than they knew, a safe haven.

Dinner was concluded before nine, and a casual stroll back
to the St. Rita put a perfect punctuation point on the night.

"Leigh, we have to go tomorrow; we have to. I'm going to go
back to work. I'm not going to listen to Gerry. Adam was murdered, and they found out who did it. I'll let the guys who know
how to do it find out who ordered it, why it was done, all that.
But we're going home."

She nodded her head, though in the dark he couldn't see it.
"I understand and I guess I agree," she said. "We're married,
and we have to do this together. We can't hide and run scared.
I won't go back to work for Drexler. He's dirty. He's weak. I
couldn't possibly trust him again, and I think Gerry has already
contacted him. So yes, we'll go back tomorrow."

They went upstairs, to their second-floor nest and decided to
throw things into the suitcases, everything except what they'd
need for the morning. That didn't take long. Ed carried the two
suitcases downstairs to the rented car, unlocked the trunk, and
deposited them. They'd leave early. Get to Manhattan by ten,
unpack, sort things out, and be ready for work the next day.

It was only when he was returning to the entrance of the St.
Rita that he saw, from the corner of his eye, a white piece of

paper, torn from a spiral notebook, under the windshield wiper of the rented car.

He took it. Scrawled in crayoned block letters were the words:

DON'T START THE CAR. CALL THE POLICE.

FORTY

ED carried the piece of paper into the room and held it out for Leigh to see. Then he called the Ship Bottom police, asked for Sgt. Andrew Rollo.

"This is Rollo."

"This is Ed Buck, Sergeant. You stood up for us at our wedding the other day?"

"Oh, yes. How are you, Mr. Buck? Surprised you're still here."

"Sergeant, I need to see someone. Right now. I'm at the St. Rita."

The policeman noted the urgency, something just short of panic, in Ed's voice. "I'll be right there."

"We'll be waiting outside, next to a gray Buick, with New York tags."

"Fine. Three minutes."

And it was probably three minutes exactly when a cruiser pulled up, lights flashing but no siren waking the neighborhood. Rollo stepped out and approached them.

"What's the problem?"

"This is." Ed handed him the paper. "It was on the windshield. It wasn't there at six when we went to dinner. It was there at ten, when we came back."

Rollo paled. Then he walked back to his car, picked up the radiophone, and called the station. "This is Rollo," he said. "I need the bomb squad here. Now. St. Rita Hotel. Gray Buick."

He returned to Ed and Leigh, huddled against the oncoming chill of the night, a biting wind slicing in off the ocean. "Somebody will be right here," he said. "Let's go sit in my car. It's warm," he offered, glancing at Leigh, who was trembling, though he wasn't sure whether it was from fear or the cold. "Is there somebody you want me to call?"

"Yes," Ed said. "Detective Sergeant Joseph Keegan, New York City, Seventeenth Precinct. Just tell him it's me. He knows we're here. And if he isn't in, tell the switchboard operator to find him. Tell him it has to do with the case he's working on."

Keegan was in. He told Rollo not to touch anything, not to allow the Ship Bottom police to tinker with whatever explosive device was found in the car. That brought a mild protest, quickly squashed when Keegan said it was part of a murder investigation and anyone who touched the car would be guilty of compromising possible evidence. Even Rollo's boss, Chief Bill Hudson, who had already shown up at the scene, agreed. "We'll leave it the way it is, Detective," he said. "But get somebody down here fast. I don't like the idea of a bomb in a car parked next to one of our hotels."

"Already on their way, Chief, and thanks," said Keegan.

And about an hour later, a bomb unit truck and an unmarked New York police car were screeching to a halt next to the small crowd gathered at the St. Rita. Keegan was in the unmarked car, and first he went to Ed and Leigh.

"You guys all right?"

"Yeah, just scared to death," Leigh said. Ed just nodded.

"Not to worry. Whatever there is, we'll find it. You've got a ride home. Now. Not tomorrow. Go upstairs and get the rest of your stuff."

When they emerged again, the car's hood was up. Two men were on sliders underneath the chassis, bright floodlights illuminating their efforts. Two more had their heads in the engine. A fifth was kneeling next to an open door, slowly checking the seats, the steering column, anywhere and everywhere a small amount of explosive could be secreted, because combined with the explosion of the gasoline in the car's tank not much was needed to incinerate those in the auto.

The skilled team went through everything, from the starter to the fuel pump, from the cables leading to the battery to the wiring needed to activate the radio, the cassette deck, and the CD player. The seat cushions were pulled out, eliminating the possibility of pressure-sensitive detonators. The underchassis search proved equally empty. The driveshaft was clean.

But not the brake pads. Once the car got up to fifty miles an hour, the Bucks would have been gone—instantly, blindingly, unavoidably.

The bomb unit's leader, Boomer Reilly, nodded. "If you ask me, these people have really pissed off somebody important."

"Yeah. But with the note being found, somebody was telling them to be careful, to be aware that they had been found. Whoever wrote the note wasn't an enemy, yet I don't think he was a friend."

The device was disconnected, five ounces of plastic explosive that would have triggered the gas tank like a Fourth of July firecracker. The police would tow the car back to New York, check it over, dust for fingerprints that no one expected to find, and then call the rental company to take possession.

The Bucks drove home with Keegan. "I didn't want you coming back yet," he said, "but somebody obviously knows where you are, so it doesn't make much difference. I'll have people with you around-the-clock."

"Gerry, what's going on? Ellsworth confessed, right? He did it, right? You've got him. It's over. Why would somebody want to kill us now?"

"I don't know for sure, but no, it's not over," Keegan said, shaking his head, watching as the Garden State Parkway came closer to turning into the New Jersey Turnpike. "We got the mechanic, we don't have the guy who ordered it, and we don't know exactly why, except that Benson wanted out, and now we have at least a dozen guys in the National Football League who are doing the same thing. Ellsworth'll turn them in. He's looking for some kind of break, and he'll probably get something.

"But we need to know who, and why, and how. And you two are right in the middle of it, I'm afraid. You are the ones who blew the first whistle. This is very big. This afternoon a man named Anthony Assante, a man so important he called the private telephone number of Commissioner Fox, dialed it and just told him he wanted a meeting. I can't tell you everything, but he turned on a man we only suspected even existed, maybe the biggest catch in the history of organized crime."

"The McDonald guy?" Ed asked.

"Yeah, but it isn't McDonald. That's a cover. The guy's whole life has been a cover. We aren't even sure who he started out being, but the McDonald story covers a guy named Giovanni Impelliteri, once known as Johnny Imp, except our records say that he has been dead a long time now. Assante is giving him to us because he's afraid for his life. He says there are about five people in the world who know McDonald's real name, who know the whole thing. He owns half the fucking United States, and it's getting more and more fuzzy every day.

"There's a son, a son who doesn't know he's the guy's son, and he works for him, for God's sake. He was taken away as an infant and brought up by one of Impelliteri's oldest friends. Nobody knows why, exactly, but he keeps going. He doesn't need money, he doesn't have many, if any, friends, and the closest to that was this guy Assante, and they worked together for damned near fifty years before this suddenly fell apart.

"Why? Because Assante was in charge of the pro football deal, because he assigned Impelliteri's 'secret son,' some goon named Rico Scalzi, to off the little worm DeSalvo and now Impelliteri thinks it has put him in a compromising position. So he has ordered a hit on his son and Assante figures he isn't far behind. He's right, of course, which is why he came in."

Ed thought. "God, what a great story," he finally said. "It's mine, isn't it?"

Keegan smiled. "Yeah, it's yours. Tell me something; aren't you even a little bit scared?"

"Shit, yes. I'm scared to death. But the best way to get past being afraid is to go right at the fear. It's an old football thing, maybe. Like you go right at the other team's best defensive lineman to get your running game working. If you defeat him, the rest of them give up. It works."

Leigh fell asleep on Ed's shoulder as they cut through the darkness, stirring when the car passed the vile stench generated by the chemical and gasoline refineries at Exit 13 of the Turnpike. "I have a friend who lives in one of the nicest parts of the country, right here in New Jersey," Keegan said. "Right on the ocean, quiet little town, nothing but money, and he says that he loves it when people think the state is made up of the Turnpike, a connection between New York City and Philly, and this exit. Keeps away the riffraff, so to speak."

FORTY ONE

IMPELLITERI knew that Assante had turned. He had expected it, because Anthony was smart enough to know that a hit on Rico was a hit on himself as well. Impelliteri knew that a first meeting had already been held, and he was as sure as anything in the world that he had been named, had been delivered to the police. He knew that Nick Conti had been paid and the hit had been put in motion. He knew that the Novak girl had been spirited away from the safe house near Gracie Mansion and he was in the process of locating her again. He knew that Buck and the woman had left New York, because he knew they had rented a car. He assumed from that they planned a somewhat local destination; one does not rent a car to drive to an airport.

Impelliteri knew all these things and more. He knew that the black, the football player, had been arrested and brought to New York and formally charged with the murder of the other football player. Everyone knew that. It was impossible not to hear that story, told and retold and on and on and on. He knew, further, that Ellsworth knew nothing more than what he had been told and all that added up to nothing. He knew that the detective had discovered the method of murder, although, of course, not the weapon. He knew the professional football thing was over, absolutely and positively.

But Assante had turned. He had walked into the arms of the police and made his deal. He had given them everything, most especially the name.

He knew all this and he knew one thing more. For the last time in his life, he would have to disappear. Arthur McDonald, now unmasked, was going to have to be found dead. He had enough money secreted around the world to live out his years in great comfort, and because of the wealth he would find people to protect him, to hide him. They all wanted a piece of the fortune. It had always been easy to deal with people, because if you had money, you had what they wanted.

He would rescind the contract, if he could. He would let Rico live without ever knowing the truth. But he could not. Conti was never reachable when he was on an assignment. To be able to be contacted would compromise his anonymity, and Nick Conti was the consummate professional. Of all the things Impelliteri had done with no thought or conscience, issuing the contract on his son was the only one that hurt him. He was logical enough to see the wisdom in it. There were few men who would understand the need. But logic, which had always ruled his life, along with a ruthless determination to succeed, was suddenly being tweaked by passion.

It surprised him, somewhat, to know he still had the ability to feel. He thought of Maria and what she would say when they were together again. He thought of Rico, who would also be there, waiting, accusing. Giovanni had always thought that the next life, or the afterlife, would be one of joy. This would not accomplish that.

He reached for the telephone and dialed Rico's number. There was no answer, nor was there an answering machine. He dialed again, to be sure he had not erred, but there was no answer again after ten rings.

So he dialed another number. A man at an airport in Newark he had bought a long, long time ago, a man whose job was important, a man who was influential and able to override all the petty airport/airline rules and regulations.

The man answered on the first ring.

"This is your friend from New York, I need a favor."

"Name it."

"I want to find a traveler. He probably left last night, or early today. There are three possible names. Rico Scalzi. Rick Stone. Michael Prince. It is very important."

"Hold on."

A pause.

He heard the faint sound of fingers hitting keyboard strokes, a short beeping sound, then another. Then a repeat of the combination.

"Sir, I have Rico Scalzi. He left New York last night, from La Guardia. He went to Fort Lauderdale."

He had been warned, probably by Assante. Good. It was something his father should have done.

"Thank you. I am in your debt."

Another call.

"Yes?"

"I would like to speak to Angelo."

"This is Angelo. Who is this?"

"Your friend from New York."

Silence. Then, "It is my honor that you have called. How may I help you?"

"Rico arrived last night in Fort Lauderdale. Track him. Find him, but do not let him know. Then guard him."

"Yes."

"This is of the greatest importance. If anything happens to him, it will be on your head."

"I understand."

"Nicholas Conti is looking for him."

"Sweet Jesus. I understand."

Giovanni placed the phone back in its cradle. Angelo Bartoli would find Rico and would put enough people between him and the assassin. He would save Giovanni's son. He was very good at things like this, which was why he was given the South Florida area as his own. Rico was probably headed to the Keys, not to Miami Beach, where his mother lived. He would not do that. He would not bring anything on his mother. Giovanni knew that Rico had purchased a house a long time ago well down the road to Key West, on Little Duck Key, quiet, protected, with limited access. It would be difficult for Conti to reach him; conversely, it would be difficult for Rico to get off the key if Conti did get through.

But Bartoli's men would almost certainly stop Conti. And if he had to be killed, it was long overdue anyway.

FORTY TWO

RICO never left New York. He knew, felt, that something was wrong. So he did what he had been taught and what he probably never had been taught as well, which was to act defensively, turn on the trouble and surprise it.

He bought the ticket for Fort Lauderdale and gave it to a friend. It was the first thing they would look for and, having found a record, the single greatest subterfuge possible, one that would convince them he had acted just as Assante had suggested, that he had done just what they wanted him to do.

Instead, having rented a car the morning after the flight, he drove upstate New York, to a town named Corning-on-Hudson, where he owned a small cabin no one knew about. No one. He spent two days there, waiting. Then he drove back, timing his return so that he would arrive just after midnight in Pound Ridge—at the home of Giovanni Impelliteri.

There was no problem gaining access. The guards knew him. He was one of the two or three most important people in the organization. No one would question his sudden appearance, even at such an unusual time. When the leader of the bodyguard team offered to notify Mr. McDonald that Rico had arrived, there was no disagreement.

"Yeah, good idea," he said. "We don't want to surprise him in his sleep."

The man looked at him. "Rico, house rules. I have to search you."

Scalzi smiled. "Of course you do. I would have turned you in if you didn't." He calmly lifted his hands over his head, spread his legs, and allowed himself to be frisked. There would be nothing found. He had learned a long time ago that he needed nothing more than his two hands, if murder was on his mind.

"He says to wait upstairs for him, in the sitting room," the man said, returning the in-house telephone handset to its hook on the wall. "I'll show you."

"I know the way," Rico replied, still smiling. "I've been here before."

"No, I'll show you."

Another smile. "Sure, Frankie. I understand. It's your job."

He was led to the sitting room. Frankie indicated he would wait with him until McDonald arrived. Once again, Rico had no problem. He sat on a large overstuffed armchair, crossed his legs, and tried to make small talk.

"Tough job, being on the road at this hour of the night." He smiled. "But you know how it is. You do what you're told to do."

Frankie nodded. "Yeah, all the time. No choice."

They heard the old man enter, and he looked as if he had just walked in from a night on the town, aside from the fact that he was wearing a bathrobe and leather slippers. His hair was tightly combed. His eyes were alive, his moves belying the truth his age told.

"Rico, Rico, what a pleasure," he said.

Rico rose, approached the old man, dropped to one knee, and lightly touched the hand offered by McDonald, who turned to the guard. "Frankie, leave us," he said, and took a seat facing Rico, who had returned to the upholstered armchair. Impelliteri's sense of poise and grace impeccable, he smiled benignly. "What brought you here, Rico? What can I do for you?"

"Why did you put a contract out on me, Giovanni?"

That startled the old man. In one sentence, Rico Scalzi had told him two things he wasn't supposed to know, Impelliteri's real name and that he knew about the Conti contract.

"What are you talking about?" Impelliteri asked, allowing his voice to remain calm.

"Don't treat me like a fool, I'm your son. Assante told me to leave, but he didn't tell me why. He didn't have to tell me. I knew when I got the call. Why?"

Reacting as if he had just taken a blow to the stomach, Impelliteri began to crumble, to lose his composure. "My son? Contract? Rico, Rico, what has happened to you?"

"My mother . . . my real mother . . . found out what happened, what you had done. She knew. For the last fifteen years of her life, she knew. And she never told you. But she told me. I knew. I loved Maria Scalzi as if she had been my mother, but I loved my mother as well, my real mother. Your wife. I didn't see her much, because you would have known. I wanted to tell you I knew, a hundred times, but I didn't. I knew you had reasons, had to have reasons. It was my life, my place in the family. I was grateful for what I had."

He didn't think there were actual tears in his eyes, but he did feel an unaccustomed dampness.

"But you put out a contract on me. With Nick Conti. To have your own son killed, that is something I cannot understand. You tell me why."

It was really at an end, all the lying and the pretense. What to say? What to do?

"It was business, Rico, foolish business. When Assante had you execute that piece of shit, that DeSalvo, he involved you more than he should have, more than was safe. The football player was a mistake; the project was a mistake. We made a lot of money, yes, but it was a mistake nevertheless. You don't know the size of the organization, the amount of money, the responsibilities and the obligations, and the impossible need to act coldly, ruthlessly. It was the most efficient way. I am sorry, truly, truly sorry, for having made that decision. I will call it off. I have already tried to do that."

"You can't stop Conti," Rico said.

"But he can be killed," Impelliteri replied. "I have spoken to our man in Florida. He has people surrounding your home on Little Duck Key. Yes. I know. I have made sure to keep up with everything you have done, all your life. And I am proud of you, Rico. I don't think you can believe that, and I know you can never love me as your father, because no father would ever have done what I did. But I am proud of you, and now I am in your hands, at your mercy. What will you do?''

Rico thought about that. He got up, walked to the bar against the wall behind his father, and poured scotch, straight, no ice, no water, into a tumbler. He walked back to his chair, swirling the drink, staring at the amber liquid as if searching for an answer.

Finally he spoke, looking up, staring straight at Impelliteri. "Nothing."

"Nothing. What do you mean, nothing?"

"I plan to do nothing, Father. I am going to leave. I am going to disappear. No one will ever find me, not even you. I have prepared many identities, homes, ready cash. I will never be found. Rico Scalzi will no longer exist. Or Arthur McDonald. I have no mother now. I have no father. I have no identity."

The overwhelming sadness penetrated Impelliteri's normally stone-cold shell. "You are my son. I would like to know there is still something we can have together."

"No, there is not," Rico said solemnly. "It is much too late for anything like that. We have never been father and son, although I wanted it from the moment I learned the truth. I waited for you to tell me, to open your heart. You chose not to include me in any part of your life, not even to acknowledge that I was your son. I accepted that. But it hardened me, Father. I cannot go back. I cannot go where I have never been."

He rose to leave.

"Is there nothing I can do, then?" Giovanni asked. "Is there no way to save any of this? It was all my fault, my mistake. Is there anything I can do now?"

Rico, towering above his aging father, nodded his head. "There is one thing," he said.

"What is it?" the old man asked, grasping at this proffered straw.

"You can die for me," Rico Scalzi said, withdrawing a small pistol successfully hidden from the cursory pat-down administered by those who knew and feared him. "You can die for all the pain and suffering you brought to my mother, not for anything else. Just for her.''

Then, calmly, he shot Giovanni Impelliteri in the forehead. One bullet, penetrating the brain. The most powerful man in organized crime was dead before he could blink, dead well before his crumpled body softly struck the carpeted floor.

Rico closed the door behind him quietly, not once looking back, and walked down the staircase. He nodded at the chief of the bodyguard unit.

"The old man went back to sleep," Rico said. "I would leave him alone. He looked very tired. Even I hated to bother him, but it was important."

Frankie nodded, aghast at the thought of bothering this powerful old man. "No problem," he said. "The morning crew will wake him at the usual time. He usually sleeps until ten these days."

Rico nodded. "Thanks, Frankie. See you around. Oh, Frankie, you missed something before."

"What?"

"This," he said, taking the small pistol from his jacket pocket and shooting the guard, just once. Once was enough, and Rico wanted the noise to bring the other two men running. It did. They were dead two shots later. The morning staff would find the three dead men downstairs and the most important dead man they will have ever found upstairs in the sitting room of one of the most expensive safe houses in all of Westchester County. As things turned out, however, it wasn't quite as safe as advertised. The son of the most powerful man in organized crime had had no trouble penetrating all the protective devices and ending the reign of the man who lived there surrounded by secrets.

FORTY THREE

NICK Conti arrived at Miami International Airport early in the morning. He rented a car, using one of the dozens of credit cards in his possession, along with one of the dozens of driver's licenses, this one identifying him as Mark Pearl of Des Moines, Iowa.

He knew the way, leaving the rental lot, turning left on Biscayne Boulevard, then left again, then right on 836. Soon after that he found himself on the Florida Turnpike, and that flowed into southbound Route 1, the only road access in and out of that special area of the state of Florida called the Keys.

They sped by, Key Largo turning into Marathon Key, to Tavernier Key, to Islamorada, and finally to one of the smaller ones, Little Duck Key, a high-income, low-profile spit of land surrounded by water. It was one of the most expensive sites in the United States as well as one of the most secure and relatively unknown. Men from New York and New Jersey, from Philadelphia and Atlanta, from as far west as Chicago and Kansas City and Dallas, had acquired property on Little Duck Key years ago. It was a haven. It was possible to register ownership under corporate names or false names. The homes were Caribbean-style—meaning tropical elegance. Open verandas led to giant heated pools, to boat slips and second-floor master bedrooms under a canopy of retractable glass. Tiled kitchens, from floor to walls to counters. Living rooms and dens that stared out into the Atlantic.

Rico's home, bought with cash and owned by Americo Impelliteri Enterprises, sat at the end of the key, with nothing around it but water on three sides. This morning the water was particularly blue, azure blue, reflecting white-fluffed clouds chasing each other across eternal skies. There was a staff, full-time and well paid, composed of those who knew nothing about the home's owner and those who knew almost everything. The latter group, of course, was in charge. His privacy was their first priority. They kept secrets the old-fashioned way: they would die before relinquishing any information to anyone.

It was the biggest estate on the key, located at 1 Tarpon Run, stupendous in white stucco and white brick. A magnificent property, valued together with the land and the home on it at more than $10 million.

This morning, while its owner was still in New York, a visitor arrived. The man in the gatehouse at the entrance to the residential portion of Little Duck Key politely asked for identification, and Mr. Mark Pearl of Des Moines, Iowa, eagerly presented his driver's license.

"Sure is pretty here," he said.

"Where are you going?" asked the guard.

"To see my friend Rico. He lives here."

"Rico who?"

"Rico Scalzi," said Nick Conti.

The man shook his head. "No Scalzi here. Maybe you have the wrong key."

"This is Little Duck Key?"

"Yep, but no Scalzi. Here, see for yourself." He held out a two-page list of names of those who owned the homes on Little Duck Key. Conti, confused, scanned them, and one popped up as if it had suddenly become alive.

And lethal.

"Rico Impelliteri?" he asked out loud, but to himself. "Impelliteri? Who the hell is Impelliteri?"

The guard smiled, although not benignly. "Maybe it was the gentleman who called last night from Fort Lauderdale and told us you might be coming our way, Nicholas Conti. Maybe it was that man."

Before Nick could reach for the Walther-PPK in his shoulder holster, the passenger side door was pulled open and hands grabbed his arm. Big, strong, hairy hands.

"You'd better come with us, sir," said the man, who might have been banned from the NFL for being too big or for having too many muscles. "And I think that maybe you'd better do it quietly."

Conti relaxed every muscle. This was not the time for bravery. He nodded and stepped out of the car, and the guard held a gun on him, the muzzle pointed at his face and only a foot away. The biggest man Nick Conti ever saw slid across and drove the car up one of the winding roads on Little Duck Key. Conti was left standing just outside the gatehouse, the guard still inside, the gun pointed directly at his face.

"Many of us have respected you for years, admired you, and tried to be like you. I am glad to have the chance to meet you, Nick Conti," the guard said.

"Thank you. Is there anything I can do to change your mind? Is there enough money to let me get back in my car and drive out of here? Or just walk out of here and hitch a ride?"

The man didn't respond. He looked as if he was deep in thought. Finally, sadly, he shook his head. "There probably is enough money, Nick," he said, "but there would be no way I'd have a chance to spend it. All the big guys want you. They are all looking for you."

"All of them?"

"Yes. Assante pulled the contract. You know what that means."

Nick nodded.

He offered no resistance as the man led him to the rear of the gatehouse, nor did he have any regrets when the bullet from the .38 special, its sound nearly inaudible, tore through the side of his head.

The contract on Rico Scalzi had been canceled.

FORTY FOUR

ANTHONY Assante was shaken, ashen.

"Impelliteri is dead? How?"

Police Commissioner James Fox nodded. "He was shot. Once through the forehead. He was found this morning by a man we are holding for his own protection. Three men downstairs were found dead, too. Each shot once. There were no witnesses; we found no fingerprints, nothing. Someone came in and did it, then left and didn't leave a clue."

They were together in Fox's office on Varick Street, not the normal public display office up near Gracie Mansion but the place where Fox did most of his work, away from prying eyes and media attention. It was sparsely furnished, mostly in government-issue metal-and-wood desks and chairs, gray filing cabinets, standard-issue telephones. A working office, stripped of the trappings of a man of his importance and stature.

"Rico Scalzi," said Assante, quietly, while feeling his immunity slipping away. If there was no Impelliteri-McDonald, then he would not be needed as much. Oh, sure, there were mysteries to unravel, crimes to be solved by putting a name to the deed, but without McDonald, without Assante's willingness to testify, there were significantly fewer reasons for the police and the Feds to need him.

"Who?" Fox asked.

"Scalzi. Rico Scalzi. He killed DeSalvo. I told you that. He was always close to the top. He was my lieutenant. Giovanni liked him, liked him a lot. His father was one of the best plate men in the world. You know, plates? Money? Stocks? Counterfeit stuff, you know?"

"Yes."

"Rico had two brothers. Both of them were killed working for me. When his father died, I sent his mother to Florida, set her up big. But it was McDonald's idea, McDonald's money. He just didn't want anybody to know, and that wasn't unusual, because he never wanted anybody to know anything about what he did. He bought that old woman a $4 million house in South Florida. I couldn't figure out why. He was never that generous, even to people who did great favors, who gave their lives."

Fox nodded. "But why do you say Rico Scalzi is responsible for this killing?"

"Because he would have been the only one, besides myself, who could get past the guards in that house without too much suspicion. It was him. There could not have been anyone else."

"Why would he do it?"

"Because two days ago, right before I called you and gave myself up, I was ordered to put a contract out on Rico. Only Giovanni could have issued that big a contract. I was really surprised, but he was running scared. Once Rico murdered De-Salvo, which was my decision, he was afraid there would be too much attention focused on the business, on all the other parts of it. And I was shocked, because I thought he really liked Rico."

"Who did you give the contract to?"

"Nick. Nick Conti. Best one I know, aside from Rico himself."

"Where is Scalzi?"

"Now I don't know. I thought he was going to Florida. He has a house down there, hidden in the Keys. I checked the airlines. He took a Continental flight the other night. So I gave Conti the contract, but then I changed my mind. Once I decided I was coming in, I put a cancel on the contract. I owed Rico that much."

"How do you cancel a contract, Anthony?"

"You kill the assassin. I called somebody in Fort Lauderdale who works for us, who knows everybody and can do anything down there, and told him there was a contract that had to be canceled. I gave him all the information."

Fox thought about that. "But Rico never got there, not if you say only he could have walked into McDonald's home and done the killings. So Conti went on a wild goose chase anyway, didn't he?"

Assante nodded. "I guess so, yes. But it doesn't matter."

"Why?"

"Because Conti is dead by now. He would have had no chance, once the area was alerted, once all those people were looking for him. I told them where he would go. I know he's dead."

Fox thought that was a bonus, not a disaster, except for the fact that Conti might have provided crucial information about his involvement in other killings that had never been solved.

Now it was Assante who looked at Fox, not nearly as authoritative as he had been moments ago, not as arrogant, not as sure of himself.

"What about our deal, Commissioner?"

"I think we still have a deal, Anthony. It will take a long time for us to find out everything you know. Until then, you'll be safe and comfortable. No one will get to you; no one will know where you are."

"And then?"

"Then? What the hell, Anthony, without McDonald around we can't pin anything on you. Once we're finished, you will be free to leave. We'll take all the information you give us, and, in return, we won't press any charges. You'll be a free man."

It was a death sentence, and Anthony Assante almost admired the sophistication, the irony, and the finality of it all. In fact, it brought a tight, hard smile to his face when he looked at Fox, the hard edge back in his voice, the cold stare back in his eyes. "I think I'd like to stick around, Commissioner," he said. "When you're finished with me, find a place to keep me. But if you decide not to do that, I will ask for transportation out of the country. There are a few places I can go and be able to live with some comfort, with a minimum of time spent looking over my shoulder and in darkened doorways. I will not cooperate on any level until you assure me of at least that much.''

Fox nodded. ''I don't think there'll be a problem with that, Anthony. And I think it is a wise decision.''

FORTY FIVE

DESPITE all Keegan's misgivings and warnings, Ed went back to work. The sports department held a quick little surprise party for him, a sort of postmarriage bachelor party, and that surprised him, because usually there wasn't much closeness in that office, just guys doing their jobs and paying their bills. The management and ownership of the newspaper purposely created that attitude and made it flourish. Too much fraternization, they felt, led to less than total efficiency. The older employees, both desk guys and reporters, were periodically offered a buyout or convinced to take early retirement, whether they wanted to or not. Refusing meant, in most cases, a warning that there would never be another raise and that those who were assigned regular beats would be taken off and assigned to the most menial jobs, covering local high school sports or harness racing or bowling.

People got the message. And the company earned its reputation on merit.

But for now, Ed had no concern about being told it was time to leave. He had, in fact, planned on staying only another few years and then beating them to the punch by resigning, taking a job with another newspaper or settling in to write the books and freelance magazine articles he had never been able to pursue before.

So he went back to work. The Giants were scheduled to play Philadelphia the next weekend, down there in Veterans Stadium, and he told his bosses that he was going to go. No problem. He did the best job of anybody on the staff, and his return was welcomed. He was told not to touch on the Adam Benson death, since it was a news section story now and Ed's closeness to the victim was viewed by the often-skewed management as a liability, a distraction from unbiased journalism.

Leigh had resigned from DD Ads by phone, but having learned that David Drexler was under investigation by the police and was about to be indicted for his involvement in gambling and conspiracy, she agreed to have lunch with the firm's vice president, now its president, a good guy named Jack Sutton. He pleaded with her to stay, at a better position and more salary and the choice of managing whichever accounts suited her fancy.

She accepted. Despite her misgivings and the bad experience at DD Ads, the money was too much to pass up and her new and broader authority was satisfying in that it propelled her right up and through that glass ceiling that still existed, in spades, up and down Madison Avenue.

She talked it over with Ed late one night, and he agreed that it was too much to pass up, on various levels and for several reasons. So she went back to work, Sutton moving into Drexler's office and she taking over Sutton's, which was right next to it and attached by a connecting door. One of her most satisfying early decisions was to respond to a call from Gene Medici of the Skeezixs Candy Company, who wanted DD Ads to take over his billing again.

Sutton gave her the choice. She told Medici to go fuck himself.

"Jack, I just threw away millions of dollars in billing," she said when that conversation ended abruptly.

Sutton smiled. "I bet myself that's what you'd do. I won dinner for you and Ed and me and my wife at an expensive restaurant of my choice."

Leigh accepted with a laugh.

Harlan Ellsworth's trial was scheduled to begin in a month's time. He planned to plead guilty, to tell everything he knew and perhaps make some kind of deal for himself. But the murder was done by him, clearly. It was premeditated, carefully planned and executed. At best, he would spend the rest of his life in jail.

Some of O.J. Simpson's Dream Team defense staff, including its chief, Johnny Cochrane, offered to take on the Ellsworth case pro bono, seeing the chance to fight organized crime, its infiltration into legitimate businesses, the high-profile nature of the NFL's involvement, and, by the way, the fact that Ellsworth had been coerced by the "white criminal establishment" to commit the murder in the first place. As things turned out, the Dream Team's contribution to the Ellsworth case was to provide the best laugh line heard in years.

Ellsworth was found guilty. Quickly, definitively. He was sentenced to life without parole in Dannamora. Three years later he would be killed in a fight with three other inmates, late at night in the laundry room. He was stabbed to death, ironically, by an ice pick in his jugular vein.

Assante was under wraps and would be for months. No one besides Gerry Keegan, Commissioner Fox, and a half-dozen handpicked members of the NYPD and the FBI knew where he was. Keegan was in charge of the Assante debriefing, somewhere deep in a remote area of Delaware. It was time spent away from his office, his job, his friends, and Sherri Novak, maybe especially Sherri Novak, who had been moved out of Keegan's mother's house and put into a true safe house, a federal location for those being prepped to begin new lives in the Witness Protection Program.

McDonald's death had been headline news for a week, especially when it was discovered (with a little help from the commissioner's office) that the man was really Giovanni Impelliteri, thought to have been killed in World War II. Information provided by Assante resulted in the arrest of more than twenty organized crime heads, many of whom had been suspected of various indiscretions for years but had never allowed themselves to be touched. It would take years to find all the money, all the holdings, all the hooks he had placed into all the various legitimate enterprises in the country, but early information had already projected his net worth at more than $2 billion.

The FBI, sharing information provided by Ellsworth and con-firmed by Assante, arrested eight professional football players, charged each with racketeering and gambling. They were promptly suspended for life by league commissioner A. Scott Small, and a study was soon under way to determine whether all the games they had allegedly fixed could be identified. The Dallas Cowboys lost a star wide receiver and a defensive tackle; the New York Jets lost their starting quarterback. Also indicted were a Miami running back and an Oakland quarterback. It would take a long time for the NFL to recover.

It was a Friday night. Ed was going to the Giants' game in Philadelphia the next morning, taking the train from Penn Sta-tion. Leigh was going to spend the weekend home, catching up on her work files, planning her week.

Just after eleven o'clock, the telephone rang.

Ed answered.

"Ed Buck?"

"Yes."

"My name is Rico Scalzi. We need to talk."

"Talk about what?"

Leigh, just half-listening, suddenly snapped to attention when she heard the strange edge in her husband's voice.

"About Sherri Novak. About your friend Adam Benson. About how easily I found you and your new wife in Long Beach Island and how easily I will always be able to find you and your new wife, wherever you go, wherever you are."

"Who the fuck do you think you are?" Ed barked, and sur-prised himself when he did. Why wasn't he afraid? Why wasn't he trembling? Why wasn't the tightness in the pit of his stomach reflecting in a wavering, quavering voice? "You're a fucking hoodlum, you ran off when it got hot, and now you're probably sitting in some fleabag hotel room jerking off, playing these games on the phone. What's next, you call some massage parlor or escort service and come all over the wall when you hear the girl answer the phone?"

It was Scalzi who was taken back. "You don't understand, Buck. Before you get yourself in real trouble, shut your fucking mouth and just listen to me. Who do you think it was who arranged to leave that note on the car windshield in Long Beach Island that night? Assante had ordered it to be wired. You and the woman were supposed to become millions of pieces of fish bait when you pushed it up to fifty miles an hour. I didn't want more deaths on my conscience. I wasn't there. But I have friends all over. It was not difficult to find and to plant the sheet of paper—it was lined notebook paper, torn from a spiral binding, in case you aren't sure we're talking about the same thing—so that you'd call the police and they'd decide to wait for your friend Keegan and the New York bomb squad clowns to show up."

Calmer now, but still tight, Ed responded, "Thank you. So what do you want?"

"I want you to call Keegan. I want to meet with him, alone. I am going to leave the country and I want to clean up a few things. Get in touch with him. I'll call later tonight. And if it works, I promise that will be the last time you ever hear from me, and the last time you ever have to worry about this thing again."

The line went dead.

Ed quickly pressed *69, which was supposed to provide the number of the last call received. But all the electronic voice said was: "The last call placed to this telephone number is not within the allowable callback distance."

Leigh, her face white, her hands cold, clearly and obviously frightened, asked, "Who was that?"

"Rico Scalzi," Ed said. "He wants to meet with Gerry."

"God, isn't this thing ever going to be over? He's the one who killed DeSalvo. He's the one who killed McDonald. All those bodyguards. He helped to fuck up poor Sherri. What would that animal want from Gerry?"

"I don't know, baby, but I have to tell him."

Finding Gerry Keegan was more difficult than Ed thought it would be. He wasn't home. He wasn't at the police station. A call to the special number from which he could always retrieve messages, especially urgent ones, took two hours for him to return. It wasn't until two in the morning that Ed's phone rang.

"Ed? What's going on?"

"We got a call from Rico Scalzi, Gerry. He wants to see you. He says he's leaving the country and he wants to talk to you. Tomorrow sometime. He said something about cleaning up a few things."

"What's supposed to happen?"

"He'll call me back. You're supposed to tell me when and where you can meet him. Gerry, I didn't know what else to do."

"You did the right thing. When he calls, tell him tomorrow morning. Six o'clock. There's an all-night diner on Hudson Street, down near the Holland Tunnel. Cabbies and truck drivers go there. Cops. Bums. Limo drivers. It's called Metro. Just Metro. Tell him to be there."

"Gerry, he said you alone. Just you."

Keegan paused. "Yeah, right. So tell him I'll be alone."

"Where are you? Why was it so hard to find you?"

"I'm with Assante. You don't need to know where. But I'll be at the Metro in the morning. And don't you dare show up; don't you be anywhere near there."

FORTY SIX

KEEGAN turned to his FBI counterpart, Alex Henley. "It was my friend the sportswriter," he said. "Scalzi just called him. He wants to talk to me. In the morning. Says he's got some stuff to spill before he vanishes."

Assante was within hearing range. He smiled. Giovanni's son was coming in, too. And at this moment, only he and Rico knew he was the son of the terrible man. "You'll never get him," Assante murmured, but Keegan heard him. So did Henley.

"We will, Anthony. Why is he so fucking special?"

Assante fixed Henley with a cold stare. "He was DeSalvo's lieutenant, big guy, did some killings for me. Not too bright, but loyal. Very loyal. I took care of his parents. His father worked for us. When he died, you know we sent his mother to Florida. His brothers, two of them, died working for me. Got caught in that situation at the piers fifteen years ago. I always took care of Rico; he was always loyal."

"So how would he know it was Impelliteri who put out the hit?"

Assante sneered. "He isn't stupid, just slow. He knew I was second in charge of everything. He knew I would not have done that to him. Couldn't, without permission, even if I had wanted to. So he figured it was Impelliteri, since he had to assume I never would have ordered it. After that, he was just acting on instinct, looking for revenge and trying to guarantee his future safety. He had to kill Giovanni. It was automatic."

"So now, why would he want to see me? What could he offer me that you can't? He must know we have you."

Assante shook his head. "That the part I don't know," he said. "I really, honestly don't know. He has some information. Not big stuff. Not important stuff. He was never involved in the business end. Just the mechanics of it. I don't know. Maybe he's looking for a deal."

"I'll see him," Keegan said. "Should I send your regards?"

"Yeah, my regards. Tell him it was nothing personal, never anything personal. Tell him it was me who put out the contract because Impelliteri ordered it, but tell him it was me who canceled it. On my own."

"Right."

Keegan got up from the chair. "Get me a ride up to New York," he said to Henley, who nodded in agreement. "But you aren't going alone, Gerry. Nobody is that stupid."

"I know. But I don't want him to know. Please, dress up some bums or something. It's an easy place to be anonymous in; that's why I picked it. A guy in a limo driver's suit, maybe a guy looks like a cabbie. Just place 'em around the area; there's lots of small tables. Single tables. Most people in there that early are singles."

"OK, I'll take care of it. I'll get Johnson to drive you up. From here, what, about three hours? You'll have time for a shower."

Keegan chuckled. "Yeah, but I wish I had time to sleep. I guess that'll come later, when this is all done. I don't think I can be wired, but I'll use one of those little coin recorder/transmitters you guys invented."

Henley smiled. "You have them? They aren't police-issue yet."

Keegan smiled in return. "The police didn't issue them," he said. "But I have them. It's what I used on Leigh when she met with that piece of shit Drexler."

He got up and went to the small dormitory-style room down the hall, where he had been staying during this debriefing vigil, splashed water on his face, threw some things into a small duffel bag, and changed into clean clothes. "I guess I'm ready," he said to himself. "Just me and my toothbrush and clean underwear."

FORTY SEVEN

THE drive north was uneventful. It was dark, with a tinge of the light that would come in another hour or so. The driver knew not to talk, figuring maybe Keegan would catch a few hours of sleep, and he made sure it looked that way, closing his eyes, hunkering down with his head against the door, but he didn't sleep. He was thinking about Rico Scalzi, about what would transpire, what would come out of the mouth of this man when he sat face-to-face with him.

He was thinking, too, about Sherri. He had decided, and he hoped she had, that there was something there worth going for, some connection they both recognized but were afraid to verbalize.

Yet.

He had decided to tell her when this was over, when whatever her involvement in this thing had been was fleshed out and flushed away, when she had been cleared—which he knew she would be—and when there was a chance that they might try for a normal life. He recognized the Sherri behind the Sherri, and maybe nobody else ever had, as an intelligent, warm, tough woman with a wide streak of survivor mentality and an acceptance of reality enough so that she could deal with whatever came along in order to keep herself going forward.

They arrived at the mouth of the Holland Tunnel, on the Jersey side, at five-thirty. They'd be there before six. Johnson was to drop him off and just leave. The two men put in place were already there, or should be. Not even someone as street-smart as Scalzi would be able to pick them out, even if they were the only other guys in the place. He was sure of that.

The coin recorder/transmitter was hanging from a chain around his neck, under his shirt, which was buttoned at the collar because he was wearing a tie. It was typical plainclothes apparel—wrinkled, nondescript blue blazer, white shirt, solid blue tie, dark gray slacks, black shoes with shoelaces. You could buy the whole outfit for under a hundred dollars: In fact, he had. Clothes were way down on Keegan's list of priorities, although maybe that would change soon.

Johnson dropped him off a block before they reached the Metro. No exchange of words, no final message to be carried back. Keegan just opened the door at a traffic light and got out, nodding. Johnson nodded back and continued driving, going to a designated uptown office building where he would wait until summoned.

Keegan walked the block quickly, observing the not-only-homeless-but-drunk sleeping in the doorways. Home sweet home.

The Metro had glass windows from floor to ceiling, maybe fifteen feet high. It was a big, bare, cold room, cafeteria-style counters in the rear, waitresses if you wanted them lounging against the far wall, small, cheap tables, with one or two chairs, scattered in an obvious random placement, maybe forty of them.

Six of the tables were occupied by single men. Two others had been taken by couples, the stay-out-late residue of a Friday night. There were four kids at another table, in jeans and sweats, loud and still halfway drunk, laughing and drinking coffee and each of them determined not to say how tired he was.

At one of the six single tables, the farthest away from anyone else, was a big man, had to be six-six, had to weigh 250, 260. He was "dressed down," but that was obvious to a trained detective. He was wearing jeans and a pullover gray sweater. Boots, black and simple, untooled. He looked up and nodded.

Keegan nodded back and walked over. "I'm Keegan," he said.

"Scalzi." It was a deep voice, and its timbre and resonance belied Assante's description of the man's lack of mental acuity. There was intelligence there, Keegan felt it, and a cold, hard

edge that he suspected was always there and not just affected
for this meeting.

"What did you want to tell me?" Keegan asked. Clearly, there
was no basis nor reason for small talk.

"I want complete immunity," Scalzi said. "I want to be allowed to leave the country. I want to visit a few banks first, make
a few wire transfers, and then I will be gone."

"Yeah, right. And what do I get in return?"

"All of it. Every place where Giovanni Impelliteri had
money. Every company that he had a hook into. Every person
who ever cooperated with him. Every fix and every stock market
swindle and all of it. Every fucking detail of the man's life and
holdings."

"And how would you know all this? All of our information
puts you as just another soldier in the organization's army."

Rico smiled mirthlessly. "No, I'm not just another soldier. I
am Giovanni Impelliteri's only son."

The words *holy shit* came instantly to mind, though of course
they were not verbalized. Instead, Keegan sat still, staring at
Scalzi, formulating a response.

"We have no record of Giovanni Impelliteri having had a
child," Keegan said, finally. "How do I know you're telling me
the truth?"

Scalzi smiled, his huge hands wrapped around a coffee cup.
"First, why would I claim to be the son of a monster unless it
was true?"

"For the money," Keegan shot back.

"No, not that. I don't care about his money. I have money. I
learned my history fifteen years ago, and I've been preparing
ever since. I want to trade this information to guarantee my privacy. I'll make three promises. First, I will leave the country.
Second, I will provide you with everything I know about my
father's dealings. Third, I will never return to the United
States."

"And we have to do what, exactly?"

"Actually, not much. I won't allow you to question me, like
you're doing with poor old Assante right now. And I won't be
locked up, not even temporarily. I've spent the last five years

recording everything I know, everything I ever heard. Names and addresses, telephone numbers, and bank account numbers. The entire network, all of it, from the drugs, to the gambling, to the stock market, to the banks that cleaned his money, to all the cops in about twenty-five cities who were on his payroll. There are some incredibly important and well-known politicians on the list, with enough documentation to burn them. It is the biggest, most important collection of information ever put together. I guarantee the accuracy of it. And it's worth my freedom."

He paused, and a small smile visited his mouth, one best and perhaps only capable of being described as ironic.

"The pro football thing was peanuts, didn't matter," he said. "My father and Anthony allowed that stupid little man, DeSalvo, to sell them on it. They didn't make more than nine, ten million on the whole thing. Shit, they made that much in a week with the drugs and ten times that much in the stock market, with construction contracts, rigged bids, government jobs. Shit, it was stupid. I tried to tell Assante, but he wouldn't listen. It was pro football that brought down the biggest and most profitable organization in the country."

Keegan spoke quietly. "I have to talk to my bosses," he said, "tell them the offer. I feel pretty strong that they'll accept it. How can I reach you?"

Rico Scalzi/Impelliteri shook his head.

"No, the answer comes now. I know you have two men here. The guy who looks like a cabbie at the table off to my left. The other one, older guy with a belly, dressed like a limo driver, behind us, middle of the room. What you don't know is that I have people here, too. One guy has a gun trained on your cabbie; another is locked into the limo driver. And those four young guys? They're mine. They are freaky, but they do wonderful things with explosives. Make a decision. Do it now. I'll tell you where the tapes are. There are more than one hundred of them in all, and you have my word that everything on them is true and, even better, can be proved."

This was not a decision Keegan could make on his own. He was being asked to set free potentially the most important wit-

ness ever reined in by any law enforcement agency in history.
He was being asked to let someone who had killed repeatedly,
who had done the dirtiest of dirty work for organized crime,
waltz off untouched, leave the country with enough money to
live like a king for the rest of his life.

Sitting in a dingy diner, early on a Saturday morning, gray
and dreary, chill and cold, he was being asked to reach well
beyond his authority, well past his parameters, and he had to
do it now.

Rico sat, motionless, staring directly at him with dark, fiery
eyes. Was he really willing to give a signal, which might be as
simple as a finger crooking or a leg being crossed, and cause the
deaths of everyone in the diner, including his own? Was he that
cold?

Yes, he thought.

"Yes," he said. "Where are the tapes?"

Scalzi smiled. He reached into his shirt pocket—and Keegan
knew that at least eight pairs of eyes were watching intently,
that eight men were tensed, focusing on what would happen
and what their next move would be—and extracted a folded
slip of white paper.

"It's a safe-deposit box," Rico said. "Salvation National Bank,
Madison and 18th. You go to an assistant manager named Richard Brightley. You tell him that you are the man Rico Scalzi
sent to pick up the material. That is all you have to do. He will
take you to the boxes, unlock it, and hand you a large metal box
that is locked inside the safe-deposit box. You will find all the
tapes and notebooks filled with more information. Good hunt-
ing. I'm leaving now. When I get up now, I will smile and shake
your hand. That will be the release for the men I have here. Then
we all leave. You won't try to follow me or have me followed.
You will never hear from me again. I have given you my word.
Tell Assante I said thank you for pulling back the contract. Tell
your friend Buck I didn't mean to frighten him. I was the one
who arranged that note to be left on his windshield. I didn't
know for sure whether my father had ordered him hit, and he
didn't deserve that."

He paused, prepared to rise.

"And tell Sherri Novak, wherever she is being held, that you are a good man and that nothing was ever personal."

He smiled then, stood, extended his hand, and shook Keegan's. And when he left the dingy diner, the two singles casually exited, and the four young guys, still laughing and making noise, started arguing about who was going to pay the bill.

It was over.

Keegan went back to his apartment for a shower and breakfast. He could not call Sherri yet, nor did he want to speak to his immediate superiors yet, either. At nine o'clock, he was at the Salvation National Bank as the doors were opened for the normal half-day Saturday business.

He walked in, found a tall, gangly man at the desk with the nameplate Richard Brightley, identified himself, and was ushered to the safe-deposit box vault.

"Mr. Scalzi said you were his brother-in-law, and even so this is very irregular," Brightley said. "But he has been such a good customer for so long that, well, I'm doing him the favor. I have his key here"—he reached into his pocket—"and I am to keep it when you leave. It is bank property, you know."

"I certainly appreciate all you have done, Mr. Brightley," Keegan replied, playing out the role. "This is very old and sentimental stuff. You've done us a big favor."

Richard Brightley saw no reason to mention the $5,000 in cash that Rico Scalzi had handed him, in a plain white envelope, when he agreed to do him this favor. Nobody would know; nobody would care—it was just a favor to a good and loyal bank customer.

Keegan took the metal strongbox Brightley extended, having extracted it from a large safe-deposit box. "Oh, Mr. Keegan, Mr. Scalzi said to tell you the key for the box is taped underneath."

So common, so ordinary, so harmless.

"Thank you, Mr. Brightley. I'll be going now."

And Gerry Keegan walked out of the bank, onto Madison Avenue, with enough information to bring down corrupt policemen, politicians, and corporations, not to mention bringing a hopefully fatal blow to the world of organized crime.

He was reasonably sure his bosses, and especially Police Commissioner Fox, would agree with his decision.

He stopped another taxi and went back to his apartment, from where he called the private home telephone of Police Commissioner James Fox, who lived in a brownstone in the Bay Ridge section of Brooklyn.

"Yes?"

"Detective Keegan, Commissioner. I have to see you right now."

"Now? Where the hell are you, Detective?"

"At home. In Manhattan. I have something you won't believe, and I have a story to tell that I hope you'll believe."

"I'm sending a car, I know the address. And, Keegan? This better be good."

Keegan smiled to himself. "Commissioner, I think it's very good. I'll be there as soon as your car arrives."

"It's already on the way," the commissioner said, hanging up.

Then Keegan called Ed's apartment.

"It's me, Gerry. It's all over."

"What? Tell me? Did you see him? What's happening?"

"Tonight, Eddie. Don't go to Philly. Fuck the game. I just made you a Pulitzer Prize–winning crime reporter."

Finally, he called the number where Sherri was being held.

"This is New York City Detective First Class Joseph Gerard Keegan," he said, "and I must speak with Miss Sherri Novak. Immediately. It is police business."

"Yes, Detective," said the male receptionist at this intensely private facility.

A long pause ensued, and Keegan knew that the beeps and whirring noises were designed to prevent eavesdropping and recording. Finally, he heard Sherri's voice.

"Gerry? What's wrong?"

"Something very serious, Sherri."

"Oh, God. What is it?"

"I'm in love with you."

There was stone silence, and it dragged on for more than sixty seconds. Finally, the noise he heard sounded remarkably like someone softly weeping.

"Detective, I think I know how to remedy the problem," she stammered. "Yes, I will marry you."

FORTY
EIGHT

FOX was furious that Keegan had allowed Scalzi to walk. His face turned red. His voice rose well above acceptable decibels. Small droplets of spittle gathered on his lips.

"How the fuck could you have done that?" he bellowed. "It was well beyond your authority. I am going to put you on suspension, and there will be an investigation, and I wouldn't be a bit surprised if you lose your badge and face criminal charges."

"Commissioner, here, take this strongbox," Keegan said, surprisingly calm.

"What's this?"

"Oh, thirty years or so of answers. Numbers, names, dates. Everything on the empire Impelliteri built. Tapes. Notebooks. Proof of everything. It was the deal I made with Scalzi."

Fox was dumbstruck. "Where did you get this?"

"From Giovanni's son."

"He had no son."

"He did. Rico Scalzi."

Commissioner Fox had nothing to say.

Later that night, Keegan was sitting in the Bucks' living room. Ketel One was pouring freely, and a few contraband Cuban cigars were fouling the air. He told the whole story, gave all the information to his friend Ed, assured Leigh that it was really over, that nothing more could be expected.

"Well, there may be one more little inconvenience," he said.

"Such as?"

"I need you two to be witnesses. Sherri and I are getting married."

Leigh, her eyes moist, looked up at him and said, "I know a great place. It's down at the Jersey shore. It's called Ship Bottom. And there's a wonderful little hotel. It's called the St. Rita. And . . . oh, damn it, Gerry, what a wonderful thing."

EPILOGUE

ABOUT thirty miles north of George Town, the capital of Grand Cayman and the Cayman Islands, is an area called Rum Point. It is the northernmost tip of the island, situated at the junction of Bowse Bluff and Cayman Kai, well past Sparrowhawk Point and Long Coconut Point, Old Man Bay and Grape Tree Point, past Spanish Bay and Boatswains Point.

The ocean cracks against the shoreline, its breaking waves and frisky whitecaps belying its Caribbean identity. It is perhaps one of the most peaceful, isolated spots in the Western Hemisphere. The weather, which is almost always placid, ranges between sixty-five and ninety degrees. There is almost always a prevailing west wind, offshore breezes that flog the ocean, and the sun's coloring is, impossibly, closest to washed-out pastels. In eternal spring, but with a small break for torrid summer, this part of Grand Cayman has an idyllic quality not found anywhere else.

There are only a dozen homes there, each built into the beach on a small, protected hillock, each parcel of land no less than twenty acres. Each of the palatial homes, built by expatriates, mostly from the States and Great Britain, bears a nameplate, a shingle swinging in the mild tropical breezes, identifying themselves to the precious few motorists who wander out that far. The nameplates bear names such as Road's End and Heaven's Gate and Windfall.

One of the homes, the most simple yet somehow the most elegant, all startling white and, to the knowing eye, clearly the most expensive, is called My Father's House.

No one ever came to visit its single occupant, and only an occasional glance at the local newspaper, the *Daily Caymanian*, told him of the continuing upheaval in the United States—famous politicians resigning in disgrace or being indicted or both, banks being forced to close, organized crime leaders being arrested and, for a change, having the charges stick, at least two major New York Stock Exchange brokerages being forced to liquidate and close.

He learned, weeks after the fact, of the promotion of Detective First Class Joseph Gerard Keegan to assistant police commissioner of New York, his invaluable help in bringing down the corruption boosting him rapidly up the ladder.

He learned of a Pulitzer Prize being awarded to Edward Kalman Buck of the *New York Express* for his investigative reporting leading to the disclosure of much of the incendiary information.

Only occasionally did the single occupant venture into George Town, usually stopping at one of the banks and then for a solitary dinner at one of only two restaurants, the Brasserie or Hooks. He never needed a reservation. When he appeared, a table was made ready for him. It seemed many people knew him, welcomed him, and fought for him to sit with them. He almost always declined, politely, and with a smile, choosing to sit alone, on the periphery of the crowded dining room.

Once, he was seen with an old man, white-haired, stooped over, feeble, and infirm. They assumed it was his father. When they left, the two embraced, as if having just seen each other for the last time.

Mostly, those who sought his company were bankers and real estate brokers. Banking, as everyone knew, comprised the single most profitable industry in the country, one that made the tiny Caribbean nation the fourth-wealthiest in the world. Caymanian banking rules demanded confidentiality and offered no exchange of information with any other country in the world. Monies deposited in Cayman banks were totally and completely safe from prying eyes. It was a criminal offense for any banking official to discuss any client's finances with anyone, even other bank employees. The banking system was billed as a tax haven, and it was. There was no income tax on the island, nor was any contemplated.

Every once in a while someone was arrested and charged with violation of the Cayman Banking Laws, the result of a sting operation conducted by the banking commission to ensure the integrity of this unique financial structure.

The solitary occupant had learned, from sources he never lost in the States, that Ed and Leigh Buck owned property on Key West. There were a few times he was tempted to call one of the old guard, to see if they could be found. No malice was intended, just a curiosity about how their lives were going, since he, and he alone, was responsible for them being alive at all.

But he resisted the impulse. He had disappeared. It was better that way. He had a lifetime of atonement to earn for all he had done. He would forever be grateful to Keegan and Buck and, in a way, to Assante.

He was Rico Impelliteri, and he was alone.